THE MISCHIEF MAKERS

Also by Elisabeth Gifford

Secrets of the Sea House
Return to Fourwinds
The Good Doctor of Warsaw
The Lost Lights of St Kilda
A Woman Made of Snow

THE MISCHIEF MAKERS

Elisabeth Gifford

Published in hardback in Great Britain in 2024 by Corvus,
an imprint of Atlantic Books Ltd.

Copyright © Elisabeth Gifford, 2024

The moral right of Elisabeth Gifford to be identified as the author
of this work has been asserted by her in accordance with the
Copyright, Designs and Patents Act of 1988.

All rights reserved. No part of this publication may be reproduced,
stored in a retrieval system, or transmitted in any form or by any
means, electronic, mechanical, photocopying, recording, or otherwise,
without the prior permission of both the copyright owner
and the above publisher of this book.

No part of this book may be used in any manner in the learning,
training or development of generative artificial intelligence technologies
(including but not limited to machine learning models and large
language models (LLMs)), whether by data scraping, data mining or use
in any way to create or form a part of data sets or in any other way.

This novel is entirely a work of fiction. The names, characters and
incidents portrayed in it are the work of the author's imagination.
Any resemblance to actual persons, living or dead, events or
localities, is entirely coincidental.

Letters from the Daphne du Maurier archive at the University of Exeter
quoted by permission of Christian Browning

10 9 8 7 6 5 4 3 2 1

A CIP catalogue record for this book
is available from the British Library.

Hardback ISBN: 978 1 83895 982 1
Trade paperback ISBN: 978 1 83895 983 8
E-book ISBN: 978 1 83895 984 5

Printed and bound in Great Britain by TJ Books Limited, Padstow, Cornwall

Corvus
An imprint of Atlantic Books Ltd
Ormond House
26–27 Boswell Street
London
WC1N 3JZ

www.atlantic-books.co.uk

To Josh

Exceeding the boundaries is part of creativity.

Jung

PROLOGUE

MENABILLY CORNWALL 1947

Daphne lay in the dark, her heart still thumping. She'd been dreaming of Michael again as he and Rupert walked towards Sanford Pool, the long summer grass in the meadows brushing their feet, the murmur of the weir growing louder as they pass the blistered wooden sign with its black lettering: *Beware. Danger of drowning.* The sudden burst of a thrush from a hawthorn tree.

At the edge of the water, they strip down to their bathers. No sound from the halls and quads of Oxford can reach them here. One goes in first, she can't see which, and the other follows, wading deeper until the meniscus of the pool laps their chins and their feet lift from the bottom, water splashing as they strike out to the middle – more of an effort for Michael who's only recently learned to swim.

They pause, treading water. Around them, the pool is a mirror of sky ringed with upside-down trees. Moving closer, Rupert's arm goes around Michael. Michael wraps both arms around Rupert. An intake of breath, the water churns, and they rise up, shoulders gleaming like fish leaping. A shout and they disappear under the water.

The stillness closes over them.

A minute, two minutes. A lifetime.

Gasping, she'd woken from the dream, the anguish of the news as fresh as ever. *Please God, let it have been an accident. One boy with cramp, panicking, the other trying to save him. Don't let it have been suicide.*

But over twenty years had gone by since Michael died, and there were still no answers. Sanford Pool had had to be dragged – that odd detail of how one body had fallen from the other's arms as they came up out of the water.

She groped for the alarm clock on the bedside table. Five o'clock. She put it back down on top of a book she'd been reading: *How People Go Mad*. Little chance of getting back to sleep now. She got up, pulled on Tommy's old worsted dressing gown and belted it round her waist. Over at the window she pushed back the curtain. It was that brief, liminal moment before dawn, the rhododendrons a barely perceptible shade darker than the fading night air, their humped shapes rising in a ring around the lawns of Menabilly.

She leaned her head against the icy glass. How strange that the very thing Michael had so desperately feared as a child should come to pass. He had always been terrified of water. Refused to learn to swim for years. On a family holiday when she was about five and Michael eleven, she'd been woken up several times at night by the sound of him shouting. Gone out of her room to find him at the top of the stairs, a small figure in a white nightgown waving an imaginary sword at whatever it was that sought to pull him under the water. Uncle Jim would be there, standing behind him in the shadows. Uncle Jim always sat with Michael through his nightmares.

That was the year that Uncle Jim had adopted Michael and his four brothers, after both Uncle Arthur and Aunt Sylvia had died of cancer. He'd written *Peter Pan* for the five Davies boys when they were smaller and the family came to stay with him at his cottage in Black Lake Woods.

Of the five boys, Michael had been the most beloved for Jim. The boy's death at the age of nineteen had all but finished him. He had hung on for another twenty years, but he was never the same man, an exhausted spectre waiting to go and join Michael.

The window sash gave a sudden rattle, a cold draught of air. She pulled the dressing gown tighter.

But why should she be dreaming of Michael now, and with such vivid urgency? As if he had some message for her.

For months now, ever since Gertie's death, she'd had a feeling of life being suspended, everything stale and static. No inspiration, no ideas, no new book to lose herself in. That had never happened to her before.

The first hints of red and green were beginning to bleed back into the shrubs, the black shapes of the trees beyond them moving in the wind. She opened the window, leaned out into the chill air, wanting to be more a part of what was happening outside, and for a moment she had the ridiculous feeling that Rebecca might still be out there, dancing on the lawns, a heartless, disembodied sprite, thumbing her nose and mocking her.

Rebecca, Rebecca, Rebecca. Would she never be free of her? Daphne had had a string of hit novels since she wrote that damned book, but it was always *Rebecca* that people wanted to talk about.

The chill was beginning to bite. She hurried back into bed and lay watching the white roses of the faded Victorian wallpaper appearing in the grey light. Midway along the wall a door led through to her husband's room. What she would love now was to see it open, for Tommy to put his head round it with his old smile, climb into bed beside her. They'd lie back on the pillows and tell each other the funny things that had happened that day, Tommy making her giggle helplessly with his impressions and jokes – like they always used to do. But for the past few years she and Tommy had not shared a bed once.

When he had come home after six years of war service she'd put him in the adjoining room to give him peace to recuperate for a while. She hadn't meant it to be for ever. She'd assumed they'd come together again in time, share their old passion.

It was a shock when she realized that no such thing was going to happen. Here she was, barely forty and that side of their life was over. It made her feel horribly old and unwanted. And with not a clue as to how to get back the old intimacy.

What if she were to tiptoe over now, turn the handle and sneak in beside him? He'd probably not even wake.

They'd settled into an unsatisfactory status quo, but lately, there'd been an odd, uncomfortable feeling of something approaching, some sort of crisis, waiting just behind her shoulder.

As she lay in the accruing light of early morning, a conversation she had had recently with Michael's brother Peter came back to her. They'd been having lunch at the Café Royale. As always, they'd ended up talking for hours about family. Incredibly, Peter had suggested that Uncle Jim might have been to blame for Michael's death.

'You do realize,' he'd said, 'that Uncle Jim wasn't always the benign influence people assumed he was when he adopted us five boys. Think of it, two of us dead now and two of us clouded over with depression. Only Nico escaped.' Peter had leaned forward. 'And you do see, Daphne, that we weren't the only ones affected by Jim's morbid mind?'

She hadn't seen it that way at all. Had no idea what he was driving at. She resolved to quiz Peter about it next time they met up.

She'd always adored Uncle Jim. He wasn't their real uncle, of course, but Daphne could not remember a time when he hadn't been part of the family, whispering tales of Peter Pan as if he'd written them only for her. What would she have done without him? He had taken the trouble to encourage her when no one else understood how desperately she wanted to write.

Perhaps she should have stayed alone in her world of books and stories because in the real world it seemed that she left nothing but a trail of damage and regrets behind her.

She could never tell Tommy exactly what she'd done to survive the long, empty years while he was away.

CHAPTER 1

LONDON 1911

Daphne watches Nico tear a bit of paper from the *Peter Pan* programme and drop it over the edge of the royal box. It twirls down like a tiny feather and lands on the head of a lady below, lodging on her little tiara. Daphne giggles. Nico tears off another bit, gives it to Daphne. She leans over the edge with its ormolu embellishments, ready to drop it on the people in evening dress below, but Michael frowns and shakes his head.

'You'll make people look up at us,' he says.

Daphne takes her hand back. Michael has shrunk down in his seat as if the whole theatre is glaring at them.

Of her five boy cousins, Nico may be nearest to her in age, but it's Michael with his elfin features and that way he has of seeming to guard a secret from another place that Daphne is most in awe of. She glances behind to see if Mummy has noticed anything but she is chatting with the older cousins, oblivious. The three older boy cousins are almost grown-ups now, George and Peter in white tie and tails, Jack in his naval cadet's uniform. Peter smiles at her. He's seen but doesn't tell Mummy.

Something changes in the air and Daphne realizes that the lights in the theatre are beginning to dim. She feels a prickle of anticipation as the people in the rows below begin to fade away into darkness. The heavy curtains part as if by unseen hands and the brightness of the stage eclipses all else. She can see a nursery spread out below, a large dog very like Uncle Jim's Porthos trying to herd three children into their beds. She blinks as Daddy comes on to the stage to a round of applause. He's dressed as if about to go out for the evening but his face has been emphasized with paint, his hair shiny with pomade. He sends Nana the dog off to her kennel outside for barking too much. Daphne's chest tightens. She knows this is a mistake. Nana can feel that the children are in danger – that Peter Pan is coming. And yet at the same time Daphne's longing to see him appear.

Her heart gives a jump because there he is, outlined in the window just as the children are falling to sleep. He leaps down into the room in all his brazen glory, dressed in a green tunic and cap, crowing around the nursery because he's captured his shadow again, then furious and tearful because he can't stick it back on to the ends of his feet.

Wendy wakes up and helps him sew his shadow back on – as the jealous fairy Tinkerbell rings out angrily in the background. Daphne grips the edge of the box, because the best bit is about to happen. There's a sprinkling of fairy dust and she's no longer sure if she's still sitting in her seat or down on the stage with Peter Pan and the children. She can feel the lightness in her body as her feet leave the stage and she flies through the darkness of the theatre with them, swooping over the lights of London and away into Neverland.

Two hours of adventures pass as quickly as a dream. Daddy appears in Neverland too, only this time he's a sneering pirate in a red frock coat and curly wig, who gets eaten up by a crocodile – which makes Daphne scream even though she knows it's coming.

At last, the children fly back to their nursery, Mummy and Daddy and Nana all waiting for them, but when Peter Pan leaves, this time for ever, it's Peter whom her heart follows as he flies away to a land where children never have to grow up.

The lights come on and she's shepherded out of the theatre among a moving forest of long skirts, grey trouser legs and polished shoes, dazed by the cold and the hurrying crowds outside, snow falling, cold slush seeping into her satin shoes as she and Angela hold hands and look up into the swirling flakes and Mummy in her fur cape and long dress frets about finding their cab.

Her five cousins wait with them on the pavement, tall and glamorous in their cashmere coats and white opera scarves, the older ones holding top hats. George goes off to find their cab. Nico, and even Michael, put their tongues out to catch the falling snowflakes and Daphne copies them, tasting the drops of coldness that almost seem sweet.

Mummy clucks around the boys as she always does since they have no Mummy or Daddy of their own – are they getting cold? where is that carriage? – in a way that gives Daphne a feeling she can't name. The same feeling she gets when she sees how Mummy clucks around Baby Jeanne. Mummy never fusses around Daphne in that cosy way. Daphne shivers and Cousin Peter with his long, serious face bends down and wraps his white silk opera scarf around her neck.

Uncle Jim appears from across the street, a small figure in a too-big coat, his bowler hat and shoulders sprinkled with snow, a twinkle in his eye and a drooping moustache.

'So was it terrible?' he asks, looking towards Michael.

'It was awful,' says Michael, laughing. 'Worst play ever.'

'It was wonderful,' says Daphne indignantly. 'Didn't you come in to see it, Uncle Jim?'

'Jim never comes in to see a first night,' says Peter. 'He paces up and down in front of the theatre, smoking, don't you, Uncle Jim?'

'That way, I can have a head start on everyone when they chase me down the street wanting their money back.' She catches a wink from him that no one else sees.

So it's a joke and she's in on it.

'It was magnificent,' Mummy tells Uncle Jim. 'It gets better each year.'

'Well, your opinion means everything, Muriel. I think the changes worked. Tell Gerald I'll pop by tomorrow afternoon and discuss another idea I had.'

Daphne jumps up and down. 'And you'll come and see us in the nursery, Uncle Jim?'

'Don't be impertinent, Daphne. Jim's a busy man. He can't be expected to entertain you children every time.'

But? Mummy's wrong. He does have time for her. Daphne and Uncle Jim share many secrets.

Daphne's had lunch and her boring nap, but still he hasn't come. She can't bear to think that he might not come at all.

She's even been taken downstairs in a clean dress, her hair brushed, to say hello to Mummy and curtsey to her friends in the drawing room – ladies in smelly perfume who insist on kissing her. Eight-year-old Angela is good at this – she enjoys charming everyone, shaking hands and smiling – but Daphne hates the way people say how sweet she is, such pretty blonde hair and blue eyes. She stares back at them angrily.

'Don't be rude, Daphne. Shake hands with people,' Mummy hisses in her ear.

Afterwards, Daphne stomps back up to the nursery, longing to be left alone with her books and her toys. She opens the door and stops in surprise. There's Uncle Jim, sitting on the nursery fender. He looks too small for his crumpled suit, his dome of a forehead gleaming amid a cloud of pipe smoke.

'Thought I'd sneak up without anyone seeing me, before those fancy women can get me tangled up in their chit-chat.'

Daphne runs across the room and throws herself on him with her biggest hug. And so it begins. Jim and Daphne taking it in turns to spin the story, Daphne brandishing the wooden sword that Uncle Jim gave her as she leads the Lost Boys around the rocking horse, or swims across the floor rug, completely caught up in a breathless dream of pirates and mermaids.

Angela arranges the dolls' tea set in the corner of the nursery, long dark curls, a neat bow on one side, her pinafore always clean. Older and more sensible than Daphne by three years, she's the perfect Wendy. Daphne, however, is always and only entirely Peter Pan, fair hair cropped short, the tilt of her little square chin, a challenge in her blue eyes as she flies from island to island, leaping from sofa to chair, until she swoops out of the window in the thick blue air of dusk, gliding out over the rooftops, the gas lamps and the dark trees of Regent's Park below, the rush of air against her skin.

'Can you see me flying, Uncle Jim?'

'Oh yes. That's the thing about you, Daphne,' he murmurs in his sing-song Scottish burr. 'You're one of the very few children who can remember back to when you were a bird. When you lived on the little island in the middle of the Serpentine where birds turn into babies. All babies start life as birds.'

Daphne pauses on the sofa, reaches down her back, trying to feel her shoulder blade. 'Yes, and I can still feel the itch on my shoulders where the wings used to be, can't I?'

'Ah little Daphne. And you know you were very nearly born a boy back then. Should have been a boy.'

Daphne nods solemnly. There's nothing better than to be a boy, like Peter Pan or her five cousins. Then she could live with Uncle Jim and the Davies boys in a house filled with jokes and pranks and hallway cricket, nobody minding about the paint, and ping-pong tables and stories told by Uncle Jim.

Sometimes Daddy comes up and joins in before his evening performance, the girls squealing with laughter as he roars round the nursery with his coat-hanger hook and a scarf for an eyepatch. Uncle Jim sits quietly watching, writing in his notebook, deep-set eyes peering out of the fug of tobacco smoke, giving his deep wheezy coughs, so alarming that each one sounds as though it might be his last.

The door opens. Daphne looks up, but it's not Daddy, only Nurse in her stiff white cap and apron.

'You girls are taking up quite enough of Mr Barrie's time. Tea and bath now.'

Uncle Jim taps out his pipe, makes a cheeky face behind Nurse's back as he disappears through the door and Peter Pan and the Lost Boys begin to fade away, hiding behind the chest of drawers or under the plump sofa.

Well scrubbed, her hair in curl papers, Daphne lies in the bed next to Angela's and wishes she had been born sooner, when her cousins were as small as she is now, back when they first found Peter Pan in the woods of Black Lake Cottage as they played castaway games with Uncle Jim and his dog Porthos. She's heard all the stories, how Michael was still a tiny baby then but he was the one who spotted the light of fairy Tinkerbell flying through the evening woods. Back in the days when the boys still had their Mummy and Daddy.

How it came to be that Uncle Jim, who was not a real uncle or even a relative of any sort according to Daddy, had come to adopt the five boys after their parents died, Daphne has never really understood – did he kidnap them? She knew it was something to do with Uncle Jim being so noble and with everyone else in the family being too busy. And something to do with money, she'd heard Mummy say. Jim has a lot of money.

Daphne knows she is lucky, because she still has her own Mummy and Daddy, although she can't work out why it is she makes Mummy so irritable. Sometimes Daphne has the rather uncomfortable feeling that Mummy doesn't like her very much. Once, when Mummy was nursing the baby, she got so cross with Daphne – Mummy's hair down and streaming out like a witch in a peignoir– that Daphne had to run and hide away in the nursery, where she prefers to be with her games and her stories. Or with Daddy who will pick her up and twirl her round, or teach her to play cricket in the garden because Daddy is her best friend, just as she his favourite daughter, the one who was very nearly born a boy.

Daphne wakes early and feels her whole being expand with a sense of freedom. Each summer, Daddy takes a house in the country and this year they are at Slyfield Manor, a Tudor mansion filled with stories. Outside, the lawns and woods and fields are waiting for her. 'She's a different child in the country,' she hears Nanny telling Mummy. And today, best of all, not only will Daddy be coming down for the weekend, but her cousins will also be arriving with Uncle Jim.

No one else is awake, though the sun is streaming through the gap in the curtains. She can't bear to be inside for a moment longer. She creeps down the stairs, past oil paintings of men in flowing wigs, silk and ruffles. She's a Cavalier spying out Roundheads, trying to escape the house unseen.

Outside, her summer sandals flapping, her dressing gown a cloak, she picks up a stick from beneath the cedar tree, flies around the lawn with her sword. This is how she will lead Nico and Michael through the woods, pirates together, stalking the enemy.

Daddy arrives after lunch with two pretty actresses in large hats and gauzy dresses. A look of tightness in Mummy's face. Daphne's seen that look before, when she's been naughty.

'Thought the air here would do the girls some good,' says Daddy as he kisses Mummy's cheek.

'You might have warned me, Gerald,' says Muriel, glancing over at the girls' tight yet bosomy dresses. 'They'll have to share a room.'

In the quiet of the afternoon, the adults overcome by the summer heat and half-asleep in deckchairs, she finally hears the puttering of a car engine, a sound of scrunched gravel. Running round to the front of the house she sees a brand-new open-top Rolls-Royce in front of the house, the boys and Jim stacked up inside like skittles in a box. They get out, stretching, George towering over Uncle Jim. The cousins are wearing white flannels and cricket sweaters. Uncle Jim a white linen safari suit, a jaunty cricket hat, his droopy moustache covering a small pointed chin. He thanks Daphne for coming to greet them, as if she's a grown-up.

While the adults are served champagne in coupe glasses, Daphne asks Michael and Nico if they would like to play pirates in the woods. Tells them she has found them all swords from beneath the cedar tree. She'll be Peter.

'Sorry, Daphne, we grew out of that guff ages ago,' says Michael apologetically. A sweet smile in a neat oval face. He climbs up into the swaying branches of the great cedar and settles there, looking out over the garden.

Peter wanders off to the library where he'll stay all day, looking at books without pictures, one leg over the side of an armchair.

Overcome with disappointment, Daphne feels her eyes prickle. She'll never be there with the Lost Boys in the castaway woods. They've gone and didn't wait for her.

Nico shrugs. 'I'll play with you,' he says with a cheerful, buck-toothed smile. He follows her through the woods, supposedly looking for a crocodile around the edges of the pond, beating at the reeds with their sticks, but he's clearly bored, acting like a grown-up playing with a child, she realizes, which stings. And he's famished, he says. They go back in through the kitchen, sidle into the dim coolness of the larder and munch the gritty seed cake and drink the tart raspberry cordial. They can hear the boys' old Nanny Hodges talking with Daphne's Nurse at the kitchen table. The chink of teacups. Daphne's not sure if they should be listening in.

'It's Michael who's the delicate one, I'd say. Needs watching over closely.'

'A bad chest?'

'That yes, but the real worry is how he's plagued by terrible nightmares,' says Nanny Hodges, lowering her voice. 'Mr Jim will insist on filling their heads with the sort of nonsense that's just not suitable for children. He's not a man who understands what's good for a child.'

Nanny pours more tea.

'But he's so devoted to them.'

Nanny Hodges huffs. 'Those boys go out to dine at the Savoy with him all the time. Even Nico. Imagine. No idea of the real world.'

Daphne hears her nurse sniff disapprovingly. 'There's them who have money to burn. . .'

Nico disappears when the cake is gone. Daphne creeps back outside and finds Uncle Jim sitting alone in a deckchair, writing in his notebook.

He looks up, stops writing when he sees her. Smiles his wry smile. 'You look like look someone in need of company.' He takes her by the hand and they walk towards the edge of the gardens where the woods begin. He starts a captivating story: a girl who knew that she was really a pirate.

'Would you like to see my favourite place?' Daphne says in a whisper. 'Where I pretend I'm Peter Pan in Neverland.'

'Oh, I think you do more than pretend, my little Daphne.'

They reach an oval disk of muddy water reflecting the sombre browns and dull greens of the encroaching trees. Tangled roots and branches overhang the water. Seeing it through Uncle Jim's eyes, Daphne feels disappointed for her magic lake. But Uncle Jim nods approvingly.

'Yes. It would have been very like this, the lake in Neverland.'

'It's a shame there's no island in the middle, though.'

'I think there is,' he says slowly in his quiet lilt. 'If you half-shut your eyes now, there, can't you see it, your own island, ever so slowly, rising from the water?'

After a moment, she nods.

'And if you concentrate, but not too hard mind, can't you make out people there, little figures, growing clearer?' His Scots accent sounds even more sing-song that usual, slow and soporific.

'I think can. Uncle Jim, I can see them. And look, it's me there.'

'There you are indeed. You see, little Daphne, any time you like, you can half-close your eyes, think about the water in that drowsy way, and sooner or later your island will appear. It's a secret very few people know.'

Feeling happy, she walks back across the lawns towards the house, still holding Uncle Jim's hand.

'Uncle Jim, when I grow up, do you think I can write stories like you do, all day long?'

He nods, as if thinking carefully about what she had said. 'I'm sure you can. You know, your grandfather George du Maurier wrote books. He wrote a story about mesmerism that was very famous in its day.'

'What's mesmerism?'

'A sort of magic spell that grown-ups practise. '

'And he wrote stories in books?'

'Oh yes. And it wouldn't surprise me one bit if you'd inherited the special du Maurier gift from him. But we won't tell anyone else. They'd be jealous.'

At night, Slyfield Manor is a more worrying place. The wooden corridors and bedrooms crack and stir with the footsteps of figures that walk out of the oil paintings and into Daphne's dreams.

In the middle of the night she's startled awake, someone shouting. A thin boyish voice filled with alarm. Her heart jumping, she goes out on to the landing. A slender white figure is standing at the top of the stairs, waving an arm to and fro, as if holding a sword. It's Michael, shouting at ghosts again. She startles to see a little goblin nearby in the dark, eyes hollowed out, a white forehead. It's only Uncle Jim, she realizes. He tiptoes over to her in the darkness. Whispers to her that they mustn't wake Michael because he's sleepwalking.

'You won't get me,' Michael cries out, his eyes open and glassy. He screams and Daphne jumps. 'Water's rising.' He slashes the dark air with his imaginary sword. 'Can't breathe. Let go. They're pulling me down.'

Peter comes out. He and Uncle Jim take hold of Michael gently, slowly lead him back to his room, a small jabbering ghost.

'You should go back to bed,' Peter whispers.

The next morning, Daphne wonders if she dreamed it all. But when she peeps into Michael's room she sees Uncle Jim in his dressing gown, sitting in the armchair by the bed as if he has been there all night, which, she realizes, he has.

Michael stirs. Lifts his head up and sees Uncle Jim reading the newspaper as if all was perfectly normal.

'Was I at it again then?' he asks.

''Fraid so.'

'What am I going to do when I go to Eton?' asks Michael.

'I shall send you a letter every day that will be so boring, you will read it and sleep like a top.'

'Thank you, Uncle Jim. I'll write back to you.'

When Michael comes down to breakfast, his heart-shaped face is the colour of chalk, dark shadows beneath his grey eyes. Michael reminds Daphne of the photo in a silver frame at home, of the boys' mother, Sylvia, who died the year Daphne was born, the same small pointed face and dark hair, the same half-dreaming expression with its suggestion of a secret world.

Michael asks the maid for toast and jam, but Jim says he should have bacon and a boiled egg first, which Michael sits and stares at, barely touches. Sighing, Jim slides the bacon on to his own plate and pushes the jam and toast towards Michael.

Most of the day is given over to cricket, everyone roped in except Mummy, even the two actresses who spend a lot of time applauding George – though all the Davies boys are excellent at cricket. It's a very hot day. As the heat mounts, Daddy suggests a swim for the young people in the pool.

Daphne can feel the squish of mud between her toes, the sticks and the debris that have fallen from the trees and sunk to the bottom as she wades tentatively into cool water the colour of stewed tea. Daddy helps her swim, holding her as she kicks her legs and soaks him, both laughing.

'Aren't you coming in, old boy?' Daddy shouts towards the bank.

Daphne looks back and sees Michael clutching his knees. Still in his cricket whites.

'I can give you a lesson. Look, even Daphne's almost swimming.'

But Michael won't be persuaded. He shakes his head. The next time Daphne looks, Michael is gone.

CHAPTER 2

STANWAY HOUSE 1920

It should have been a glorious day, deep-blue sky with butterflies appearing and disappearing, the smell of cut grass mixing with the warm air, but fourteen-year-old Daphne sits confined to a deckchair next to Angela, Jeanne and Mummy, watching Nico and his Eton friends rush up and down in their white trousers, white shirts sleeves rolled up, the thrilling crack of the ball on the bat. Across the field, the small figure of Jim sitting on a shooting stick, umpiring the match.

Daphne is rather good at cricket, but she isn't allowed to join in with the boys today, with all Nico's friends from Eton. Being a girl, Daphne is beginning to realize, is simply a set of betrayals.

Not only that, but she and Angela have to wear stockings and heels for the weekend, which puts a damper on being invited somewhere as grand as the Asquiths' Tudor mansion, the sort of house that Daphne would have loved to wander around as a child, back when each morning held a hundred possibilities of magic.

There's a shout and people stand to clap.

Cynthia announces that tea is ready. The boys begin to pick up their sweaters and head for the honey-stone gables and chimneys of Stanway House. The ladies and girls follow.

There's a small car parked in front of the entrance. Jim's face lights up with a hopeful joy. Michael is standing next to the car. Another boy by his side, tall, a pleasant face. 'You remember Rupert, Uncle Jim?'

'It's a wonderful car, Sir Jim.'

Jim gives him a curt nod, turns away to speak to Michael. 'Well, what do you think? Should make it easier to get home at the weekend.'

'She's beautiful, Uncle Jim.'

As Michael unloads a bag from the boot, Daphne runs round to give him a hug.

'Hello, cousin.'

'I didn't think you were coming this weekend.'

'Don't tell Jim yet, but we won't be staying long. We're motoring down to Dorset in the morning.'

After supper they play a game that Jim has invented, a cross between shuffle penny and ping-pong. Daphne notices that Jim and Michael have disappeared. She leaves the boisterous noise of the games and creeps away to explore the passages and rooms of the house. She hears familiar voices coming from the library.

'Art and music are good as hobbies, Michael, but you need a solid degree.'

'But art and music are the only things that make life worth living, Jim. I don't expect you to understand but—'

'Yes, yes, I know I'm a Philistine when it comes to such things, a dull old wordsmith, but I can't let you throw it all up to go to Paris and paint. Oxford opens doors. You could be anything, Michael. I was going to tell you later, but I may as well tell you now. I've put a small house in your name, a cottage really, near Oxford. It's yours. And with the car you can use it as much as you like to get away from Oxford at the weekends. If you're at Oxford. Don't say anything now. It's getting late. We can talk about it in the morning.'

'I meant to say, sorry. Rupert and I will be off first thing. We're driving down to Dorset.'

'You're leaving?'

There's a tone of desperation in Jim's voice that makes Daphne feel that she shouldn't be listening.

In the morning, they stand on the steps and wave Michael and Rupert off. She notices that Jim has not spoken one more word to Michael's friend since he arrived. Walked past him as if he didn't exist. As with most of Michael's friends. Which is puzzling, and a very odd way for a grown-up to behave.

The following year, as spring is about to become summer, fifteen-year-old Daphne and ten-year-old Jeanne have developed a craze for playing cricket in the garden, wearing shorts and shirts. They are, Daphne says, two schoolboys at Harrow, Eric and David. One day they will go to university and then out into the world. They're good at everything, could go anywhere they like – being boys.

The windows of the house are open in the warm air, the clack of the ball on the bat, Daphne running backwards to catch it. Suddenly, they hear a bellowing from the drawing-room window. Daddy. An anguished sound that breaks the air in two. They race to the house in alarm. Find Daddy sitting by the phone, head in hands.

Michael is dead. Drowned in Sanford Pool.

'That man,' moans Daddy. 'I should never have left the boys, my own nephews, with that man.'

CHAPTER 3

HAMPSTEAD 1926

Early morning in the loft above the garage at the bottom of the garden. Daphne had claimed the little attic as her own after she got back from finishing school in Paris. She loved the quiet around her, a few watery notes from a blackbird outside, the scratch of her pen on the paper. She even loved the ink's chemical smell, mixed in as it was with a faint whiff of rubber shoes since the loft was used as a changing room in summer for tennis parties. In front of her, a slim notebook with green leather covers and marbled endpapers. 'To write whatever you want,' Jim had said as she had flicked through the blank pages. 'With as many crossings-out as you want. One must be brutal.'

She certainly had plenty of crossings-out.

She hadn't told Daddy whom the notebook came from. She never told Daddy when she was going out to meet dear old Uncle Jim for tea any more, pretending she was going shopping. Ever since the telegram came with the news that had broken everybody's hearts, almost killed Uncle Jim, Daddy had forbidden the girls from seeing Jim on their own – as if the tragedy of Michael's drowning was somehow contagious.

Daddy and Peter had supported Jim through the worst times, but ever since Michael died, Daddy had tried to pull away from Uncle Jim.

Daddy had set up his own theatre company as an actor manager, refused to work for Uncle Jim any more, although after a few years, the company struggling, Daddy had had to go back and ask if he could put on one of Jim's plays. With a Barrie smash hit in production, Daddy soon went back to making as much money as before. But it still wasn't like the old days, with Jim popping in cheerfully after rehearsals.

Daddy kept Jim at arm's length, for reasons Daphne couldn't quite understand.

Poor Uncle Jim, so broken since the loss of Michael, an old man overnight. She sneaked out regularly to have teas with him.

She'd always counted Uncle Jim as one of her dearest friends. He gave her advice and encouragement, the only one who understood that she had to write.

She needed to talk to him now about a new story she'd begun brewing, set among Daddy's theatre people. They came for lunch and champagne every Sunday. A glamorous set, filled with sparkling gossip about each other, but if you listened in to what they were actually saying, their affairs and the secrets, it all seemed rather sordid and shabby. Of course, she wouldn't describe anyone by name. Imagine the scandal. As Uncle Jim had said, the trick was to use real people more as a kind of hook upon which one could hang one's imagined version of them.

She heard footsteps on the wooden stairs leading up from the garden. Angela came in.

'Mummy's taking us to Selfridges. Says she wants to make an early start.'

Daphne groaned. 'Why is it that every time I sit down to write someone has to come and drag me away?'

'Well, thank you. I for one think it's rather pleasant to go to Selfridges to buy new dresses for my debutante ball,' said Angela in mock offence.

'Sorry, Piffy. You're right. But honestly, is it a sin for a du Maurier to not want to join in everything? All I hear is, "What's wrong with Daphne, always wanting to be alone. . ."'

'You always did spend your day in one of those terrific daydreams as a child, making us all act it out. Those plasticine pustules for the bubonic plague. Shame one has to grow up, old thing.'

Jammed in between Mummy and Angela in the back of the Packard, Daphne stared at the traffic ahead. She knew Angela was right: most girls would be more than grateful to go to Oxford Street and buy all the dresses they wanted, to live in a splendid Georgian pile in Hampstead, go to balls at Claridge's, but lately Daphne had begun to wake in the night gasping for breath, a feeling of being swaddled with layers of thick black cloth – with no escape from the path set out by one's very Edwardian mother, days filled with girdles and garters, with tight hats and tight shoes, and with dull conversations with dull people, until she got engaged and married to someone suitable and had to spend her days worrying about whether the bacon at breakfast was overdone or if her husband had enough collar studs.

An anguished cry of 'Stop!' came from Mummy. The car braked and Daphne slid forward in her seat. Mummy was staring out of the side window, her beaded bag clutched in both hands as if it might save her. Daphne followed her gaze, felt her cheeks flush.

Across the road was a white stucco house that she knew belonged to Daddy's latest leading lady, a rather fun and pretty actress called Maude Acre. In front of the house was parked Daddy's unmistakable maroon car– at nine-thirty in the morning. Clearly it had been there all night. Daddy might as well have put up a giant noticeboard declaring his latest affair.

Daphne looked away. It was horribly embarrassing. Of course, Daddy's string of girlfriends was an open secret, but all was well and stayed well so long as Mummy was allowed to act as though she knew nothing. Gerald would come home to his darling wife after the evening performance – unless there was something he had to sort out since he was not only the leading actor but also the director – and Mummy would be waiting in her Japanese housecoat to cook him his favourite bacon and eggs. Gerald never stopped declaring, loudly and often, how dearest Muriel was his everything. How he'd be lost without her. Adored her.

'Should I park here, Lady du Maurier?' Allan the driver asked, looking at her enquiringly in the rear-view mirror.

'We'll carry on, thank you, Allan,' Mummy's voice icily calm.

At Selfridges Mummy swept through the doors, stoutly elegant in her embroidered linen coat and wide-brimmed hat, Angela and Daphne following behind, pulling alarmed faces at each other.

Mummy took shopping very seriously. Elegance such as Lady du Maurier's did not simply happen. Seated on a silk sofa in the ladies' dressing room she looked critically at Daphne who was standing in front of a floor-length mirror in an under-slip, a blue velvet dress in one hand and a black shantung jacket and trousers in the other.

'Daphne, you simply can't wear trousers to a coming-out do at Claridge's.'

Daphne held the blue dress under her chin once again, staring glumly at her reflection. The sales assistant put her hands together and gave a bright smile.

'The dress does work very well with Miss du Maurier's fair hair and blue eyes.' She took her tape measure and nipped it around Daphne's waist. 'Especially since one is so slim. One could even consider a smaller size since it is the latest fashion to have a boyish figure.'

While Mummy consulted with the sales girl, Daphne took the chance to hold up the black satin suit once more, her small, square chin defiant. If she shingled her hair in that daring new way, then she'd be a blonde version of the deliciously dangerous actress, Molly Kerr.

She heard a loud sniff of disapproval behind her, turned to see Mummy's cold stare.

'The velvet dress will be lovely. Thank you, Mummy,' said Daphne, stifling a sigh.

Angela came out from the fitting room, a sturdy meringue in a cream satin dress, her dark hair dishevelled from trying on so many frocks.

'What do you think? I hate it. Do you think it will do?'

'Definitely the nicest yet,' said Mummy. 'With a few tweaks, I think it will do very well.'

'They'll all want to dance with Daphne anyway.' No bitterness, just a statement of fact.

'Nonsense,' said Daphne, though she had noticed the need to steer boys towards Angela at parties. 'You're the one who knows how to get on with people. No one sweeter than you.'

Another hour trailing around Selfridges – Daddy needed ties, socks. Then coffee and cake in the hum of the tearooms before the boxes were piled into the car.

When they passed Maud Acre's house, Daddy's car was gone.

Mummy went straight to her room with a migraine. She came down later to have supper with the three girls, looking older and strained.

Usually Daphne was completely on Daddy's side, but lately she had begun to feel a conflict in her loyalties, let down by him for hurting Mummy in this shabby, careless way. If only she could say something to make Mummy see that she understood how hard it must be.

'I think,' Daphne began as the soup was served, 'that if people were simply honest instead of pretending. . . I mean, the way that Daddy behaves, I think—'

Daphne jumped as Mummy banged the table with both hands.

'Don't ever speak about things you know nothing about.' Daphne had never seen Mummy so furious, such cold hate in her eyes. Her mother swept out of the room.

Angela rolled her eyes. Jeanne, Mummy's pet, stared down at her plate, pushed a long plait behind her shoulder, then got up. 'I'd better go and see if Mummy's all right.'

Feeling for ever destined to say the wrong thing when it came to Mummy, Daphne escaped back to her loft above the garage. She sat down at the table, too unsettled to write. She had thought she was long used to Mummy not liking her particularly, always shrugged it off, and yet if you prodded there was always that gap in her soul that felt sore and empty – a lack that even Daddy's outright adoration for his favourite girl couldn't fill.

She shook her head, wrote a short paragraph. Read it back. The writing seemed stilted and puerile. Put a line through everything she'd written.

The truth was that she couldn't begin to write when she felt so angry with Mummy. How could Mummy bear to collude with Daddy's secrets like that, pretending not to see – as if Mummy had made her whole life about Gerald and what Gerald needed? His welfare the only thing that filled her head. Daphne was never going to end up like that.

And to think that Mummy had once had her own career as an actress – until she and Daddy were stranded together on a desert island, night after night plus matinees, in one of Uncle Jim's plays, *The Admirable Crichton*. You could say that Jim had scripted her parents to fall in love beneath the bright stage lights, Gerald with his boyish face and expressive blue eyes, pink-cheeked Muriel with her sweet smile and cloud of blonde hair. A year later they were married. Another year and Angela was born, Uncle Jim her godfather. Then Daphne, then Jeanne had arrived.

But now, when Daphne looked at the photograph of Mummy as a young woman in a silk dress, staring directly into the camera with an impish smile, it was hard to believe this was the same woman. Where had that confident young actress gone? Was it a rule that a woman must be subsumed by marriage, even when they married someone as lovely as Daddy?

Daphne already knew that she was never going to get married. She fully intended to keep her freedom and write as much as wanted, undisturbed. But here was the conundrum: to be left alone enough to write, then she needed to make her own money, but the only way she could see for her to earn enough money herself was to be published. A real author, earning like a man did. Yet here she was with another day gone by and she'd written nothing worth keeping.

Of course, the allowance from Daddy was generous, but it came with strings. She couldn't face ending up like Angela, always running out of money at the end of the month and worrying what Mummy would think about what she had spent it on.

It was getting chilly. And late. They'd want to know where she was. She walked back up the garden to the house. Most of its nineteen windows were in darkness, but there were still lights on downstairs. Slipping in the side door she heard music coming from the drawing room. Someone was playing 'Charmaine' on the gramophone, the sultry French version, suffused with longing and romance. *'Charmaine, le plus beau roman de ma vie'* – Charmaine, the most beautiful story I've ever read.

She peeped around the door. Daddy was dancing with some invisible partner, eyes closed, a glass of whisky raised in one hand. He wore his silk Gieves & Hawkes pyjamas and a long, holey cashmere cardigan purloined from Muriel as a dressing gown. Daddy was a matinee idol but he never took himself too seriously, always elegantly dressed but with some odd, quirky detail, a canary-yellow handkerchief or a holey jumper. At fifty, he was slim as ever, the same wide forehead and high cheekbones, but when, she realized with a pang, had his hair got so grey and thin, his lips become fleshy and blurred?

And when had she started to find Daddy's behaviour rather weak and quite frankly squalid with his secret girlfriends? It had all seemed so funny when she was younger, the way he joked about his stable of actresses from whatever play he was doing – back when she had thought her darling Daddy could do no wrong.

And there was something else that rankled. She and Daddy had always been close, but of late he had become embarrassingly possessive, hanging on to her hand at parties, his arm heavy around her shoulders as she tried to supress an urge to wriggle away.

And was it normal that he should still want to know everything she did – when she was almost twenty? Whenever

Allan drove her and Angela home from some party that she hadn't particularly wanted to go to in the first place Daddy would wait up to quiz them. Where had they been? Who had they danced with? Had they kissed anyone? Sometimes, Daddy could get so angry with his ridiculous accusations that she barely recognized him.

She'd begun to tell Daddy less and less about what she was really thinking. As had Angela.

It must be nice, it occurred to her as she tiptoed past the doorway and up the stairs, to have a mother one could talk to about how very confusing life was for a girl in these modern times.

Up in her bedroom, she took out a photograph. A black-and-white portrait of an actress, the divine Molly Kerr, dark hair shingled around her delicate skull, a satin tuxedo, a diamond starburst on the lapel, a cigarette held in a long holder. It was signed, *with love to Daphne.* Daphne opened the note that had come with it, feeling that tingle of excitement once again.

Darling Daphs, Thrilled you came to see the play. And flowers! Our picnic in Richmond Park yesterday was heavenly. Sending kisses – and in a trance now thinking of you, your own Molly Kerr.

As she sat down at the dressing table, the scents and sounds of that afternoon came back to her, the bluebells she had picked for Molly, Molly's dark red lips. They'd spent a long afternoon in the hot sun, lying together on a picnic rug in a clearing of crushed bracken, hidden away from prying eyes, sharing egg sandwiches and a bottle of wine, the smoothness of Molly's cheek against her lips, a heady smell of blackberries and of the musky scent that Molly wore. She'd seen it all as if she were floating above, chuckling at their daring.

She turned over Molly's note and began to write a poem on the back, looking up from time to time to see her blue eyes and fair hair in the mirror, the gold knitted rayon dress, the slender shoulders that Molly had so praised.

A knock on the door made her jump. Daddy came in.

She quickly slid the note and photo under the embroidered runner and placed a hairbrush on top.

'Thought I'd come and say goodnight.' He walked around the room, picking up a figurine from the mantelpiece, straightening a candlestick.

Daphne noticed a corner of Molly's photo still sticking out from beneath the linen runner. She placed a hand over it as casually as she could.

'You must be awfully tired though, Daddy darling, with such a long run of *The Ringer*. I know I'm ready to turn in.' She yawned.

He carried on with his tour, peered at a painting of Paris, coming to stand next to the dressing table where her hand covered the photo. She stiffened, felt her heart starting to jump in her chest.

If he found the letter?

He went back to the picture of Paris. 'You're so like me, Daphne. We both love the old city,' he sighed. 'And just like Grandpa.' He turned to her. 'You always did understand me best. We're made of the same stuff, aren't we, darling one?'

'Of course, Daddy. We are.'

He came over and kissed her forehead. Cigarettes, whisky and sandalwood cologne, the smell that had always meant comfort and reassurance – and she did love Daddy as much as ever, but he was stifling her. She held her breath. Exhaled with relief when he went out and pulled the door shut behind him.

It took a while for her heart to stop beating so fast. Daddy could never find out about Molly. Molly stood for everything Daddy despised. She'd starred in one of Noël Coward's plays, the new actor and playwright who was taking the West End by storm, just as the reviewers were beginning to say Daddy's plays were old fashioned. 'What do they want?' Daddy fumed. 'For me to bring the filth of a sewer to the stage like Coward does, with blatantly open hints of men falling in love with men? The man's ruining the theatre.'

If Daddy found out about her and Molly he'd probably burst into flames.

She pushed the photo and letter securely under the linen runner, meaning to put them away in her desk in the morning.

She lay in bed, still smarting with anger. Sometimes she felt like a half-formed creature in a chrysalis, damp wings pressing against dry walls, waiting to unfurl and find who she was meant to be – a creature that wanted to answer the wild notes that she heard in secret at night.

It wasn't until late the next day, taking off her hat in front of her dressing-table mirror – Mummy had got tickets for Wimbledon – that Daphne realized that the note and the photo were gone.

Horrified, she took everything off the dressing table, all her creams and silver-backed brushes, shook out the linen runner. Nothing. Had she moved them? With a mounting panic, she turned out drawers, emptied her writing desk. She sat back on her heels in front of the last ransacked cupboard.

They were gone. She thought of Dora the maid with her disapproving expression. More or less a spy for Mummy. What if Dora had found them and given them to Mummy who would then show them to Daddy? He would be incandescent.

She couldn't eat a thing at breakfast next morning, her stomach tight. There was no sign of Daddy or Mummy all day, Daddy at rehearsals, Mummy on errands somewhere. She took herself off to work in the attic room and had almost convinced herself that she was worrying about nothing as she changed for dinner when Dora knocked on the door. Her parents would like to see her in the dining room before supper. She felt her stomach drop. Walked slowly along the corridor as if to the gallows.

Mummy and Daddy were seated together at the long oak table beneath a portrait of Charles I – painted shortly before he was beheaded. The photograph and letter were spread out on the polished Georgian table. For once, Daphne knew she could expect no help from Daddy.

Did Daphne realize, he thundered, that once a girl's reputation is gone, it's gone for ever? Mummy silent by his side, her plump face an icy mask. Did Daphne not realize how much her parents loved and cared about her? he carried on. There were going to be rules from now on. She was to tell them exactly whom she was going out to see. She was to be home by ten. In fact, she was not to go out at all, not for days, for weeks, not until she had shown that she could be trusted.

She went back to her room, smarting. Wriggled out of the linen dress with its panels of embroidery, peeled off her stockings and threw her itchy garters on the dressing table. Sat in her under-slip by the open window, gulping in the night air with its tang of London soot, a hint of the climbing jasmine on the wall of the house below. In the distance, the glow of the town. She needed to be out there, living on her own terms, finding out what life was really about, writing stories that would burrow down to the heart of people, shocking and real.

Which all came back to money, her own income – and that meant her stories published and paid for.

She went to her drawer and took out some pages she'd typed a few weeks earlier, an odd enough little story about a man who can only fall in love with a soulless, mechanical doll.

Before she could lose her courage, she folded it inside an envelope and wrote the address of a literary agent, A. P. Watt, on the front, along with a quick note to introduce herself. She went down to the hallway, slid it beneath the letters on the silver salver waiting to be posted in the morning and went up to bed feeling as though she had achieved something decisive.

Nothing she could do now but wait for bad news, she told herself – hoping, with a tingle of excitement, that she might hear quite the opposite. Saw herself going to see Uncle Jim in his flat to tell him the good news. Or to receive his commiserations.

CHAPTER 4

HAMPSTEAD 1927

'Isn't this nice,' Gerald said one evening after supper as he poured Daphne a glass of port and one for himself. Just the two of them left at the table. Daddy hated quarrels. He'd been especially nice these past few days, wanting to smooth things over. He lit a cigarette. 'You see, the thing I ask myself is what is it that you want from life, darling Daphne? What is it that makes you so unsettled?'

She sipped the sweet liquid, half-shook her head. 'I don't know. It's as if there's something I can feel is out there. Something I need to discover. Perhaps if I lived somewhere else, in Paris perhaps, like Grandpa did. Or I could join Doodie's cousin in South Africa, on his farm.'

'Africa. I see. That's a long way away from us here.'

She went up to bed, leaving Daddy alone at the table, swirling his glass of port as if pondering some unsolved question.

The following week, Gerald had an announcement. 'What this family needs,' he said, 'is a holiday place by the sea. After all, Grandpa George used to take us all to Whitby for the entire summer every year. *The Ringer*'s done so well we can easily afford it – if Mummy doesn't mind looking for somewhere, since I'm tied up with rehearsals. You girls can go too. I was thinking the Cornish coast.'

Daphne was in no mood to go on a tour of the West Country with Mummy and Angela. She needed to be at home in case a reply came from the literary agent. What if they replied to confirm that there was no hope? What if she was nothing but a talentless amateur with a compunction to scribble down words for hours?

She sat in the back of the car feeling slightly nauseous as Allan drove along narrow roads buried deep between fat hedges. Angela had already stopped them twice to be sick. The car rounded a bend and began a steep descent and at the same moment the hedges opened out into an expansive view of jade water. Fowey Estuary. The car stopped at the foot of the hill to wait for the ferry to Fowey. Daphne got out of the car. The wind was alive with the cries of seagulls, a thin layer of bright cloud moving apart to reveal a dazzling blue sky. On the far bank Fowey's grey cottages looked like a Breton village, the crenulations of a small castle, a church tower in grey granite, mysterious wooden gibbets and boatyard cranes along the waterfront, an old three-masted barque in for repair. The river was filled with life, small rowing boats, fishing vessels with brown sails, large ships sailing upriver to the china-clay wharves or setting out to sea, gulls swooping and crying.

Hands on her hips, her thick blonde hair combed by the breeze, Daphne felt a rising excitement bubbling up. A recognition. Here. This was the place.

Mummy was looking across the water with a frown. The ferry, a flat wooden boat with two men sculling long oars, had just left.

'It will be an hour before it's back,' she sighed. 'Might as well try to find somewhere for lunch here.' As they set off up the hill towards the Bodinnick Inn, Angela pointed out a *For Sale* sign fixed to a wall by the ferry. Beyond it they could see a stone building with a protruding upper storey made of wood, like an alpine cottage.

'Oh yes, the old boatyard's for sale,' the publican told them as he brought over pie and mashed potato. 'We call it the Swiss Cottage. I've got the key if you want to have a look.'

Tall wooden gates pushed open to reveal an abandoned stone boathouse, a third storey made of wood protruding out over the water. It was partly built into the cliff, steps and stairs leading to the steep terraced gardens. On the ground floor, a long room with mysterious boatbuilder's tools still hung along one wall. Upstairs, a loft, a brown sail still trailing from one of the poles. The top floor had been living quarters, a wood-burning stove, a dusty table and a broken chair.

Daphne leaned from the window of the overhanging room and took in the wide water. A great ship with a tar-black funnel was passing only a few hundred yards away. The air filled with scents of rope and salt. With a strange, rising feeling of excitement, Daphne knew that if she could stay here and write, she would be able to begin in earnest.

Angela came to join her, her curly dark hair tousled, a streak of dust down the side of her sleeve, smiling broadly. 'What do you think? Isn't it fun?'

'I absolutely love it.'

'Enough to stop you leaving for South Africa or for France? You do know that's what's behind Daddy insisting we need a place in the country – because of how delicate Daphne is.'

'Delicate being code for badly behaved. I know.' They clomped down the wooden steps to the gardens and stood at the top of the slipway leading down to the water.

'All the same, you really did have pneumonia last winter, in that draughty old finishing school in Paris. Mummy does care about you, you know. Cares about all of us, in her own way.'

There it was, the bond that Daphne and Angela shared. All their mother's love went to Jeanne, the baby of the family, and to Daddy of course. Affection for Daphne and Angela had to come from various nannies and governesses who tended to disappear without warning – and from each other.

Mummy had completed her inspection. Daphne prepared herself for disappointment as she watched Mummy picking her way across the planks and lobster pots left in the garden.

'If this is to be our summer cottage,' her mother said, threading her arm through Angela's and Daphne's in a way that was surprising but rather pleasant, 'then we must change the name. Swiss Cottage sounds far too like that dreary underground station. What if we called it Ferryside? I think we could make something very special here. If they'll sell it to us.'

*

By summer the house had been transformed. Where there had once been a boat shed there was now an elegant sitting room with linen-covered sofas and simple antique furniture in keeping with the atmosphere of the place. In the long sitting room, a row of arched windows looking over the Fowey Estuary.

Daphne's bedroom was on the top floor, a corner room overhanging the sea. She loved to sit at her desk in the window, the light from the water moving around the room with the hour and tides, the feel of accumulated history that resonated in the walls and in the weather-beaten boards.

Each morning she set out to walk for miles along old byways through ancient woods, following green tunnels where the trees met overhead, noticing the rich array of plants, honeysuckle and foxgloves, the wind moving in the trees. Or she walked along the cliffs and bays, absorbing the quality of the light and the colours of the sea. She found a new sense of peace in immersing herself in the landscape, trying to find the words to capture what she saw, the sounds and the light and the scents.

Early in the morning she loved to row across the estuary and walk through the narrow, winding streets of Fowey before any brash tourists arrived, buying a loaf of warm brown bread from the baker's. 'That'll be sixpence, Daphne, me dear.' She learned the fishermen's names along the wharf and would sit and chat with them, listening to the cadence of their Cornish speech and learning about their lives.

Here, she wrote to Daddy, was the freedom she had longed for, to walk and to think, to write and to discover who she was.

Dressed in shorts and shirt, she learned to sail with old John Adams who owned the boatyard that was going to be looking after Daddy's new boat when it arrived. She loved the wind and spray on her face, proud to show John Adams that she could tack into choppy water and manage the heavy canvas sails by herself. *This London girl*, she wrote to Daddy, *cares only for fishing and for pollock and mackerel brought home by the bucketload.*

At evening, dressed in waders and a seaman's jumper, she went with John Adams to catch eight-foot-long conger eels, a sou'wester on her head and a fearsome grappling hook in her hand.

All the while Daphne had been looking out for a reply from the literary agent, trying not to think about it too much but rifling through the mail that was forwarded from London each day. When the letter with their address on the back finally came, she took it out into the strip of garden overlooking the water, imagining the worst.

It was neither good news nor bad news. They did not feel able to represent her, but they thought she showed talent. They said that she should keep working and try again. She was disappointed, but more determined than ever to prove to them that she really could write.

There was a more pressing matter to worry about, however, over the following days. Daddy was finally coming down to see the house. She had clear memories of Daddy altering holiday plans and insisting they all return home because he had found his hotel room unsatisfactory, or the resort they were staying in too dull. Going on holiday with Gerald had always been a military operation for Mummy, with his aftershave and bath salts and row of favourite suits and shoes, his binoculars for birdwatching, his hats, a pile of books, with added magazines from the railway stand and bars of Fry's chocolate. What if Daddy decided he didn't like Ferryside, that they would have the house for just one season, sell it to some other family?

But Mummy had arranged everything just as Daddy might like it. As he walked in, he found his binoculars hanging by the door, his walking sticks nearby in a Chinese pot. The oil painting of the three girls as children with blue silk ribbons and white dresses faced him across the sitting room. Around the walls were framed prints from Grandpa's *Punch* cartoons

They sat on deckchairs on the slip of garden overlooking the water, a smell of rust and pond water, the estuary in front of them a theatre of fishing boats and ships. Would Daddy think it too busy? Too near the water? Daphne, in a dress for once, the stray Westie she had adopted by her side, waiting for a clue from Daddy, while Mummy supervised a large picnic of sandwiches with thick-cut ham and mustard, split scones and clotted cream with jam.

'I have to say, Muriel,' he began, 'you girls have found the perfect spot.'

Daphne felt herself breathing out.

That evening Daphne lit a fire of logs that she had chopped herself, a stool for Daddy's feet, a glass of best brandy. She sat on the rug, her arms round her knees, staring into the mesmeric rising and falling of the flames.

'So you've found something you like here?' Daddy asked with a half-smile. 'What is it that you like so much?'

She rocked a little, hugging her knees tight. 'There's space to dream and to think. You can walk for hours. And life seems different here, more open and honest. I've felt at home here since the moment we arrived.'

As September approached and the time came for them to return for Daddy's opening night, Daphne begged to stay on for a few more weeks. She was amazed when Mummy agreed – so long as Angela was willing to keep Daphne company.

The bliss of a quiet house as the two girls took breakfast with the windows wide open, the distant sound of a ship's horn, the warm weather conspiring with the girls to make summer last into October. So much still to explore. Daphne spread a map out on the table.

'Apparently there's a rather mysterious house over towards Gribben Head that's been shut up for years. John Adams says it's so hidden away in the woods that few people have seen it. She pointed to a grey square. 'That must be it. Though it's not clear how one approaches it. Perhaps this path here from Four Turnings through the woods. Should be a nice enough walk.'

'Won't we be trespassing, wandering through someone's gardens?'

Daphne went through to the kitchens to ask Agnes what she knew.

'Menabilly, miss? I hear the house is all closed up. It belongs to the Rashleighs but the heir as owns it lives away in Devon these days.'

'But do you think we could visit the grounds?

'There's no one there to stop you if that's what you mean, though they do say a blue lady looks out of a window upstairs when it gets dark.'

'Ooh, a ghost. How perfect,' said Angela.

They set out under clear skies. Banks of blue mop-headed hydrangeas crowded along the lanes. Reaching Four Turnings they came to a dilapidated gatehouse that they had driven past often but never paid any attention to before. The thatch was thick with moss. Peering through the streaky window, Daphne could see that all furniture was gone.

A broken chain hung down from the rusty gates. Daphne creaked one side open. An overgrown driveway led down to a valley filled with trees. Soon, they entered a dense wood, the path narrowing, shrubs and trees crowding in on each side. Strange specimens planted by Victorian gardeners had been left to grow into vast, twisted giants, their branches twining overhead, hung with creepers and vines. Every so often a great tree lay fallen across the path and they had to scramble over its mossy trunk. Birdsong in the trees.

Daphne felt herself holding her breath as they walked through the ancient and overgrown trees, imagining the people who had once walked this path, almost palpably still present in the damp air. She could almost hear the echo of Victorian coach wheels rumbling by. The muffled clop of a cavalier's horse still reverberating.

And something else, she felt, deeper in the darkness between the trees, watching them, an ancient presence emanating from the wilder parts of the crowded woods. She shivered, half-afraid and yet almost wanting to plunge in and follow it against her better judgement. Calling her in. Once or twice, she glanced around, almost expecting to see something, or somebody, there.

On they went, picking their way through brambles and reeds along the ghost of a path. Still no sign of the house. The light was beginning to fade, a chill rising from the ground with a tang of wet leaf mould. A blackbird semaphored a sudden warning of approaching twilight, making them jump. The path hard to find, the garden shrubs grown into enormous shapes against the twilight, laurel and rhododendrons fifty feet high.

'It's getting dark,' said Angela.

'Just a little further.'

An owl hooted, then others, the woods filled with the eerie calls bringing in the night. With a sudden whoosh one flew across them in the gloom, large and white, disturbing the air.

'I don't like this,' said Angela. 'I think we should go back.'

There was nothing for it but to give up. The path had disappeared in the gathering dark, both before and behind. They found themselves climbing over fallen trunks, slipping down holes, hoping to finally get out of the beastly wood. When they came out on to fields they found themselves much further along than they had expected, with at least three miles to walk before they got home.

They tramped home along the cliff paths, reaching Ferryside at two in the morning.

'Never again,' said Angela, kicking off her walking shoes and rubbing her feet.

Daphne went up to bed filled with the memories of the mysterious woods, vowing to go back and try to find the secretive house the next day. But as they slept a storm blew in with lashing rain. A phone call came from Mummy reminding the girls that they were booked on the sleeper that weekend.

Daphne stared out of the train window as they crossed the River Tamar and Cornwall disappeared from view. In front of them, a winter back in London. How could she feel homesick for a place where she had only lived for a few months?

'Do you think I'd ever be allowed to live at Ferryside all year long?' asked Daphne.

There was no answer. Sitting next to her, Angela was looking worried. She had her own reasons to feel apprehensive about going back. 'Do you think I was right to say yes?' she asked. 'I know Daddy thinks I should play Wendy again, and Uncle Jim is very sweet about the things that went wrong last season, but I can feel the others in the cast thinking I'm a bit plain for the part, wondering why I'm really there, Jim's god-daughter and all that. And I don't know if I can face getting up in that harness for the flying sessions after what happened last time.'

'It wasn't your fault, Piffy. The mechanism broke.'

'And landed me in the orchestra pit. Lucky I didn't break something. Oh God, I feel sick just thinking about it.'

'You'll be marvellous. You've always been the ideal Wendy.' Daphne gave Angela a hug, and Angela nodded, slightly pacified.

But Daphne felt an odd sense of unease as she sat watching the countryside slide away past the train window. She thought of another accident, five years earlier, the quiet waters of Sanford Pool closing over two figures for the last time. When Jim's life had stopped, an old man overnight with the ravaged face of one who never sleeps, waiting out his days in the gloom of his lonely top-floor apartment.

CHAPTER 5

LONDON 1926

Longing to be allowed to return to Cornwall after Christmas, Daphne was on her best behaviour. She helped decorate the tree. She even offered to sit with poor Daddy so that Mummy could go out to run some errands.

He was suffering from one of his nervous depressions and hated to be left alone. Daphne had noticed that these breakdowns often happened at the end of a play, as he came out of the role he had been playing and returned to being Gerald again, a man blinking in a room where the light has suddenly been switched on.

Daphne had an idea that it was also partly related to Maud Acre finally giving up on him – along with the resultant tippling. But this time the despair seemed deeper, more existential. It was heartbreaking to see him shaking and haunted, clinging on to her arm, a hand over his eyes.

'What have I done with my life? Nothing but ephemeral plays that the world will forget one day. Nothing that will last.'

'You're one of the greatest actors of your generation, knighted by the King, Daddy. And you've starred in some of

Jim's greatest plays. You're his favourite actor for a very good reason. Think of *Dear Brutus*.'

'No one understands what Jim takes from your soul with his damned twisted plots.'

However, Daddy was a professional. He pulled himself together for the special performance of *Peter Pan* that was to be held in aid of the charity for orphans of actors that he headed. Transformed by greasepaint, a Charles II wig and a red frock coat, his Hook was magnificent, a sneering Etonian pirate hounded by the ticking of time – and thwarted by Peter Pan out-foxing him at every turn.

In the darkened theatre, watching Daddy play Hook again, Daphne smiled to think of an earlier Christmas performance, sitting in the Royal Box next to Michael and Nico. At four years old she had not been sure if Daddy really had become Hook and, confusingly, also Mr Darling. Uncle Jim would be there in the background as ever, but unseen, hovering just outside the theatre doors, still young and mischievous.

The play had evolved year by year to reach its final version. That year, Uncle Jim had added an exciting new scene where Peter Pan was stranded on an island, the waters rising around him, the mermaids singing him to his watery grave, Peter bravely calling out how it will be a great adventure to die.

Uncle Jim said Michael had helped him write the new scene, which had impressed Daphne greatly.

A sudden memory came back to her now: noticing nine-year-old Michael crying in the dark, cowering behind the seats, hands over his eyes as the waters rose around Peter Pan. There had been a warm salty smell and Daphne had realized with a jolt of shame that Michael had wet his trousers.

And she thought of all the years that had gone by since Michael was lost. Thought of the young man who should have been sitting beside her now, perhaps, Jim no longer so broken and reduced. All the ghosts of people who should have been.

'Of course you can't go back to Ferryside on your own, Daphne,' her mother said as New Year came round. 'The house is shut up for the winter. And whatever would you do?'

'I'd write.'

'But you can do that here.'

How could she explain to Mummy that it was only in Cornwall, in the freedom of the woods and the sea, that she was beginning to find what she wanted to say?

'Daphne, you are coming to the party for the Edgars tonight?' asked Angela. 'So much nicer than going on my own. Please.'

Angela adored parties as much as Daphne hated them. 'Just for you, Piffy. Why not?'

It was a birthday party, held at the Connaught. Daphne stood at the side, refusing partners and watching Angela in her new beaded flapper dresses dance with a succession of interchangeable young men. As the evening wore on she noticed a boy also standing alone, leaning against one of the marble pillars at the edge of the room. He had a long, sensitive face, eyes a little close set in a way that gave his gaze an intriguing intensity. She took her champagne and boldly stood alongside him, gazing out as if watching the dancers.

'You've a button missing,' she nodded to his shirt.

He put a hand to his chest. 'I was hoping no one would notice. Is it really so awful?'

'I think it's sweet. But I'm the last person to worry about clothes, really.'

'You look very nice.'

She shrugged. She was aware that the lilac of her dress made her eyes almost the same shade, that her blonde hair was newly washed and curled around her face.

'I'm Carol Reed, by the way.' He held out his hand. She took it, gave a firm shake. 'Daphne du Maurier.'

He narrowed his eyes. 'The granddaughter of George du Maurier?'

'Indeed. Though most people mention my father, Gerald.'

He became animated. 'My father was Max Beerbohm. He played Svengali in the first stage adaptation of your grandfather's book *Trilby*. We're practically cousins.'

'But you don't go by the name Beerbohm?'

'Born on the wrong side of the blanket, I'm afraid. It's not so bad. Forces one to be a self-made man. Look, I'm sorry, can I get you some punch or a drink of some sort? Or would you like to dance? I'm hopelessly bad at being civilized, as you can see.'

'I'd rather talk. Though perhaps some champagne.' She held out her now empty glass.

He came back, holding two full coupes.

'So what does one do, as a self-made man?'

'I'm working as a lowly runner in a studio, but I want to make my own films one day. Direct them. And you?'

She was rather pleased he didn't assume she did nothing. 'I write. Hoping to get published one day. I've just sent a couple of stories off to the *Bystander*.'

'The *Bystander*'s very good. You must tell me when your stories come out.'

'If they do.'

'They will. I have a feeling.'

The band struck up a jazz foxtrot, 'I'm Sorry Sally', with its crooning trumpets and violins, the plucking beat of a snare drum. Hearing a foxtrot had always made her feel like dancing. She took Carol's hand.

'I can't resist this one. Shall we?'

'I should warn you, I'm not the world's best dancer.'

They joined the swirl going around the floor. Once they had settled into the beat, with Daphne leading, Carol proved a nimble dancer and they flew across the floor, laughing as they turned in circles, holding each other close. A singer in black tails crooning about lost love.

When Angela came to tell her that it was eleven o'clock and Allan was waiting to drive them home, Daphne felt annoyed. She picked up a match book and wrote her telephone number on it, slid it into Carol's top pocket.

Seeing Carol each day became the only thing that made life in London bearable. Neither of them cared a fig about smart clothes or restaurants. They liked to drive out to Limehouse

Docks and linger in steamy greasy-spoon cafés with mugs of dark tea, making up stories about the people they saw around them. Or sit in the upper balcony of the Kit Kat club where the jazz singers' lyrics were thrillingly scandalous. Carol was a dreamer, still a boy at twenty with his buttons missing or a shirt collar fraying, which made one quite want to take care of him.

One spring night they wandered through misty London until late. They climbed up the scaffolding of a half-finished building and sat and talking all night. It wasn't until Daphne noticed a red line growing at the foot of the night sky that she realized it was almost morning.

Carol drove her home as fast as he could, Daphne silent by his side.

'It won't be that bad, will it?' he asked.

'I'm afraid it most probably will.'

Carol dropped her off at Cannon Hall.

'You'd better not stay,' she told him. She could see the lights on in the hall, the curtain twitching. She found Daddy waiting inside in his dressing gown, his eyes puffy, his hair uncombed.

'Daddy, you didn't have to wait up.'

'Like hell I didn't. And let me tell you, this is not the behaviour of a daughter of mine,' he was yelling, beside himself with anger. 'Behaving like some common tramp. And I have no respect for your friend, keeping you out all night. Mark my words, you will never see him again.'

Mummy appeared at the top of her stairs in her Japanese robe, her greying hair in a long plait. 'If this is how you carry on,' she said icily, 'then we can only hope that you are not pregnant.' She turned and walked away.

Speechless, Daphne ran up the stairs, shut herself in her room, her face flaming. How could they throw such accusations at her, treat her as if she was some sort of prostitute? She and Carol had never even done 'it', for goodness' sake.

She began to meet Carol in the afternoons, which was easy to do since he lived alone in a room in Kensington, a small stove to cook on. For Carol's birthday she bought a gramophone, crept into his room and set it up before he got back from work at the studio. They lay on the creaky bed and smoked and talked as the jazz music twined around the room.

'Don't you think,' said Daphne, leaning on one elbow, 'that perfectly sensible people like you and me ought to treat the whole making-love thing as being on a par with tennis or skiing?'

Carole leaned on his elbow facing her, his eyes wide. 'I suppose so, though it seems a little brutal.'

She stubbed out her cigarette. Took his away also and slid a hand inside his shirt. She might as well find out what all the fuss was about – especially now they seemed so certain that she had already committed the act.

Later, lying on the bed and listening to the cars pass by outside, she thought that it wasn't entirely disappointing. Certainly didn't merit all the fuss of marriage so far as she could see.

The following day, something far more exciting happened. The maid brought a letter up to her room. A London postmark. Daphne tore it open. Read the letter and let out a whoop.

'Whatever's happened?' asked Angela, laying her plump arm on Daphne's shoulder to scan the letter.

'Ten pounds,' said Daphne excitedly. The *Bystander*'s going to pay me ten pounds for two of my stories. I'm going to be published.'

Angela kissed her cheek. 'My sister, the writer.'

A few days later a letter came from Michael Joseph at Curtis Brown. The editor of the *Bystander* had alerted them to Miss du Maurier's work and they would like to represent her. Daphne hugged the letter to her chest. At last, she had a literary agent. And he would like to discuss whether she had plans to write a novel.

She explained to him over lunch at the Savoy that she most certainly did although the subject matter was still unclear. No matter, he told her. He would be willing to take whatever she wanted to write. She went home walking on air. She couldn't see its shape, but she knew with a fierce determination that the book was waiting for her to find it as she sat and wrote each day.

It was embarrassing having to have her photograph done in a studio. Alarming to think it was going to be on the cover. She wore trousers and a knitted silk top that showed off her narrow shoulders elegantly, her hair daringly short, her blue eyes clear and piercing even in a black-and-white photograph.

A couple of weeks later, Daphne woke early and dressed, set out alone to the newsagent's. There were few people about, the morning's papers still being thrown from the back of a van, a man and a boy taking them inside and cutting the strings.

'Can I help you, miss?' asked a man in a brown apron.

'I don't suppose you have a copy of the *Bystander*? It's out today.'

'Should be here somewhere.'

He split open a couple of parcels and pulled out a magazine. He looked at the cover and then at Daphne.

'Well, I never. That's you, isn't it?'

'I'm afraid it is. Very embarrassing. How much do I owe you?'

'On the house, miss, not often we have a famous author in here.'

Holding it against her chest, she walked up the hill to the coffee shop. She felt elated and changed by a new reality. One that she needed a moment to get used to. She ordered a coffee and sat drinking it, the magazine lying on the table. A new companion stared at her from the cover with a cool, appraising gaze. *Miss Daphne du Maurier*, read the byline, *an exciting new writer.*

She began to notice a certain dampness to Carol's hand, how intent and meaningful his gaze. As the summer went by, he began to develop a grateful, hangdog look, started to talk about marriage being rather a good idea – for the right people.

She was horrified. They were friends and she cared for him, but that was all. How ever was she going to let him down without hurting his feelings terribly?

She was saved when Mummy announced that they would finally open up Ferryside for the summer. It was wonderful to be back, light reflecting from the water on to her bedroom ceiling, days wandering along the cliffs, calling out greetings to the people in the little town who now knew her.

And this time she was determined to find her mysterious abandoned house, Menabilly.

Five a.m. Not yet light. She dressed in cords and a jumper and untied *Annabel Lee* from the steps leading down to the water. The air smelled sharp with salt, the water glass-like and reflecting the last lamps still alight along the harbour. She began to pull towards Readymoney Cove, cries of seagulls scissoring the dark, a glow rising from the horizon. By the time she reached Polridmouth, the whole sky was pale rose, the sea sheened pink. Somewhere, in the woods rising up beyond Polridmouth Cove, her Menabilly was sleeping. She pulled the boat up on a curve of sand. A shuttered cottage stood next to a small lake fringed with rushes. A wooden gate across a path into the woods, a faded *No Trespassing* sign. She climbed over it. The path led up through trees filled with birdsong, beeches and ash trees and many-trunked sycamores. Everything growing madly, undisturbed and unkempt. Ferns and foxgloves studded the banks. The ancient trees, damp with sea air, carried forests of moss on their trunks, boughs laden with fantastical lichen and creepers.

As she reached the top of the hill, the woods began to thin out. To the left was a high stone wall engulfed in greenery; beyond, glimpses of sloping fields and the sea. The path swept around to the right, through knee-high grass interspersed with silver-trunked beeches, slender and grown to an enormous height, curving on until she had lost sense of direction. Surely she must have passed the house by now. She came upon banks of scarlet rhododendrons, forty feet high. Still no sight of the house. Overhead the susurration of trees, rising and falling in the wind. A pheasant's rusty bedspring call.

As she walked she discovered what must have been a lawn among the rhododendrons, the grass waist high, curving as if it might lead somewhere, but smaller bushes of camellias blocked the view each time she though she might spy Menabilly.

She caught a glimpse of grey stone, the corner of a building, a lower window glinting in the morning sun. She carried on walking, more of the house appearing and then vanishing among the camellia bushes, partial and tantalizing, playing hide-and-seek.

At last the bushes opened out and she saw Menabilly in its entirety. It was all but covered in ivy, a sleeping princess under a thick green blanket. She stopped, sank down to her knees in the wet grass. A strange feeling of trespass overcame her. She could see a low roof of silvery slate, corbelled chimneys and a pointed bell tower. No sound except for birdsong, the morning clear and shimmering with sunlight on the dew.

She got up, brushing down her damp clothes, and began to walk around the house. She knew it was ridiculous but her heart was beating fast, as if she were visiting some forbidden lover. The black oak doors were carved with classical reliefs, worn but still there: Poseidon and his mermaids, a Roman chariot, urns filled with flowers. She pushed on the door gently, but it was locked.

In the gaps between the ivy, she could see that the house was built from a crystalline granite that seemed spun from sugar, pale tones of viridian, honey and faded magenta. How she longed to remove the ivy, stems thick as saplings, see the house as it should be. Could one fall in love with stones?

If only she could live here, make the house and its secrets hers.

She pressed her face to a window and made out a dim wood-panelled room, a fireplace large enough to stand in. All the furniture was still inside, family portraits staring down at a long dining table covered in dust. A wine bottle on a sideboard. In another room, she made out shelves filled with books.

What could have happened to make someone leave such a house and all it contained so unloved and neglected?

She walked round to the back. One of the sash windows at floor level had been left open. Pushing it up a little further, she clambered inside and found a shadowy corridor with dark brown fungi sprouting along the ceiling.

The back of the house was starting to rot and fall down. How long before it reached the rest of the house?

Through a pair of double doors she found the rooms she had seen from the front, filled with sheeted furniture. She came out into a hall with a twisting oak staircase. At the top, an oil painting of a woman in a red silk gown looked down at her sternly.

It was strange that she didn't feel afraid; she felt at home, rather.

But the chill damp was undeniable. She retraced her steps, climbed back out of the window. A sudden whooshing sound above her head made her jump as a white owl glided from a top window.

Daphne rubbed her arms, feeling like someone who had stepped back from another time. No wonder she felt light-headed and fanciful, she thought. She hadn't eaten for hours.

She cast one long look back, that odd feeling of being watched by mischievous eyes, and the house began folding itself away among the woods as she followed the path back to the beach.

As she rowed back she felt a rising conviction. She had no idea how it was going to happen, but she knew that one day she was going to make Menabilly hers, bring it back to life and live there. So is this how it felt, she wondered, to fall in love at first sight?

CHAPTER 6

FERRYSIDE 1930

Sitting at the oak table at breakfast with Mummy one morning, the estuary and Fowey across the water framed in the arched windows, Daphne peeled an orange as she glanced down at the unopened letter by her plate. It was alarming how Carol managed to write to her every day. She, however, was a little ashamed to find that once he was out of her sight he evaporated from her thoughts entirely. And he was worryingly obsessed about this marriage thing. How on earth was she going to let him down when they returned to London?

Mummy took a piece of toast from the silver rack, eyeing the letter.

'From Carol again?'

'Yes.'

'How does that boy find the time to write so often? Has he no work to do?'

'He's making films, Mummy. He's working as a runner.'

'My point entirely.' Mummy spread butter on her toast, then marmalade.

'Daphne, I was thinking, if you can really make enough from writing to support yourself one day, Daddy and

I might consider allowing you to live here at Ferryside permanently.'

Daphne looked up. She couldn't believe her ears. Couldn't think of anything she wanted more than to be here all the time, long days immersed in the green countryside or sailing out on the blue planes of the sea. So much to explore. Could it be she'd misheard?

'You mean I really could stay in Cornwall and not have to go back to dreary London?'

'We could try this autumn and see how it goes. There'd be rules. You couldn't sleep at the house on your own, of course. I've enquired with Miss Roberts at the cottage behind the house and you could board there, work in the house during the day.'

Daphne was even more flabbergasted. So Mummy had thought it through. Even talked to Miss Roberts. She must really mean it. Mummy must be very keen for her to drop Carol then, but she hardly cared about all that, desperate to stay on. She could feel there was something bubbling up into a book if they'd just leave her to mull on it.

'Yes, yes. Anything. Whatever rules you like.' Feeling a rush of love, Daphne ran and flung her arms around Mummy – felt that instinctive shrinking back she'd always had from her, even as a small child, a physical pulling away. And once again the quick thought that there must be something very wrong with a girl whose Mother disliked her so much that she couldn't bear to be touched by her.

But what did it matter when she had the chance to stay on in Ferryside by herself?

*

Daphne stood waving off the family with a feeling of great weight falling from her shoulders. It was a ridiculously high bar for her to earn a living from writing given that she'd only earned ten pounds so far from her two short stories in the *Bystander* but she felt the most ridiculous certainty that she could do it. She ran up to her room that jutted out over the estuary, her desk in the window with water and air beneath her feet, birds' cries and boats' horns in the distance, sat down and picked up her pen.

A few months earlier, walking along Pont Pill Creek at low tide, she had come across a Victorian barque abandoned on the mudflats; the name was still legible, the *Jane Slade*. There was a figurehead on its prow, a woman with long black hair and a blue dress. Was she Jane Slade? Intrigued, Daphne had climbed on to the boat and walked the damp and rotting decks, imagining the people who had once stood where she did, the boat's sails full of wind, looking out over the sea. Perhaps old John Adams would know more.

Daphne sailed out with John Adams most afternoons. Being out on the sea was mesmerizing, feeling the play of the water against the boat, the calm expanses of silky blue stretching to the horizon. She wore tweed shorts and an Argyle jumper, woollen socks to the knees and gumboots, looking, she had to admit, like a smarter version of a schoolboy – though with her delicate face and bobbed fair hair no one would have mistaken her for a boy. Nothing could beat the feeling of flying across the water towards the horizon on a silver-and-blue morning like today.

'Jane Slade?' said John Adams when she asked him about the abandoned barque. That will be Jane, my grandmother. The figurehead was carved for her. She were tougher than any man when it came to the hard decisions, but the kindest of souls. We miss her to this day. We still have a box of her old letters and account books at home.'

'John, you don't think I could look at those letters some time?'

'Don't see why not.'

Alone in her room, Daphne read through the letters, imagining Jane Slade a lifetime ago, her blue dress and a small jaunty hat as she walked the same paths and byways that Daphne did today, hearing the cries of gulls, the smells of tar and sea as she oversaw the Polruan boatyard. A story began to form in her mind, a saga following three generations.

Some days, Daphne wasn't sure if she inhabited her own body, or that of one of her characters in the story in her mind. As she stood on the cliffs beyond Polruan one evening, the sun setting red and gold, the wind blowing gently, she imagined herself as a young man, Jane's son, left to manage the boatyard after her death. She could feel his confusion so acutely, not knowing what to do with such a heavy task, and in the same moment there was a sense of a presence by his side, comforting him and speaking to him, the boy's mother whispering to him in the wind. In the rays of the sun and the buffeting of the wind, it seemed as though she were detached from the earth, transported into a moment from another life.

She hurried back to her room to write, her pen flying across the paper. Jane Slade would become Janet Coombe, the head of a shipbuilding dynasty, a woman doing a man's job. After her death Janet would come back as a benign ghost to guide her son and grandson as they fought to keep the business alive.

But she needed a title. A poem came to mind by Emily Brontë, how our spirit longs to remain in the world with our loved ones, even after we die. That was it, it would be called *The Loving Spirit*.

'Oh gosh, you mean a bit like Jim's ghost play, *Mary Rose*!' Angela said, slathering jam and cream on a split, as Daphne outlined the plot in the upper room of a Fowey tearoom overlooking the churchyard. 'The one where the mother comes back as a ghost, trying to find the baby she left behind, only to find he's grown up and doesn't recognize her. And she doesn't recognize him. Gosh, I cried so much when that happened.'

'No, nothing like *Mary Rose*,' Daphne replied. 'Jane Slade was very much a real person, the grandmother of the man who's building a boat for Daddy. I've even walked up the hill to Lanteglos church, and visited her grave. It's perfectly original as a story.'

'But she comes back as a ghost.'

'At least you'll be going back to London tomorrow,' said Daphne, dabbing a bit of cream on the end of Angela's nose.

*

Each evening, after spending the day writing, Daphne shut up the house and climbed the hill to Miss Robert's cottage where she found a meal waiting for her.

'I hope you don't mind if it's sausages again, Miss Doreen,' the old lady said as Daphne warmed her icy hands in front of the fire.

'Nothing better,' said Daphne. Even after several weeks, she didn't like to tell her that her name was Daphne, Miss Roberts was such a dear. Or that she disliked sausages. She ate them anyway. She revelled in the privations of having to take a hip bath in her bedroom in chilly water, or battling the winds and the autumn frost to go outside to the lavatory. Each morning, after a cooked breakfast, Daphne returned to sit at her desk in Ferryside, wrapped in a blanket and relishing the storms that battered the house as she sailed the seas with Janet Coombe and her sons, free as any man to roam the waves or cut deals.

Daphne had never been happier. Cornwall, its land and its people, had got inside her bones. In rubber boots and a tweed coat, she strode out along the cliffs, the story playing out in her head, talking aloud, holding conversations with people long dead.

It was a wrench when she was summoned back to Cannon Hall for Christmas. She packaged up the finished manuscript of *The Loving Spirit* and posted it to her agent, feeling jubilant – finally, a finished book.

But as she returned to London, a few days later, an anxious feeling set in like incoming bad weather, any view obliterated by a cold mist. It was one thing to get a couple of short stories published, but a novel was the real test if one were to have a career as a writer. What if Michael didn't want her book after she had poured everything she had into it?

She saw herself for ever stuck at Cannon Hall, an adult child with pocket money from Daddy – very generous, of course, but always the appendage to his and Mummy's world. A society wedding swamped beneath a guest list of two hundred people and yards of white tulle, no longer free to immerse oneself in the delicious world of a new book.

Back in her childhood room, after a couple of weeks of such despair, Daphne could barely get out of bed.

A knock on the door and Angela came in, a letter in her hand.

Daphne raced over and tore it open and read. She froze, couldn't breathe.

'What is it? Is it bad news?' said Angela, trying to read her face. 'What's happened?' Daphne couldn't speak for a moment. She looked at Angela in astonishment. 'The book's been taken by a publisher. And they're going to take my next book as well, pay me seventy-five pounds, if you can believe it.' Angela squealed and gave her a huge hug, Daphne beaming. Then her face fell. 'But whatever am I going to write for my next book?'

A few weeks later, on a visit to friends in Paris, an idea came to her, a tale of benighted modern love, *I'll Never be Young Again*. It was probably going to shock people, but if there was one truth that Daphne stood by it was that romance was overrated – and generally ended with a bad deal for the girl.

She sat at a table outside a café, ordered a coffee, a roll filled with butter and ham. Bit into it, savouring how far she had come. Her first book was about to be published both at home and in America. Her publisher was predicting a hit, the reviews so far good.

It was ten in the morning, but why not. When the waiter passed by she called him over and ordered a glass of champagne, sat sipping it with the sun on her face.

As soon as *The Loving Spirit* came out, she took a signed copy to Jim's flat. It was hard to see how much frailer he had grown, his frame stooped under a grief that had crushed him, his face wizened and birdlike. She knew that he was writing less and less now, occasional stories of loss and nostalgia. In the decade since that fateful day when he had learned of Michael's death, Jim's world had grown smaller. He sat for long hours alone each day, smoking his pipe in the bleak penthouse flat with its distant sounds of foghorns along the Thames.

'I salute you, dear Daphne,' Uncle Jim had said as she gave him the book. 'I am proud to see your literary talents take flight.' He flipped through the pages with an approving nod, put the book down on the small table by his side.

'And I've begun my next book,' she told him. 'I'm afraid some people are going to be horribly shocked by this one too, but I refuse to be just another lady novelist peddling romantic nonsense.'

He nodded thoughtfully, lit up his pipe, spasms of hacking coughs.

'You see, Daphne, whimsy and humour and fairies, that's what I'm known for. But the truth is you and I are among the few willing to look behind life's facade and it's rarely pretty what one finds there.'

She left feeling disturbed by Jim's speech. She'd never heard him sound so cynical and gloomy, but after all that had happened, losing his beloved George and then Michael, he could hardly be blamed. She resolved to telephone him more often, check that he was keeping as well as possible.

For the next two years, Daphne worked steadily, whether at Ferryside or back at Cannon Hall. She knew from Jim how important it was to have a writing routine. Beginning each morning at ten, she wrote for three hours, took a walk after lunch, then wrote for another two hours before supper. The evenings she spent reading and making notes. Bed by ten.

She was finally in a place where she was able to support herself, free to write and live in Cornwall, to choose her path ahead. A freedom that she had no intention of giving up, and certainly not for some man bearing a sparkly ring. Flings and adventures, yes, why not, but she was never going to exchange books for nappies, and never play second fiddle to any man.

CHAPTER 7

FOWEY 1932

'I say. Do come and see,' said Angela. She was hanging out of the stable door overlooking the Fowey Estuary, peering through a pair of Daddy's birding binoculars. 'There's the most splendid man going up and down the harbour in a white motorboat.'

Daphne was curled up on the sofa making notes for a scene in *I'll Never be Young Again*. She was writing as the hero – if hero was the right word – when he tells his lover, a rather pathetic young girl, that there was sex, yes, and there was friendship, marriage even if you must, but as for romance, she couldn't expect that from him because it didn't exist.

'Daphs, hurry up or you'll miss him.'

She got up reluctantly and took the binoculars. Adjusting the focus she saw a tall man at the helm of a new motorboat, a slim, athletic build, thick brown hair brushed back. A relaxed and confident bearing as he steered the boat with one hand, half-turning to talk to someone seated in the stern.

'Hmm. Yes, he is rather good.'

The boat passed closer to the house. Daphne ducked away.

*

The following day Angela burst into Daphne's room and plumped down on the bed.

'Guess who they were gossiping about in the post office in Fowey? That stunning man in the motorboat. And I've got a name, Major Tommy Browning. Youngest major in the army, Mrs Pridstone says. Received a medal for bravery in the last war. Can you imagine, he must have been hardly more than a boy at the time? She says he's thinking of laying his boat up in the Hunkins' boatyard here. Ever so charming, according to Mrs Hunkin. Took part in the winter Olympics, bobsleigh run I think. Oh, and listen, he was a Grenadier Guards, red uniform and everything. Remember when we used to watch them from the nursery window, when we lived near the Palace. Don't you think he sounds like a dream? Though I spotted him first,' Angela teased, wagging her finger.

'You are most welcome. I'm so glad you've found your crush of the week,' said Daphne with a wry look. She was making notes for the bitter quarrel when the heartless Dick would abandon his adoring lover, but realizing she was not going to get much more done with Angel gushing about Major Browning, she closed her notebook.

'I suppose I may as well start packing now that Mummy's decided to close up Ferryside for these wretched repairs. Daddy says there's a room at his theatre I can use to finish the book, but it won't be the same.'

'Cornwall's your big pash really, isn't it?'

'And Major Browning yours, I can see.'

'One of these days, I am going to meet the one,' said Angela, picking up a cream scarf, draping it on her head and going over to the mirror.

'I wish you well,' smiled Daphne. 'I can't imagine being at the beck and call of some dreary man.' Daphne stopped, gave a little groan.

'I say Daphne, are you all right?'

Daphne clutched her stomach, a sheen of sweat on her brow.

Travelling up to London on the train was agony. By the time she reached Cannon Hall it was clear that Daphne urgently needed a doctor. She was admitted to hospital to have her appendix removed.

Her recovery was slow. As she rested, half-dozing by the fire in Cannon Hall with cups of broth, she sometimes recalled that little cut-out silhouette on the water, like a motif in a tune that recurs unbidden at odd moments, but she dismissed her curiosity each time as frivolous. What she needed to do now was to focus on completing her third book.

By April Daphne was back at Ferryside. She sat on a steamer chair in the strip of garden overlooking the estuary, watching the boats coming and going, frustrated that she was still too weak to be out on the water.

She heard the postman calling out from the garden gate and got up to take the mail from him. A letter from Mummy, and another which looked far more interesting, *Miss D. du Maurier* written on the front in bold and flowing cursive. She ripped open the top, unfolded a sheet of notepaper.

Dear Miss du Maurier,

My father attended the same club as your father, Sir Gerald du Maurier, and I believe they knew each other at the Garrick and I feel that we have been introduced, so I wondered if I might take the liberty of introducing myself in person. I am a great fan of your recent novel, 'The Loving Spirit', and was inspired to visit the area through your descriptions, which did not disappoint. I was very sorry to hear that you are not able to row at the moment while you are recuperating, and I wondered if I might be of service in taking you out in my own small boat.

Yours, Major Tommy (Boy) Browning

She turned the letter over, as if to find more clues on the back. So this was the mysterious Major Browning. He sounded pleasant. And he was certainly a pal if he understood how much one missed sailing. The nickname, Boy, was intriguing, she thought, with its frisson of Peter Pan and the glamour of the boy's world of adventures that she'd loved so much as a child. She realized she was rather looking forward to meeting this Tommy Browning.

Two days later, Tommy's boat moored at the foot of the stone steps leading down from the garden, an exhilarating April breeze troubling the water, white gulls up on the air currents. As Tommy handed her into the boat with a steady grip, she noted laughter lines at the corners of his eyes, the tan of someone who likes to be outdoors. He made sure she was comfortable with a rug, then the boat sped off towards the open sea. It gave her a good opportunity to study him, shirtsleeves rolled up, arms lean and athletic, every so often turning his head towards her as they shouted a conversation to and fro above the noise of the engine. Eventually, Daphne threw off the rug and got up to stand next to him.

He was thirty-six to her twenty-five. He smelled of sandalwood and leather, clean and male, and a hint of something subtle and unexpected. Lavender, perhaps? Examining him sideways when she though he might not notice, she took in an aquiline nose, a high hairline that gave him the air of someone wise for his years, undeniably tall and handsome in a refined way – the type that girls must fall for a lot, she guessed – but fortunately she was inured to that sort of thing.

A good sort to have as a friend, however. There was something solid about Tommy with his erect, lean posture and brown limbs. Carol and other boys she'd met had had a quality of modelling clay that she could push this way and that, without resistance. But Tommy was himself, fully formed and sure of whom he was. He had the delicious allure of a tall and vital Peter Pan who had matured to live in the real world and gone forth to have grown-up adventures, a decorated major who skied and rode and competed in the Olympics. And yet also seemed to care for books – her books.

'I was surprised when you mentioned that you came to Fowey because of *The Loving Spirit*,' she called out above the engine. 'Wouldn't necessarily have pegged you as someone who might read a saga written by a lady novelist.'

He turned a smile on her. She heard a voice inside saying this was the smile, the face, that she wanted to see every day. Which was ridiculous. Dismissed it immediately.

'I adored it, ' he said. 'All my favourite things – boats, the sea, history. And your descriptions of Fowey and the land around, they were spot on. As good as being here, which helped an awful lot when one was stuck in army barracks in the middle of a gloomy winter.'

'I expect you imagined someone rather more glamorous, though, as the writer,' she said, looking down at her trousers and jacket.

He gave a sheepish smile. A tiny bit wicked. 'Not disappointed one bit. Quite the opposite, if you don't mind me saying so.'

She shrugged as if it was no concern of hers, looked out across the water and felt ridiculously pleased. 'So do you read novels often? You can't have much time, being in the army.'

'I read a lot in fact. Very keen on old legends. The sagas and Norse mythology.'

'I was wondering how the boat's name came about, *Yggdrasil*.'

'It's old Norse. After the great ash tree in the sagas, the Tree of Life.'

She stared at him, impressed and charmed. 'That's quite lovely.'

'*Iggy* for short. Do you mind if I open the throttle now we've cleared the harbour? Might be fun to pick up a bit of speed.'

'Oh gosh, yes. All I can do is hobble about slowly these days. I love the feel of skimming over the water, nothing but the sea and the sky.'

'Only thing that beats that is flying down a luge run. Bob-sleighing can be a bit dangerous, but it's very addictive.'

'I know. Adored it on a winter holiday in Caux.'

He gave her an appraising look, whistled. 'Never met a girl who liked to luge. I am impressed.'

The sea was becoming choppy, the boat hitting the waves and sending up showers of spray that soon had them both drenched and laughing. They had to shout loudly to be heard above the engine and the slap of the water.

'So your nickname, Boy, where did that come from?'

'My father and I were in the army at the same time. Two Major Brownings is a bit confusing, so I was known as Boy Browning and it rather stuck among my army pals. You must find it odd.'

'No. I like it. A boy is a lovely thing to be.'

'In fact, Tommy's also a nickname. I was christened Frederick, but only my mother uses that one. I prefer Tommy.'

'Tommy it is then.'

She found herself reluctant when he suggested it was time to go back. He swung the boat round. She had to hold on to the side rail.

As the boat slowed to a steady pace he noticed that she was shivering. He went down and found a spare jumper in one of the lockers below. She pulled it on, the scent of leather and sandalwood and something more male. It was deliciously soft, darned at the elbows like a garment her father might have worn.

'But you didn't really come to Fowey just because you read about it in a book?' she said, pulling the jumper straight.

'I absolutely did. Very strange to recognize a place I'd never visited before. A bit like the feeling I had when you came out to greet me – as if we'd already met.'

She almost blurted out, but that's exactly how I feel.

'I have to confess, though,' he went on. 'I had in fact seen your photograph in the *Bystander* a while back.'

'Oh no, you saw that awful photograph. Ridiculous how one has to get scrubbed up for the publisher's sake. A holey fisherman's jersey and an old pair of shorts is far more me.'

'I know exactly what you mean. There's an awful lot of buckle-polishing in the army, and it does matter, all part of army discipline, but I'm far happier in an old fishing sweater and gumboots.'

They motored back, Fowey coming into view, an enjoyable feeling of agreement between them.

By the time they reached Bodinnick, a gold-and-amethyst sun was setting behind the hills. The boat came to a stop at the bottom of the Ferryside steps. There was the feeling of a conversation half-finished. She hesitated, the boat rocking gently on the water as it lapped against the stone wall.

'I have to warn you that I'm the proverbial girl who can't boil an egg, but why don't I make us something for supper? The least I can do after such a lovely afternoon out on the water. You must be famished. I know I am.'

'I don't want to impose. . .'

'Please do.' She realized she was holding her breath.

'Well, if you're sure.'

Jeanne who was also staying at Ferryside was away at a friend's that night. There was no one else in the house. Daphne ran upstairs to change into dry clothes, linen slacks and a cream shirt. Added a necklace of amber beads. He was standing in the sitting room looking out of the window towards the harbour, the long line of his back. How right he looked there.

He turned when she came in, gave a smile that made her heart flip.

'What a charming house this is.'

'They used to build boats in this room. Come on, I'll give you the tour.'

He followed her through the rooms, her arms sketching out where the sails would have been, the tools that once hung along the wall.

'Can't think of a nicer history for a house,' he said.

Daphne nodded.

'Here, I'll just light a fire,' she told him. 'Pour us a drink from over there if you don't mind.'

She enjoying showing him how at home she was taking on a task normally done by a man as she set the fire and watched the logs catch flame, a sweet tinge of apple-wood smoke in the air. They sipped their whiskies, the lights of Fowey coming on across the estuary as darkness fell, little trails of lamp light running across the dark water.

'I can imagine this must be a wonderful house to live in,' he said, looking very much at home in the armchair by the fire.

'I do love it here. But there's another house that's for me.' She told him how she had found Menabilly, his head nodding slightly as he listened. 'I'll take you there one day. If I haven't made you expire from hunger. I should do something about that supper I promised you.'

He'd taken over the omelettes pretty quickly when he'd seen what she was doing with the eggs. She watched him moving between the kitchen table and the stove, an apron tied neatly around his waist, army style she supposed.

She rather liked this feeling of being taken care of by a tall handsome man.

They sat on the rug in front of the fire with their plates of eggs, opened a bottle of one of Daddy's reds. The heat of his body palpable as he reached forward to fill her glass, his arm near hers. Daphne felt her stomach flip – due to sipping wine on an empty stomach most probably, she told herself.

'I only wish I was fit enough take you out on the *Marie Louise*, my father's boat,' she said. 'Not that he sails her. She's a sixteen-foot schooner. When the wind fills the sails it's marvellous.'

'That would be my dream, a sail-rigged schooner. Out on the water with the wind kicking in.'

She took a sip of wine. 'Well, it's a deal then. We'll go out on the *Marie Louise* as soon as I'm able to manage the rigging. Though I have to admit I'm a pretty grumpy captain if the crew aren't up to the mark.'

'Quite right,' he smiled. 'Sadly, however, the army doesn't give us a lot of time for sailing. I'm in Pirbright most of the time.'

'That's a shame. I mean, not having much leave to sail.'

'I'd certainly love to spend much more time in Fowey.' Said quietly, like a confession.

They had so much to talk about. Daphne told him about the old schooner abandoned on Pont Pill that had inspired the book he had liked so much, promised to show him Lanteglos church on the hill above where Jane Slade was buried.

They had the same opinions on dogs and books and finding beauty in nature and music. There was so much she wanted to ask him about himself. At one point, they both sighed at the same time, a pause where they stared into the flames quietly like old friends in easy contemplation. She thought how natural it would be to move over and lean against his side, how much she wanted to. What if she were to take his hand that lay so near to hers on the rug?

'I should get back to my lodgings before one of us falls asleep,' Tommy said. 'You need your rest.' He stood up, stretching.

'There's no need to. We've got plenty of spare beds here if you like.'

'You're too kind, but I couldn't possibly.' He seemed a tad embarrassed by the suggestion. 'But why don't I come by in the morning? You can show me the best places for a spot of fishing, if you like?'

As his boat set off for the lights on the other side of the estuary, she stood in the garden and watched him until he disappeared.

Daphne barely slept that night. She felt excited, bewildered. Could this be the madness that made girls throw everything up in the air and bind themselves to some male for the rest of their lives? Was this what they called love at first sight, this undeniable attraction, finding everything he did so right and fascinating?

She needed to keep her head.

She was up early, her favourite blue roll neck tucked into her neatest slacks. Hair brushed out and a touch of lipstick. What a fool she was.

He appeared shortly after breakfast. They set off for a day's sailing and fishing, vying to see who could catch the most pollock. Stayed out again until the sun began to sink, casting its long gleams across the water.

Heading home to Ferryside, standing behind him, as naturally as if she had always done so, she slid her arms around his waist, rested her head against his shoulder blade, felt her body relaxed and at peace with the rightness of it, breathing in the smell of his woollen jacket. Feeling the strength of his back, the pull of unstoppable attraction.

Did he feel the same? Did he mind?

He turned, drew her gently alongside him, holding her there comfortably, steering the boat with his other arm, easy and peaceful, with a big grin on his face. His eyes, she realized, were the clearest green.

Another evening talking non-stop in front of a flickering fire, bacon and eggs with potatoes and buttered cabbage, cooked by Tommy again after Daphne had offered to open a tin of soup. He had gone into army mode, rifling through the larder and assembling utensils. She sat and asked more questions as he cooked. His father had died and left the family with debts. He adored his mother and sister. He went to church, had an old-fashioned belief in serving God and country, which seemed admirable and sweetly charming.

Tommy was the book that she wanted to read for the rest of her life.

As the fire sank and settled into glowing embers, the wine almost gone, nestled together against the chintz sofa, Daphne felt a thrill of anticipation as he moved towards her and they kissed for the first time. She could think of nothing else for those moments, had experienced nothing so right and so powerful in her life.

The silver clock on the side table chimed two in the morning.

'Impossible,' laughed Tommy. 'I should go before I ruin your reputation in Fowey.' He smoothed her hair back from her forehead and kissed her brow. He collected the plates, carried them up to the kitchen and began to wash them, ever the soldier. She took a tea towel, drying a plate thoughtfully. Did she dare say what she was going to say? What would he think?

'Look, I don't see the point in playing games, darling Tommy. It would be the most natural thing in the world if you would stay tonight. With me.'

His arms still in the soapy water, he turned and stared at her. She read shock in his eyes. Her heart gave a thump.

'Daphne, sweet girl, of course I would love nothing more. But this is a small place, people gossip. And you see, I've always thought that one should wait, until one is married.'

She let out a short laugh. 'Bit late for me on that score.'

He flushed, wouldn't look her in the eye as he dried his hands and rolled his shirtsleeves back down, buttoned the cuffs. 'Daphne, I don't think you understand what you are saying.'

She followed him downstairs to the sitting room, feeling stupid and forlorn. He found his jacket.

'Look, it's been the most marvellous day. Thank you,' he said.

She couldn't reply, a lump in her throat because she'd blown it. She watched him walk away across the dark strip of garden, heard the motor start up and saw him cut a wide curve back across the water.

He knew that he had to go back to Pirbright in the morning. And he'd made no suggestions to keep in touch.

Daphne sat down in front of the fire. Trust her to fling herself at the only man left in England who still had high moral principles, she told herself angrily. Was he right? She didn't know any more. A kiss had flipped the world and all her ideas about love and men upside down. She saw now that what she had felt for Carol had been a mere game. She had come up against something as undeniable as rock, as elemental as wind over the sea. She was powerfully, and inconveniently, attracted to a man from a world quite different from her own. A man who felt like her true soulmate. After just two days. Whom she longed with all her being to see again.

Small hope of that now.

She heard nothing from him next day, but he'd told her how little chance he had to be in touch from his barracks in Pirbright. But as the days went by, with still no message, she felt increasingly hopeless.

She decided some physical work might help. She set to sawing logs in the garden, heard her dog Bingo barking madly. Someone the dog knew was coming. Turned to see Tommy at the gate, hatless, a brown leather jerkin, grey flannel trousers tucked into sea boots. He strode over and hugged her, a kiss on her forehead. Those clear green eyes, a smile that curled at one corner.

'Come on you, enough with sawing logs. We're going out on *Iggy*.'

Had anyone ever given Daphne an order before? She realized that she liked it very much. They sailed out beyond the harbour and with nothing around them but the satiny blues of water and air they kissed with a passion while the engine lay still and the waves rocked them.

Over the next few weeks, Tommy came down on every leave he had, plus some more borrowed from a pal, Daphne unable to think of anything but Tommy while he was away. They took *Marie Louise* out on the water, calling to each other as they manoeuvred the ropes and sails. Daphne, dressed in white linen dungarees with green trim, bare arms tanned and lithe, standing at the helm as the boat sailed like a white bird, wings wide to the wind, and they shouted companionable instructions to each other. 'Mind those bloody lobster pots there.' Two old shipmates. Or sitting on the deck as a dome of stars rose above them, then sailing back under a shining moon.

She loved the scent of his skin, his laugh and his deep and reassuring voice, his long, capable hands, his knightly courtesy, his ease, old trousers tucked into boots ready to walk for miles or sail in *Iggy*. The way he towered a good couple of feet above her. How they laughed about the same things, had the same sort of off-beat humour, wicked and mocking the pompous.

If she looked into the future, she wanted Tommy to be there. Couldn't bear to think of a life without him.

They were out beyond Gribben Head one afternoon when

she told Tommy about a writer who lived on the banks of the Helford River. 'He has the most adorable wooden shack overlooking the water where he lives with his girlfriend. So in love but not married. Don't you think that's about as romantic as it gets?'

Tommy frowned. 'What if they have children – how would that affect the kids? To be honest, I think that sounds rather foolish and young as an idea, not to take one's responsibilities seriously. And why wouldn't one want to commit to one's love?' He paused. 'Don't you think of having children one day?'

'I suppose I have always rather pictured myself with a whole troop of little boys one day. Five boys at least. Me at the head of all their mischief like Peter Pan. Yes, I think I do.'

They sailed home in a quiet and reflective mood.

Over the following days, Daphne realized that just at the moment when she had achieved the freedom she wanted, all she could think about was Tommy. To throw their lot in together, creating their own world as they sailed into the blue in the small wooden boat. She could not believe that this was what she was thinking.

One afternoon she and Tommy sailed out toward the Fal, the engine a soporific song. She leaned her head against his back, sheltering from the breeze.

'You know, sometimes,' she began, 'I don't think it would be such a bad idea to make a life together with someone. With the right person. I don't suppose you'd like to marry me?'

He stopped the engine, let the boat float with the swell of the water. He turned, his face confused. 'I'm sorry, I thought. . . Daphne, did you just ask me to marry you?'

'I did.'

'But I should have proposed to you.'

'So is it a yes?'

'Yes and yes, a hundred times yes, with all my heart.'

'I don't know what it's going to mean,' she told him, 'but this is all I want. Throw our hats up in the air and let everything fall where it may.'

And if she had any doubts, the intensity of his kiss put them to rest.

A few weeks later, she travelled up to his battalion headquarters in Pirbright. Tommy said that she must have the chance to understand what life in the army was going to mean before she took him on.

Tommy in full major's uniform was both impressive and alarming, his hair polished like varnished wood, moustache trimmed, high on a gleaming black horse, although sitting in the stands to watch the parade passing, she found the constant marching and stamping and shouting absurd. At the cocktail parties in the mess she realized that she had little in common with the army wives who seemed to have given themselves over completely to serving their men and their infants. How was she ever going to live here in the barracks, on top of everybody else, not a moment's privacy, trying to write to the sound of shouted orders and bugles? Far from her beloved Cornwall.

'Look,' she told Tommy over a supper of ham and potatoes on the last evening as she poked her salad with its vinegary dressing. 'I love you, darling, and always will do, but I think that you are right – I'm just not cut out for this kind of life. I want to be with you for the rest of my days, Tommy darling, but I absolutely don't see why one has to marry – why we can't carry on more or less as we are.'

Tommy folded his napkin, his face stricken. He stood, bowed his head and left for his quarters. She waited miserably until her hosts, Tommy's pal Chink and his wife, got back. Tommy had evidently spoken to them.

Chink poured a drink for Daphne and himself as they sat in the sitting room. He pulled off his dinner jacket, leaned forward, elbows on his knees.

'Daphne, Tommy is so crazy about you that he'd be prepared to live with you under any circumstances rather than lose you, but you have to realize that the army is his life. An affair would ruin his career. It would be the end of him as a soldier. Would you really make him give up the army so that he can be with you? Is that the price he'd have to pay? And as you know, Tommy is also a man of deeply held beliefs.'

'I know, Chink. That's the Tommy I love. I don't want to change him. But living here on top of everyone like this. It would kill me.'

Daphne travelled back to Ferryside with nothing settled between Tommy and her. Coming home with no prospect of seeing him again hit her like a bereavement.

She sat down to write but nothing came. She walked and rowed, but she couldn't outpace the fact that nothing meant anything without Tommy. Here was the life she had worked for and so wanted, but without him it had lost its appeal.

At last, a letter came from Tommy.

You know I wouldn't want you to stop writing, or to change anything that makes you the wonderful girl I love so much if we did marry. I don't want an ordinary kind of wife, darling, I want you. I'm not sure how, yet, but I believe we love each other enough to work things out so that you can still write, even if I stay in the army.

She took his letter and walked out along the cliffs, the view of the town changing its position among the hills the further she walked. Sitting down to look out over the sea, she realized that if she listened to what she really wanted, deep in her heart, then it was Tommy.

What if she did take the plunge, a church wedding, making sacred vows for life? Would she mean it? All she knew was that she couldn't bear to think of a world without Tommy.

She walked home, almost running, called Tommy on the telephone. She had to see him. Please could he come down to Ferryside. He sounded guarded but agreed to drive down for the weekend.

He arrived late afternoon, looking thin and weary. Had she done this to him? They took Bingo for a walk up to the headland, a sea flecked with gold along the ridges of the waves, lilac shadows near the rocks.

She stopped, took his hands in hers. 'You ask me this time.'

His head whipped round. He studied her face. 'Ask you. . .? You mean. . .?'

'Yes, darling, ask me.'

He went down on one knee, took her hands, Daphne laughing.

'Darling one, will you marry me?'

'Yes. For ever and ever.'

A bust of the sun's rays as it began to dip below the horizon and they kissed. They walked home with their arms around each other, deliriously happy, Bingo jumping around them and barking madly.

Tommy felt exactly the same way about a big society wedding as she did. No, thank you to twenty bridesmaids or a battalion guard of honour. No, thank you to a guest list of two hundred people.

Early one morning in July, Daphne and Tommy left Ferryside in *Yggdrasil*. Muriel and Gerald followed in *Marie Louise*, Mr Adams from Hunkins' boatyard sailing with them to act as best man. Daphne was wearing her blue serge suit, carefully ironed the night before by Muriel. They sailed up the Pont Estuary, a heron setting off before them above the limpid water. At Pont Pill Bridge they moored and climbed the footpath to St Wylow's Church, hidden in a cleft of the hills above the sea – the same church where Jane Slade had married. They walked in single file through tall, slender trees trailing mazy ivy. Wild roses and honeysuckle growing on banks of shaded ferns. The ancient fishermen's church stood silver grey against the deep-blue sky. Daphne waited outside with Gerald while Tommy and the others went inside, then holding Gerald's arm, a posy of white roses in the other hand, Daphne stepped down into the cool light of the white church. The roof above an upturned boat with sturdy ancient oak beams hammered in place, the ancient oak pew ends carved with dolphins and ships. A warm smell of polish and pitch pine as the vicar in his vestments began the marriage service.

As she and Tommy made their vows, Daphne was overcome with a solemn feeling of taking part in something ancient and holy, yet also deeply personal and private. They promised to love each other for the rest of their days, their kiss charged with a sweet significance like no other kiss before it.

Back in Fowey Harbour, they found the houses along the front now hung with bunting, sirens and horns sounding, almost every boat in Fowey out on the water. Fireworks set off from the quayside. They sailed through, laughing and waving and holding hands.

At Ferryside they had a brief wedding breakfast with Mummy and Daddy and read out telegrams from family and friends. A sweet one from Uncle Jim. Then they changed into their favourite old sailing clothes, loaded the stores into *Iggy* and set off for their honeymoon on the Helford River.

Tommy steered the boat into a secret cove he knew, Frenchman's Creek, where the boat was completely hidden among the bright green banks of trees. They moored between the trees overhanging the water's edge, evening mist rising from the river, snuggled together on eiderdowns lain down over the deck and watched the stars come out through the interlaced trees. Brown and naked they lay together, mapping each other's contours to the sound of an evening song thrush and the cry of a nightjar, sleeping as the river rose and fell, woke to a pale pink dawn and a silvery mist floating above the river. Nowhere more beautiful.

For Tommy's next posting they were able to stay in the cottage in the grounds of Cannon Hall. Daphne was relived to be able to avoid life in barracks. She began work on a tale of smugglers and fog-drenched moors, *Jamaica Inn*, but a few months later, she was shocked to realize that she was already pregnant. Tommy was delighted.

She knew it was going to be a boy. She had always seen herself at the head of a troop of five little boys, leading the games of Castaways, climbing trees and making campfires, all dressed in matching red sweaters.

She had the nursery painted blue, little blue cupboards, the name Christian stencilled on the door.

Barely a year after she and Tommy were wed, a strapping, healthy girl arrived. Tommy wanted to call her Tessa, which Daphne agreed to since she didn't have any strong opinions on girls' names.

'No, thank you,' an exhausted Daphne told the nanny. She wasn't one of those fussy mothers who need to hold the baby all the time. She'd leave Nanny Margaret to get on with things without disturbing her schedule. Daphne did give it her best shot at feeding the baby herself, but was mortified to have to admit defeat. Everything about the baby left her feeling incapable and guilty. She'd no idea one had to buy a pram, or what else one needed. She had managed two yards of flannel from Selfridges and some small nighties. Nanny had given her a list of all the things that were missing.

As soon as she was recovered, Daphne headed up to her study to work, leaving Tessa in the care of Nanny, which seemed the best thing for the poor child – and was, after all, how Daphne herself had been brought up.

CHAPTER 8

ALEXANDRIA EGYPT 1936

Daphne's fingers had started sticking to the keys of the typewriter again. She wiped away the sweat on a handkerchief. What wouldn't she give to walk in the misty Cornwall rain instead of being cooped up in this stifling heat? Ten in the morning, and the thermometer already showing eighty degrees. Thinking, let alone writing, was a constant battle. A mechanical whirring of cicadas in the palm trees of the scrubby garden rose and fell all day long. A distant call to prayer from the medina in the old town drifted through the air like smoke. She lit another cigarette in an attempt to calm her nausea, the breakfast tray untouched except for tea. It was impossible to eat in such heat.

And it wasn't only the heat that was stifling. Now that she was living on top of the battalion there was so much that she was expected to do as the wife of a commanding officer. For the past three years she'd been able to hide away and work, but here she couldn't ignore the endless dinners and cocktails and parades one was supposed to attend. And what on earth did one wear as an officer's wife in such wilting heat?

Walking along the concrete seafront past the army buildings one afternoon, wearing shorts and a shirt, a gingham headscarf to tie her hair out of the wind, she'd been whistled at by a troop of new squaddies. Mrs Wainwright-Thompson had been there to see it. Scolded the men roundly. She'd offered Daphne a little advice. 'And I know you won't mind me saying this, but one needs to look the part, my dear. One is, after all, the highest-ranking officer's wife. Not some recruit's girlfriend.' She'd felt so embarrassed about it that she hadn't even told Tommy.

She was trying. She wanted to be at Tommy's side and support him, but it was exhausting. Last night there'd been a party for three hundred in the mess with the most incredible quantities of champagne consumed, plump army wives outdoing each other in wearing extraordinary dresses and bright lipstick, wanting to talk to her about Manchester. Her head was soon throbbing with the noise and the worry that she would do or say the wrong thing – disgrace Tommy in some way.

'Darling, you shouldn't fret,' he'd told her, after he had driven her home in tears at the end of the night. 'Everyone thinks you are charm itself. They want to help you settle in, that's all.'

Poor Tommy. He had enough real worries, convinced that there was a war on the horizon, wanting to talk about Hitler and his thuggish Nazis, and the rise of the Fascists in Italy in a rather alarming way. 'Of course, we'd have to make sure they don't take El Alamein,' he tells the darkness as he lies awake, the sweat on their skin keeping in the heat rather than cooling them, leaving her to wonder what he thought about in their moments of greatest passion. 'We could hold on, so long as we kept the port.'

Was he really talking about another war? She didn't realize it before they married, but Tommy had never really recovered from the last war. Who would have imagined that tall, suave Tommy, dazzling in his gold-braided uniform, wakes many nights drenched with sweat, crying out as he tries, once again, to save his men as they try to hold out in Gauche Wood, scores of them mown down by machine guns? Or that Tommy kept a row of small childhood teddies, the Boys, by his bed?

The heat was almost at its afternoon height, the air weighted. She wiped the moisture from her hands again, fanned herself with a notebook from her desk.

A knock on the door. Hassan entered and gave a deep bow, which she found embarrassing each time, but she could hardly forbid him. He wore an immaculate long white robe, a red fez with a tassel. She knew she should be grateful to have Hassan who managed the running of the household, for the large white villa and the garden, a rarity for officers in Egypt, but she hated it all. The house sterile, the garden a dry strip of thorny plants. And as to what instructions she should be giving Hassan regarding a supper party for two visiting officers the next day, she honestly had no idea. Hassan was the symbol of her incompetence in the kitchen.

'Perhaps fish, madam?' suggested Hassan.

'Ah yes, fish.'

'Though perhaps an egg for Miss Tessa's supper since she dislikes fish.'

'Indeed.' Did Tessa not eat fish? Margaret would know.

And so the game went each day, Hassan's suggestions giving a veil to her incompetence, politely leading her towards the evening's menu. It was a relief when he closed the door and she was alone again.

Tommy couldn't believe how clueless she was about running a house, no idea of how much milk costs or how to manage a linen cupboard, have clean shirts ready. 'But one would save so much money if one did one's own cooking,' he'd suggested when they first lived in London. She tried. She gave the cook notice and wrestled with turnips and lamb chops. Daphne's meals were so inedible that he had finally suggested that since she was so busy perhaps it was best if they rehired Cook. There were a lot of surprising things they'd found out about each other since they got married. Who would have guessed that tall and strong Tommy, known for his iron discipline in the army, clings to her in the middle of the night as he slowly emerges from the bloody carnage of Gauche? It's only her arms around him and her whispered words that bring him back to the present. Poor Tommy. He tried to do all he could to shield her from army life and let her carry on working, but he really needed someone who could manage things the way a proper wife should.

She read what she'd written. Pulled the sheet of paper from the typewriter, crumpled it up and hurled it in the waste-paper basket. If only there were somewhere one could go for a proper walk in this damn place to clear her mind. Jim had always said that walking in Scotland had given him his best ideas. Walking in Alexandria, however, was an ordeal rather than an inspiration. The heat that pushed down with such force, red dust seeping in everywhere. A crowd of children and beggars following, pleading for pennies even after she had handed out all she had. The monotonous flat sand and sea, and the shabby, hurriedly built buildings dropped down on the soulless concrete front.

Better to stay indoors, the shutters closed against the heat. To begin with she had lost herself in completing her biography of Gerald, her way of coping with the grief of losing her father so suddenly two years earlier, calling him back page by page. Eventually she had to admit that the book was finished.

All she could think about now was how much she longed to be far away from the debilitating heat. She wished she were walking in the misty woods of Menabilly again, the cool air on her skin, towards that elusive house that she could never own since it was entailed from generation to generation to the Rashleighs – who were leaving the house to rot and die.

She closed her eyes. She could smell wild garlic leaves crushed underfoot, and the salt in the air as she walked down to the cottage by the beach, hear the sea as she climbed over the silvery rocks to the rusted wreck that lay stranded on the beach at low tide.

The germ of an idea began to form. An insecure young woman who marries a widower but feels constantly overshadowed by the lingering presence of the first wife, a woman so much more competent and glamorous than she can ever be. There's a sinister housekeeper who mesmerises with sensual tales of the first wife's beauty and power of fascination. She needs a name for the first wife, something strong.

She thought back to the time she had discovered some letters in Tommy's desk from his old girlfriend, Jan Ricardo. Daphne had been struck by the bold and confident handwriting, the strong elaborate letter R. Who was this woman that had captivated Tommy before he knew her? With such an exotic name she must be far more sophisticated and darkly beautiful than a pale and English Daphne.

Rebecca. That was it. The first Mrs de Winter. As for the mousy second wife, she'd have no name other than 'the second Mrs de Winter'. It would be a tale of jealousy and obsession, and it would be set in a house very like Menabilly.

A knock on the door, Margaret with two-year-old Tessa. Could the whole morning really have gone by already? They were back from a play visit with another nanny and child, Tessa suntanned and forever full of energy. She ran over to Mummy, pressed a couple of keys on the typewriter and looked up at her.

'Darling, you know you mustn't. Margaret has so many lovely crayons for you. Why don't you go play with those?'

'Perhaps Tessa can play with them when you are with her after her nap this afternoon,' suggested Margaret. Margaret insisted that Daphne spend an hour each day with her daughter. A novel idea for one who had never spent even ten minutes a day receiving her own mother's undivided attention, but Daphne found she did enjoy these times, more than she had expected. She told Tessa stories, played dolls with her and was jolly glad to hand Tessa back to Nanny in a way that felt perfectly healthy to Daphne. She wasn't the type to be overly obsessed about her own children, nothing else to talk about except the latest thing her child had done or said, she told herself with some pride.

'I was thinking,' added Nanny Margaret more tentatively, 'that since Tessa has a slight sore throat, I'd like the doctor to take a look at her.'

'Oh really? If you think so.'

'And I was wondering if you might like the doctor to take a quick look at you too, Daphne, since you have been finding it so hard to eat anything for a while now.' Why was Margaret wringing her hands?

'No need, surely. It's just the heat.'

'I think it would be a good idea.'

The door closed. Daphne sat staring at the shuttered window, her longing for Cornwall so acute that she could smell the leaf mould, hear the twigs snapping as she walked through the tangled woods of a cooling evening. She could feel her heart slowing, attentive to every sight and sound, the overgrown path, the falling dusk, the first call of the owls that haunted the woods in autumn, the woody smell of the loam. Hidden among the woods was the house, Manderley.

She took out her blue notebook.

It was quite a shock when a knock came at the door an hour or so later and she found herself back in the heat of Egypt again. It was Margaret with the doctor.

He'd seen Tessa. Nothing much wrong but he'd left her a gargle and a tonic.

'Hear you've been off colour too, Mrs Browning.' He examined her eyes, looked down her throat, asked about her diet or lack of one. Examined her abdomen.

After he left, she sat in silence in her room until Margaret knocked timidly on the door. She could see from Margaret's face that she knew what Daphne was going to say. Almost.

'It's a disaster,' said Daphne, tears rolling down her cheeks. 'Another bloody baby.' She let Margaret lay her down, put a cold cloth on her forehead.

Later, with Tommy popping champagne, clearly over the moon, she began to come round to the idea. She wanted more children after all, five boys, but perhaps she wouldn't even mind even if it were another daughter. Tessa was a very sweet child. And it occurred to her that there might be a good side to all this. She hated to admit her treachery, and she hated being parted from Tommy, but a pregnant wife would be allowed to go home. To Ferryside. To her beloved Cornwall. For the sake of her health and the health of the baby, she and Tessa and Margaret would be allowed to go back to England.

Tommy agreed, looking bereft. Her health must come first. After all, he joked, she must look after herself. It might be strapping twin boys.

She did not find this thought amusing.

'I'll come back with the baby, as soon as it is strong enough, and we'll finish your posting together.'

But she had already left Alexandria, and was home in Cornwall, in the enchanted woods of Menabilly where someone walked ahead of her, dark-haired and laughing and rotten to the core. Rebecca, cunning as a fox, bold as a man. All the things that Daphne was not allowed to be.

Rebecca had arrived.

*

Just before Daphne sailed home with Margaret and Tessa on the *Caledonia*, a letter came from Angela with upsetting news. Uncle Jim was dying. By the time they arrived in London she was relieved to hear that he had rallied. She went to visit him in his apartment in Adelphi Terrace, a weight lying on her chest to think that this might be the last time she saw him.

She was let into the flat by Thurlston, the butler, who immediately melted away into a back room. No sign of Uncle Jim. At least his snooty secretary, Cynthia Asquith, wasn't there. Daphne had an instinctive distrust of Cynthia, the way she managed Jim and thrust her awful smirking little boy like a counterfeit Peter Pan at him, a child who made fun of Jim behind his back and asked him for sixpences.

Jim's apartment had the sepulchral gloominess of one of his ghostly plays, the walls panelled in dark oak, dark brown bookcases, a vast inglenook fireplace more in keeping with a rambling country farmhouse than a top-floor flat in London. His sitting room had in fact been used as a template for the scenery in one of his shivery ghost plays: where a young soldier comes back from the dead to talk to his father. The young man had been disturbingly like her eldest cousin George who had been killed in the Great War, almost breaking Jim's heart.

As Daphne stood waiting for Jim she noticed a photograph on the oak panelling. Michael at twelve years old, dressed for a fishing holiday in Scotland, the second summer after Sylvia died. Large eyes with a boy's uncomplicated, trusting gaze, a little sad. The small chin and tilted nose so clearly passed down from Grandpa George and Sylvia. He wore a tweed coat, a hat with a feather in the band, a fishing creel on his back. Jim had kitted all the boys out with rods and fishing gear that summer, rented an entire castle in the Outer Hebrides for two months. *Peter Pan* had made him staggeringly rich, money he poured out on the boys in fees for Eton, meals at the Savoy, the best tailoring – a sign both of his generosity and of his insecurity in raising his foster family.

She startled when a terrible, phlegmy coughing came from the inglenook. Uncle Jim had been there all along, sitting on the wooden settle inside the shadows. He got up slowly and came to join her. He'd aged terribly again since she last saw him, his face collapsed into folds of grief, his already small frame shrivelled away inside his jacket. He pointed to the basket on Michael's back.

'He wouldn't take that fishing creel off all the way over on the boat to Harris, wore it for days, ready to jump off and start fishing the moment we got there. That was the summer we first caught the ghost of Mary Rose. Found her on a tiny island on Loch Voshimid. Though it was a few years before I wrote the play.'

'I remember *Mary Rose*. It was so moving. And the music.' She gave an involuntary shiver, as if there were a cold draught from somewhere.

'Ah well, that was down to Michael. I know nothing about music so I had to ask Michael if he thought it was going to do. He was always my best critic.'

Daphne recalled sitting quietly on a sofa with Nico in the flat, the two of them turning the pages of a comic while Michael and

Uncle Jim listened to a gramophone recording of the haunting, ethereal music that was meant to conjure up the ghost who came back looking for her lost baby. She remembered thinking how she didn't like it much; the music made her feel the way she did when her bedroom was full of shadows. And yet there was something alluring and exciting about it.

The gramophone record crackling, Michael had picked up the needle, and said he liked it. It was mysterious and beautiful. Captured the mystery of the world beyond very well.

Jim stared at the photograph of Michael in silence, then wandered slowly back to the settle. Daphne joined him on the chair opposite, the fire every so often glowing brighter with a backdraught from the chimney. Thurlston came in with a tray of tea. Jim added a nip of whisky to his from a hip flask, offered it to Daphne who shook her head.

'And here's to the new child,' he said, raising his cup. 'May he or she be another talented and poetic du Maurier.' He put down his cup, interrupted by a coughing fit that made Daphne grasp the arms of her chair, ready to phone a doctor.

'That was the thing about my Michael, he had the soul of a poet, unlike me. Everything I write dry as dust.'

'Jim, you've always written such beautiful plays.'

'Whimsy written by a dry old cynic.'

'But your plays about meeting with those from the other side, the soldier who comes back from the war and speaks with his father. As if there's something beyond this life. A message of hope.'

'The sort of thing that sells tickets. No, when I am done, that's it for me. I always wished I could believe in a next life, as dear Michael seemed to. Michael was a pure soul. When Michael went, a light went out in the world.'

He struggled with another cough. Drew in deeply from his pipe and coughed alarmingly again.

'Are you writing anything new, Uncle Jim?'

He shook his head. ''Fraid it's all up with me.'

'When you get better, you'll be writing again.'

'No, Daphne. It's MacConnachie, he's done for me. You have to beware of MacConnachie.'

It took her a moment to remember who MacConnachie was. Some legendary trickster figure Jim had invented as a warning to the young, always calling them to take it easy, turn their back on the dullness of daily life and do as they wish.

'He looks fun, skimming along on his wings to begin with.' Another bout of phlegmy coughing. 'But then he turns on you, you're left wheeling around on one broken wing, going nowhere.' More racking coughs. 'He's done for me, MacConnachie. Takes all you have.'

'Never. You have to concentrate on getting better, Uncle Jim. And next time I see you, we'll go out to the Savoy for tea.'

He shook his head.

She took the lift down to the entrance knowing he was right, feeling a pang of loss for the mischievous Jim who had been part of her life as a child. She hated to think of him sitting alone in his empty flat now, with only memories and ghosts to keep him company. She sighed, laid a hand on her stomach. This baby would probably never meet Jim, would never meet Gerald. It was all too sad. The lift bumped as it reached the ground floor. She dabbed her face with her hands, then pulled back the concertina iron gate of the lift, suddenly needing to breathe in the cooler air outside.

She'd never really though about it, but she wondered now what it must have been like for Michael to spend so much time bound up in Jim's world, on the border between this life and the next, as if trapped in one of Jim's ghostly and nihilistic plays?

Poor Jim. He had done the best he could. He loved the boys.

And she thought of Daddy's arm heavy around her shoulder as a teenager at one of his parties in the garden, trying not to give in to her urge to pull away.

Sometimes, it wasn't enough to love a child fiercely. One had to let them go.

She headed for the office of the publishing house that Peter now ran with Nico, Peter Davies Ltd.

After the Great War twenty-year-old Peter had caused a great scandal by setting up house with a married woman twice his age. 'The war's broken that boy,' Daddy said. 'Clearly he needs a mother.' Jim, however, had refused to speak to Peter, worried what such an example might do to his younger brothers. It was only after the death of Michael that Peter and Jim had reconciled. Jim had set Peter up with a publishing company, giving him the rights to his books and plays. Nico had joined the firm a few years later.

After climbing the steep staircase to Peter Davies Ltd, Daphne arrived in the office out of breath. Peter leapt up and found her a seat. Brought through a tray of tea, at home in his book-lined room. Nico was also there, fair hair flopping over his forehead, a welcoming smile, always reassuringly pleasant.

'My, you look splendid,' Nico said. 'And congratulations.'

Peter handed round mugs of dark tea, a packet of Ginger Nuts. She was pleased to see that he was on great form, no sign of the low moods that sometimes troubled him. 'Sorry we're in shirtsleeves,' he said, nodding to his jacket on the back of the chair, 'but we've been wrestling with budgets. It's marvellous to see you. The last time must have been at dear Gerald's funeral.'

She bit her lip and nodded. 'At the wake afterwards, anyway. I couldn't bear to be there for the actual thing. I went up on the heath he loved so much, set some doves that I bought free. Watched them fly away.'

'A lovely idea.'

'It helped me. To think of him up there somehow, free. But tell me how you have been. And it's going well?'

Peter leaned back in his chair, looked more than pleased. 'Very well, in fact. Helps having Jim's royalties in the mix, of course. But you must let us know if there's anything we can do, with the new baby so imminent, lifts or running errands. You'll say if there is?'

'Angela and Mummy are here. You two have enough on your plate with your own growing families. And I know you keep an eye on Jim, pop in to see him most days. It's a weight off my mind to know you're both there.'

'Poor old thing,' said Peter. 'As you'll have seen, he's in a bad way. He's not going to get any better, but we'll make sure he's not alone. After all he's done for us. . .'

*

A week later, Flavia was born and a few weeks after that, Daphne returned to Egypt. A telegram came from Peter with the sad news that Daphne had expected. Tommy came home to find Daphne crying, the telegram in her hand.

'What is it? Is it your mother?'

'No, it's Jim – he's gone. But it feels as bad as losing family. I know I should be grateful having had the chance to spend so much of my childhood with such a special person, but it's hard, knowing I won't see him again. And with Daddy gone too.'

Tommy took her in his arms and rocked her gently.

'He was a great man. Loved by all.'

The newspapers were filled with tributes to the author who had created a legend that was now part of every childhood. When Daphne heard that the cinema was showing newsreels of Jim's funeral in Kirriemuir, she crept in at the end of the feature film to watch. With a jolt she saw Peter and Nico walking behind the coffin, shocked to see how terrible Peter looked, frowning, thin as a rake. Nothing like his cheerful self from the last time she had seen him. Nico beside him grim-faced. As ever, the newsreader insisted on referring to Peter as Peter Pan in that ghastly way the news people had, which he always hated.

Then a letter arrived from Peter with a fuller account of how Jim had passed away, painting a disturbing picture.

I wanted to let you know that Jim faded away with Nico and I by his side constantly. And I believe he would have had a peaceful end but for Cynthia. My mistake was to call her to let her know that Jim seemed to be going. I thought I owed it to her to let her know since she'd been his secretary for years. She must have leapt in her car and driven all night because she and her doctor arrived with remarkable speed. Jim was unconscious by then, more or less gone. She offered to let Nico and I have a rest – we'd been up for several nights. So we thanked her and left her and her doctor with Jim. When we came back, they must have given Jim an enormous shot of adrenalin by hypodermic syringe, enough for Jim to wake up and sign his name to a will she'd brought with her. I doubt he knew what he was doing.

So now it all goes to Cynthia, all the rights to the books, the money. And since she's in with the powers that be and the top lawyers, we can't fight it. I know one shouldn't fuss about money – one isn't owed anything – but one does feel it for one's children. He'd set up legacies for the boys and for Nico's and Jack's children. That's all gone. Nico's particularly upset about losing the rights to producing the plays. Says no one else will understand how to put them on properly.

One can't begin to imagine how Cynthia could sink so low, but there it is. The aristocracy are not like us. But it's funny how these things take one emotionally. You see, I've always wanted to see Jim as a father figure after Arthur died, as he wanted us to think of him in that way. But a father leaves a legacy, and with Cynthia *cutting the knot, leaving us out completely, it somehow feels as though the whole thing with Jim was a mirage.*

I'll have to go to Jim's flat to sort out the family belongings that are still stored there, boxes and boxes of papers and photographs that must have been there for years. All rather depressing.

Daphne put in a trunk call to Peter but when she got through he sounded very unlike his usual calm self, very off, speaking slowly and carefully in a monotone voice, a man who has had one drink too many. He was coldly angry with Cynthia.

She rang Nico, who was also furious with Cynthia but more resigned to how things had turned out. He confirmed that Peter was very depressed, and drinking too much, but promised to keep an eye on him.

Daphne put down the phone with a feeling of apprehension.

Another three months before she and Tommy returned home. It felt too long.

CHAPTER 9

ALEXANDRIA 1936

For the first time, Daphne began to fall in love with Egypt. Tommy took her out to camp among the vast sand dunes along the Libyan border. They slept beneath a silent dome of stars, the only sound the sighing fire crumbling into amber jewels, as she and Tommy lay side by side at night, waking together at five in the morning to watch the dawn rise over the desert.

Sometimes, Tommy sat looking out towards Libya, a tin cup of coffee in his hands. She knew at those times that he wasn't thinking of the stark beauty of the desert, but of troop movements, the rumble of war sounding ever louder.

Please God, let that never happen.

Back in her room in rue Jessop, the shutters closed against the glaring Egyptian heat, Daphne continued to walk the damp and verdant woods of Menabilly – or Manderley as she named the house in her story. She saw the newly married second Mrs de Winter timidly meeting the mesmeric housekeeper, Mrs Danvers, who constantly conjured up the spirit of Rebecca, undermining what little confidence she had until she doubted even her husband's love for her.

There would be a drowning. A murder. It was all rather macabre. Whatever was the publisher going to think? She doubted that anyone would ever want to read such an odd, psychological tale.

Her world of Manderley became a drug, an escape from dusty Alexandria, as she followed cool pathways through ancient trees, or wandered the passageways of a mysterious house lost in time. And dancing ahead of her, always a little out of reach, the beautiful Rebecca, bold and daring as a man. Wicked, careless Rebecca, causing whatever mischief she wanted, taking whatever she wanted.

Mrs de Winter was a pale, insipid figure by her side. Rebecca was the one who fascinated Daphne, and her constant companion until Tommy's posting ended that December and they were finally able to go home.

Mummy was shocked when Daphne announced that she wasn't going to be with Tessa and Baby Flavia and Nanny at Cannon Hall for Christmas. She was going down to Ferryside with just Tommy.

'Mummy, I absolutely have to finish this book.'

'But what will the girls think if you are not with them?' she asked, evidently forgetting how Angela and Daphne had seen far more of Nanny than Mummy growing up.

'They won't even notice. They're too small,' said Daphne confidently. 'They will be more than happy just playing with some wrapping paper.'

Rebecca had taken hold of her. She wrote in a frenzy, while winter squalls battered the Ferryside windows with sleet, sitting at her desk overlooking the choppy estuary waters, hardly noticing the weather. Tommy cooked an excellent duck for Christmas dinner in the top-floor kitchen, whistling tunes as though he were in a galley kitchen on the high seas.

When the weather was mild enough, she and Tommy wrapped up in jumpers and coats and took the ferry over to Fowey to walk the three miles out to Menabilly, holding hands and walking through the pattering of wet leaves, staring up into the tangled woods with their hundred-foot oaks and sycamores against the fading light of three o'clock.

By the time they were due to return to London at New Year, Daphne had an almost complete manuscript. She packed it up, ready to finish once they were in Tommy's new quarters near Fleet. But as she tucked it into her suitcase, she had the odd impression that something that hadn't existed before was now out in the world, the fleeting figure of a woman in a red dress, Rebecca, wandering the shadows in the tangled woods of Menabilly, trailing cigarette smoke, a sneer on her lips.

CHAPTER 10

FLEET 1938

The chaos of moving to a house near Fleet where Tommy was posted meant that all writing was put on hold. 'I know you're doing your very best,' Tommy would say, 'But have you seen my blue tie, Daphs? Haven't found it since we moved in.'

As soon as the house was unpacked and in order, the furniture placed as much like their old house as possible – to give a feeling of home despite the move, an army trick, Tommy said – Daphne set up her desk in the French windows of the sitting room where she could see the girls playing in the garden and continued working on *Rebecca*.

One evening in March, she came through to the sitting room where Tommy was listening to music on the wireless. She felt drained and exhausted but elated.

'Pour me a very large gin, would you, Ducks. It's done.' She threw herself on the sofa, put her feet up on the arm. 'All this work and I bet no one will even read it. I've told Victor to expect a rather odd little book.'

She parcelled the book up and sent it off to Victor with a feeling of doom. She barely understood herself what she had written. Now, exorcised of some possession, exiled from world that she had created in her Manderley, she was left with a deflated low mood.

She knew she had to put *Rebecca* and her qualms about it out of her mind, not expect to hear from Victor very soon, but after just four days he was on the phone. 'Daphne, this has major hit all over it. A perfect bestseller. I'm ordering a run of twenty thousand.'

'Was it bad news?' asked Tommy, seeing Daphne's worried face as she put down the phone. She gave a bemused laugh.

'No, it's good news, actually. Victor thinks it will be a smash. I only hope he hasn't ordered too many copies. Twenty thousand, would you believe? How ever are we going to sell that many?' She put her hands on her cheeks and shook her head, smiling in spite of herself.

'*Rebecca*'s wonderful. Take it from your biggest fan. And look how well your last book did. *Jamaica Inn*'s a film now. Don't you worry.'

'Thank you, Ducks. You're always the first person I want to read my books.'

What she couldn't say to Tommy was how much she did worry, lying awake at night, thinking about money. Tommy's army pay wasn't nearly enough to cover their bills with the house and Nanny. Unlike most men of his rank, he didn't have a private income and Tommy had expensive tastes in cigars and bespoke tailoring, fine wines and a new car. She was the main breadwinner in the house. They would be in serious difficulties if this book panned.

*

Spring was breaking out in the gardens around the lovely old Georgian rectory they had rented. Tulips and forget-me-nots gave way to peonies and irises. Daphne spent long afternoons in the garden, wearing shorts and a sleeveless top while the children played with their wheelbarrow and spades. At thirty-one, her limbs slim and brown, her waist almost as small as before the children, she felt strong and healthy, her hair sun-bleached, her square but delicate face tanned in a way that made her eyes more blue. She loved to watch Tommy stride across the lawn when he came home each evening, tall and vital, in the prime of his life. They often lingered together in the garden in the summer evenings, reading out things that amused them from books or magazines, making wicked fun of people they knew, or simply sipping a gimlet and listening to a recording by Charles Trenet, singing in French about love and happiness – perhaps reaching out to hold hands and listen to the birds sing their last litany as the evening twilight began to gather.

But the worsening situation in Europe was impossible to ignore, casting a long shadow over the future. The newspapers were full of reports of Hitler and the Nazis in Germany, their stockpiling of weapons, their aggressive talk of war.

Tommy began looking ever more strained and worried when he returned home.

Watching him as he walked across the garden one afternoon, she could tell that some meeting had not gone well.

'Come on, Ducks. Sit down and have a drink and catch your breath,' she insisted. She went inside to fix a gimlet for them both and came back to find him sitting in the deckchair, fists on knees, not one bit relaxed and glaring at the flower beds.

'This government are fools to think we can appease Hitler,' he said, hardly noticing as he took the glass, stood up and began to march up and down with it. 'I can't bear to say it, Ducks, but there's going to be a war soon and it's only Churchill who really understands just how unprepared the army is.'

'It can't be as bad as that, surely, darling.'

'Worse than that. It's so bad we're going to have to rely on the French. They have four divisions. Germany has a hundred. I tell you, this government ought to be shot. Country's simply not prepared.' He drained his glass and went to change out of his uniform for dinner.

She walked slowly around the garden, adjusting to the realization that Tommy had moved from talking about if there would be a war to when, considering actual details and plans ready for an invasion. She felt as chilled as if a cloud had pulled across the sky, the garden reduced to monochrome. The future a tunnel leading them towards a place where real bombs and bullets could injure Tommy or might hurt Tessa and Flavia if there were to be an invasion.

A cold growth of fear began to bloom in her chest, a prickle of adrenalin in her fingers. And she was powerless. Nothing she could do to stop what was coming.

The publication of *Rebecca* in a few days felt like a small matter in comparison. She only hoped the critics would be kind. And that Victor had been right to print so many copies.

At the end of the week, Victor rang again, his voice jubilant. 'Daphne, get ready for some marvellous news. *Rebecca*'s already sold out, all twenty thousand copies, in a week. I'm reprinting immediately. I told you it was going to be a bestseller.'

'The newspaper reviews don't seem so keen,' said Daphne. 'Listen to this one. Here we go.' She read out, "A lightweight romance to take the mind away from the troubles of real life." Not a single one gets that it's a psychological study, and rather dark.'

'Pay no attention to them, Daphne. The critics never forgive a bestseller. Just look at the size of your cheques, dear.'

When *Rebecca* was published in America with Doubleday, it was the same story, record sales and snooty critics. It was certainly a relief, however, to see so much money coming in.

'Perhaps we can think about that new car now,' suggested Tommy, leafing through his car magazines.

'When we've put some savings by, Ducks, don't you think? I don't want to be like Daddy. Spent the money so fast that he had to do those embarrassing cigarette adverts before he died.'

Victor rang once again to say that they were going to a third printing, then a fourth. Foreign language rights were sold in dozens of countries, a film deal agreed with Hitchcock as the director. She was astonished that so many people had been caught up in a story spun from memories of a house that she had only seen on fleeting visits, creeping around the grounds like a trespasser.

Newspapers wanted interviews, and the more she refused, the more they clamoured. Victor was pressing her to do them though she hated to be photographed and dissected. 'Look at this one,' she told Tommy, waving a magazine at him. 'I gave the wretched man tea and cake, answered all his damn questions and then this. "Mrs Browning looks more like a pretty subaltern's wife than the wife of a major," she read out crossly.

'Nothing wrong with his eyesight,' said Tommy with a smile.

A call came from her American publisher, Nelson Doubleday. 'The good news is that you've sold two hundred thousand copies of *Rebecca* here and counting, Daphne. Astonishing. The other news isn't so good. When a book does this well, it brings the crackpots out of the woodwork. There's a woman threatening to sue you for plagiarism. It's complete nonsense but she claims you read her book, *Blind Windows*, and copied *Rebecca* from it.'

'But I've never heard of it.'

'No one has. It's unreadable, and nothing like *Rebecca*. Anyway, she wants to take us to court, but I'm going to make this go away. I don't want you to worry about it. This is just to let you know.'

In another time, she would have lost sleep over such news, but there were far more serious matters to worry about.

With the possibility of another war growing, Tommy often came home in a furious mood, stamping up and down the sitting room in his uniform about the lack of discipline in the men, the stupidity of the generals who didn't realize how important the air force was going to be in the next war.

It was stirringly impressive to see her soldier husband, so sure and passionate about defending the country, a knight about to do battle – but this was no game. Two horrible companions had moved in to live with Daphne permanently, fear and anxiety. She had grim memories of the last war as a child, wearing black armbands for Daddy's brother, Guy, and for Cousin George, shot through the head at just nineteen years old.

What was it that made people want to fight and kill each other? Something dark in the human heart, some greed or selfishness that if left unchecked grew to monstrous proportions, menacing entire countries with war. This was the evil that had to be cut out like a cancer.

If the world was to change, then people needed to change – and she should begin with herself. She began to pray and attend the village church nearby, reading the Bible for clues as to how one might become a better person. Sending for tomes on Greek philosophy from Foyles.

Each day spent with Tommy felt precious, lying against his soft jumper, his favourite canary-yellow one, breathing in his reassuring scent of cigars and cologne.

'Perhaps we should try for another baby,' she suggested one evening. The thought of new life among so much gloom had made her realize how much she did want another baby.

'Certainly be marvellous to put a notice in *The Times* one day saying one had a son,' he said.

'One's son, Christian Browning, doesn't that sound heavenly. But even if it is another girl I think I'll be happy,' said Daphne. 'Tessa and Flavia are such dears, really.'

'Another beautiful girl, like her mother.'

She thought of the little blue cupboard that she had had painted for the nursery the first time she was pregnant, the name Christian stencilled on the nursery door. Could it be possible they might bring the little blue cupboard down from the attic this time?

Hand in hand they went upstairs, the sound of a song thrush through the open window.

At the beginning of September, she listened with a sinking heart as Chamberlain announced on the wireless that Germany had refused to retreat from its invasion of Poland. The United Kingdom was now at war. She knew that from now on Tommy would belong to the army far more than he belonged to the family, and there was nothing to be done but bear it.

At least their house in Fleet seemed removed from troubles, a quiet backwater where she and the girls might wait out the war. But a few weeks later, Tommy had news.

'They are making me Commander of the Hundred and Twenty-eighth Battalion.'

'Well, that's wonderful, Ducks, but why the long face?'

'Darling, I'm afraid the barracks are on the coast and there's no married accommodation for you and the children.'

'Then we'll find somewhere very near.'

'Too dangerous. The army barracks will be too much of a target for enemy aircraft across the Channel.'

'Then you'll be in danger.'

'Shh.' He pressed her against his chest, stroking her hair. 'I'll find you somewhere far enough away for you to be safe, but near enough to drive over and visit whenever I have leave.'

'Living apart. . .'

They lay together in bed, skin against skin. She looked over at the row of five small teddy bears that Tommy took with him everywhere. One of the things that had made her love him more when she had found out about them. It struck her then that they would soon be gone, placed by his bed in the barracks.

How many nights would she lie alone in the dark, Tommy away on the coast, the barracks a prime target? She felt tears flooding on to the pillow. Not wanting to wake Tommy, she crept along the corridor to the bathroom, shut the door, sat on the side of the bath and sobbed.

At least before they had to move – still no idea where she was to go to with the girls – Daphne was able to give Tommy some good news. 'Darling, I'm expecting again.'

He was ecstatic, sure it was a boy.

But what sort of a world, she wondered, was this baby going to be born into?

CHAPTER 11

HERTFORDSHIRE MAY 1940

Daphne wasn't expecting too much, though a little garden for the children would be nice, she thought, as the car drove through fields and orchards towards their new accommodation. Tommy's batman, a rough-cut East Ender of twenty, had been in charge of finding them somewhere to stay. It was going to be horribly cramped and uncomfortable being billeted on strangers, but there was a war on and so she was determined to make the best of it.

The car followed a long brick wall and turned in through tall ironwork gates. It pulled up in front of a red-brick Lutyens mansion, elegant roofs and chimneys outlined against a blue spring sky. Getting out of the car, she felt a new respect for Tommy's aide-de-camp. The house was beautiful.

Their hosts were waiting on the steps: Patricia and Christopher Puxley. A tall, well-dressed couple in country tweeds. Daphne felt a surge of gratitude that complete strangers were willing to take them into their home, for no other reason than that they wanted to do their bit.

'You are most welcome,' said Patricia, as if Daphne were a long-awaited friend. She was a thin, angular woman with an

Irish accent, red hair in a bob. Christopher shook her hand, a gentle manner and thick dark hair swept back from his forehead. He was a little plump but tall enough to carry it off. They were both in their late forties, the same age as Tommy.

'Now, call me Paddy. Everyone does,' said her host, leading Daphne through a succession of elegant rooms. 'And this will be yours.' Daphne was shown into her own suite: bedroom, sitting room and bathroom. The windows open over a formal garden filled with roses and birdsong. Another set of rooms for Margaret and the girls.

'It's heavenly,' said Daphne. 'I really can't thank you enough.'

'It's we who should be thanking you,' said Paddy, 'with Commander Browning doing so much for the war. I'm afraid poor Christopher was invalided out in the last one.'

She couldn't wait for Tommy to arrive, see the beautiful house and meet the charming Puxleys, but three weeks passed before Tommy was given leave, and then disappointingly, only for a couple of days.

Paddy set out a supper table in Daphne's sitting room. But it was almost ten before Tommy's car drew up outside. Paddy and Christopher had tactfully already gone to bed.

Up in her room, Tommy poured himself a drink, still in his greatcoat. Sat down on the sofa, looking weary and drawn. 'I was right. We're going to have to bloody rely on the French until we can get our army into shape. Can you believe that's all that stands between us and Hitler marching straight into London.'

'Well, have something to eat.'

'Don't think I can. The old stomach playing up again.'

Since the last war, Tommy had always suffered from terrible stomach cramps under stress. How on earth was he going to manage now when he had nothing but stress?

'Do you want me to call the doctor?'

He held up his hand, shook his head. Clearly he didn't want her to go on about it.

'This'll settle it,' he said, holding up his whisky.

Her darling Tommy was asleep the moment he lay on the bed. She pulled the eiderdown up over his shoulder and lay down beside him. His face seemed older but as fine as ever. Tomorrow she would show him the gardens. Perhaps he would relax a little, play with Tessa and Flavia.

She woke to find him bending over her, already fully dressed, smelling of shaving soap. He kissed her forehead. She squinted at the alarm. Six o'clock.

'You're going?'

'Sorry, darling. They called.'

She grabbed her housecoat and followed him down to the car. He looked so handsome in his uniform and she loved him more than ever, but as the car drove away she noticed a more vinegary mix of emotions, a keen resentment for him leaving – even though she understood perfectly well that it was hardly his fault – and a cold fear for what might happen to him.

Over the next few weeks, Tommy telephoned every day, but was given hardly any leave. The news on the wireless was shockingly terrible. With devastating speed, country after country across Europe fell to Hitler. Reich soldiers entered Paris. The British and French were driven back to the beaches of Dunkirk, brought home in a makeshift flotilla of domestic boats. Thousands of soldiers were captured or killed. Two of Tommy's closest friends had died at Dunkirk, and she was profoundly shaken by the realization that it could so easily have been Tommy. Life was a bleak nightmare that could not be escaped, simply endured.

If only she could do something to help. She'd signed up for a civil defence course but the bossy woman in charge had advised against a pregnant woman doing gas contamination. Paddy ran everything so well in the house, told her to rest with a new baby on the way. The girls were either with Nanny Margaret or with Paddy who had no children of her own and seemed happy to spend hours brushing their hair, letting them sort through her jewellery box or taking them out on walks.

A phone call came from one of Daddy's old friends, Bunny Austin. 'I recall you were very interested in the ideas of Moral Rearmament last time we spoke. We were wondering if you would you consider writing a few articles for us. Something to inspire people, encourage them to listen to that voice of conscience and become less egotistical. The only way we're going to put an end to fighting and wars. And we want to give people hope and courage to keep going while this war is raging on.'

'Oh, Bunny, I don't think I could. I've never written sermons.'

'Not sermons. These are real accounts from people who've actually faced the hardships of war with bravery and selflessness, for the sake of family and country. What we need now is someone with the skill and talent to turn them into readable stories.'

Daphne set to work. Now that bullying regimes had taken over much of the world – Stalin in Russia, Hitler and Mussolini in Europe – Britain seemed like a small outpost on the edge of the Atlantic, holding on to its values of democracy, justice and freedom. She might have lightly scoffed at the Church of England and the King before, but now she saw them as beacons of hope, an example of all that she valued in the world that she wanted to give to her children, precious and vital and in grave danger.

She also began to follow Bunny's advice and spend time sitting quietly and listening for that small voice of conscience, determined to start with changing herself for the better.

She could hardly bear to listen to the wireless any more, however, with an invasion from across the Channel expected at any minute. When this baby was born, would Nazis be marching through London just as they had marched into Paris?

Each afternoon, Daphne sat in the garden, the scent of the roses soporific, feeling weighted down by the small mound of her pregnancy. From the open doors of the sitting room, she could hear Christopher playing Debussy on the piano, each languid note like a drop in a pool on a summer afternoon. She went in through the open French windows and sat beside him on the piano stool. He smiled as she began to turn the pages of the music for him. He was tall and charming in a very English way, a gentleman farmer slightly run to fat.

Christopher stopped playing. 'Fix you a drink?'

'Lovely. Very weak gin and it.'

She sat on the sofa, feet up. She found that Christopher always had a calming effect on her. Although she'd noticed that sometimes the oddest thought popped into her mind when she was with him – how his chin with its blueish five o'clock shadow at the end of the day might feel against her cheek.

He handed her a glass, his long fingers brushing hers – a fleeting reaction in her body that surprised her.

'Don't you sometimes wish one could disappear to an island far away until all this is over?' asked Daphne.

Christopher considered this, his blue eyes narrowed. He had the thickest of black hair. 'Mull,' said Christopher. 'I love Mull. Or a tiny place in the Caribbean perhaps, palm trees and sunshine.'

'Shall I tell you a secret?' said Daphne. 'I've always been able to disappear to a secret island, any time I choose. It's a game Barrie taught me when I was small.'

Christopher took out an embroidered tobacco pouch. Filled his pipe and put the stem between his full lips. 'Do tell.'

'First, you must close your eyes. No, I mean do it.'

He chuckled and shut his eyes, still sucking on his pipe.

'Now concentrate on some point in the distance. There, you see it? Now very slowly, your island starts to rise up from the sea, growing larger all the time.'

'I'm not seeing much.'

'It's there. Keep looking. No, don't open your eyes.'

After a moment, he nodded slowly. 'I think I'm seeing it.'

'Yes.'

'Is it a nice island?'

'Lovely. Somewhere near Jamaica.'

'And look, there are tiny figures on it. Growing clearer. You can see their faces now. How many are there?'

'Just two. And what do you know? They look awfully like you and me.' He turned to her with a look of mock surprise. 'Well, wouldn't that be nice?'

As summer progressed, Daphne sat with her feet up on the sofa in the drawing room each afternoon – her ankles became noticeably puffy in the hot weather – listening to Christopher play the piano rather divinely. He too seemed to have nothing else to do. And she was beginning to realize what a sensitive man Christopher actually was. Always ready to listen.

She lay, eyes half-closed as he played, imagining being held in his protective arms. She saw him dip his head to kiss her. Her eyes flew open. What was she thinking?

She missed their afternoon music for the next few days, guilty at such treacherous thoughts.

Tommy telephoned faithfully every day, but if his calls were better than nothing, his visits were almost worse than nothing, their time together snatched away before they had had a chance to relax, moods and misunderstandings on both sides in the sultry summer heat.

When she heard he was due a whole week's leave, it felt as though Christmas had arrived early. At last, they could be together as a family for a while.

He arrived in full general's uniform, important and hurried. People, especially women, she noticed, had begun to treat her tall and rather impressive husband with notable deference.

Paddy invited neighbours over for tennis. She'd heard that Tommy loved sports. The neighbours had five daughters, all in their teens and twenties. Slim and pretty in tennis whites, they twittered around Tommy who was in his most charming mode. Daphne sat at the side of the court, feeling fat and slow, her maternity smock and tweed skirt shapeless and dated.

He came over, flushed from winning his mixed doubles with Veronica. Or was it Virginia?

'Shall I get you some lemonade, darling?' he asked.

'I'm surprised you have the time,' glowered Daphne.

He poured her a glass.

'Do you want me to stop playing, sit with you?'

'What sort of a dragon of a wife do you think I am? No, go and play.' She waved him away.

The trouble was, she did feel like a dragon, very snappy indeed. Every time Tommy came for one of his brief leaves it was the same; he was preoccupied and busy with phone calls and papers to sign. She was beginning to feel entirely peripheral to his life.

It took her a couple of days to stop feeling irritable. A couple more days, then he was gone. Why hadn't she been nicer? She sat on the edge of her bed that evening and tried to listen for the small voice that helped one behave less selfishly.

Christopher and she had been thrown together a lot of late.

One afternoon, as she sat next to him on the piano stool, turning the pages while Christopher played Chopin, she heard Margaret talking out in the hallway.

'Go and tell Mummy that it's time for tea, Tessa.'

'Mummy's sitting with Christopher,' said Tessa. 'And she gets cross if I disturb her when she's with him.'

'Don't be silly, dear.'

'She does,' Flavia chimed in. 'Mummy likes to talk with Christopher on her own and we can't join in.'

Margaret put her head around the door. She looked over at Daphne and Christopher together on the piano stool as if she had never seen them until now.

'Tea's ready, Daphne,' she said in a slightly offended voice. 'If you want to join the children.'

Margaret began to suddenly appear in the sitting room in the evening as if expecting to chance upon something, saying she'd had to come down because the noise of the piano was keeping the children awake in the nursery above. So Christopher would stop playing and he and Daphne would sit and chat on the sofa.

Daphne had begun to mull over an idea for a new book. It wasn't usually her thing, but she felt that she needed to lose herself inside a romance, as did most war-weary people. Lady St Columb would fall in love with a handsome French pirate with the same dark hair and gentle manners as Christopher Puxley, and with the same long and sensitive hands. Dressed as a boy, Lady St Columb would join the pirate ship and have a passionate affair before returning to the family she dearly loved, as she knew she always would.

It was not difficult to conjure up a burgeoning romance on paper while she allowed herself this small flirtation with Christopher, the air increasingly charged with anticipation, brief caresses that left them both on edge as they parted and went up to bed.

None of it was real. It was nothing more than an escape from the day-to-day worries of war. After all, she was simply following the old Jim method of taking a real person and hanging around their neck a similar but imaginary character for the sake of the novel.

One evening, after Paddy had gone to bed early with a migraine, Daphne found herself leaning against Christopher on the sofa. She felt his lips soft against hers. His skin smelled divine. Realized she didn't want him to stop. She began to kiss him back.

A picture of Tommy, alone in his barracks, the children asleep in their beds. She felt her head beginning to spin.

'I'm sorry. I'm sorry. We shouldn't...'

She pushed him away, ran up to her room.

Alone on her bed upstairs, the bed that she shared with Tommy when he was there, Daphne finally heard that still, small voice. What was she doing? She had to leave Langley End, as soon as possible.

*

Daphne wrote to Tommy to tell him that she was moving out from Langley End. She didn't want Paddy to have to cope with the trouble of her giving birth. Fortunately a house nearby was available.

Christian Frederick Browning was the easiest birth she had experienced. Tommy drove over as soon as he could get away, delighted with the pink scrap with a ruff of blond hair.

'Isn't he perfect?' said Daphne, kissing his warm, downy head. You can put your announcement in *The Times* at last. A boy. Christian Frederick Browning.'

Margaret came in with a warmed bottle of milk. 'If you want me to take the baby now,' she said, 'I'll feed him while you have a nap. Same routine as the girls,' she said confidently.

'Oh no,' said Daphne, her face bemused. 'I shall be feeding Kits myself. I could simply hold this darling boy for ever.'

Daphne did have a twinge of worry, wondering if the girls might be jealous to see how much she kissed and cuddled Kits. She remembered how at sea she'd felt when the girls were born, desperate to hand them over to Nanny. But Tessa and Flavia seemed thrilled with their little brother, vying for the chance to let his fingers curl around theirs and to kiss him.

'That's enough now, girls,' said Daphne. 'I need to talk to Daddy about where we are going to live next.'

'Well, it was jolly good of you to move out of the Puxleys' for the birth, but I'm not sure why you did. Paddy was happy for you to stay.'

'It felt like time. I just didn't expect the owners here to return so suddenly. I suppose I could go down to Mummy in Fowey.'

'Ducks, that's far too far away. I'd hardly see you and the children. The best thing is to go back to Langley End. Don't you think so, Margaret?'

'I couldn't say,' said Margaret, who pursed her lips and looked as though she could say a lot.

Daphne picked up Baby Kits and breathed in his delicious smell of baby talc. Perhaps Langley End would be best for all the family in the end. The girls loved Paddy. The house ran so smoothly. And if she could hear warning bells going off, she firmly ignored them.

CHAPTER 12

LONDON MARCH 1941

Seated in the makeshift recording studio, a dimly lit bomb shelter beneath West Kensington, Daphne coughed, held up her sheet of notes and leaned towards the microphone. Even down here, the air had a gritty quality, filled with the dust from a thousand pulverised buildings. Bunny nodded a look of encouragement at her.

'When I say three,' said a young man sitting next to the recording machine. Daphne took a deep breath and spoke into the microphone.

'I am speaking to you today from a London air-raid shelter, but by the miracle of wireless, it is as though I am with you as you sit by your firesides across America. Eighteen months ago, our lives here were equally peaceful. But all that has changed. Five days after my son was born, my husband left for the coast and now I lie awake and think of him as he and his men keep watch, and as Hitler's barges lie ready for invasion at any moment. And yet, though life may be difficult, and food scarce, this terrible war has given us the opportunity to find new strengths within ourselves. The greater the destruction around us, the more we bear each other's burdens and work for the common good.'

*

The train back to Cornwall was late leaving the station. Everyone looked tense and tired, their clothes faded. It was a risk coming up to London with the Blitz raging, but the Moral Rearmament work was essential. She rested her head against the seat, drained of every last bit of energy. With Margaret constantly ill for the past few weeks, life had become a never-ending round of sleepless nights with a crying baby, days feeding Kits and pinning on nappies while trying to keep the two little girls from running riot. Yesterday she'd found Flavia drawing on the wall while Tessa threw a tantrum because she wanted her best frock so she could go downstairs and drink sherry. In any moment she had to herself, Daphne tried to write a few more pages of *Frenchman's Creek*, cursing Christopher in the room below, forever banging away on his piano.

The dust and the damp had left an itchy rawness in her lungs. She hoped to goodness that she wasn't starting a cold.

But the London air had done its work. For the next week she lay in bed, delirious and burning, her breathing raw and painful. Tommy must have come home on leave at some point for she had woken to find him by the bed, holding her hand, his face taut with concern. She'd heard the doctor talking about pneumonia. 'Touch and go, I'm afraid.' Wondered whom the doctor was talking about. Should she get up and help?

When she was finally able to sit up, dizzy and weak, the doctor told her sternly, 'You will need a long convalescence, Mrs Browning, if you are to avoid lasting damage to your lungs.'

She was hardly going to rush around. She could barely totter to the bathroom without feeling faint. Stairs were impossible. Thankfully, Margaret was now better, taking full charge of the children.

'You need to have a change from this room,' said Paddy when she came in with beef tea a few days later. 'You must come down to the drawing room for a couple of hours each afternoon.'

'I'm not sure I could manage the stairs.'

Paddy sent Christopher to help. He picked her up and she put her arms round his neck. He carried her downstairs and placed her gently on the sofa.

Each day Christopher would carry her down in his arms before playing music for hours as Daphne lay and dreamed of Donna St Columb and her dark-haired French pirate with his scent of tobacco.

Was it so very wrong to daydream in this way, to share kisses and cuddles when everyone else had gone to bed? Was this little fantasy perhaps nature's way of helping wives cope when their husbands were away?

The news on the wireless was a nightmare. She worried constantly. Tommy had been promoted again, to Major General, and sent down to Somerset to organize the army's first airborne division. He was now flying gliders and planes in readiness for some mission she wasn't to ask about. She saw him falling from the sky. Dreamed of burning planes.

The only time the din of anxiety stopped was when she entered into the private world between her and Christopher, the distant island where no one else could reach them –

all the annoyance of Christopher disturbing her work now forgiven.

She and Christopher began to stay up later and later after everyone else was in bed, gradually finding themselves sitting closer, Daphne resting her head on his shoulder, his arm around her. Easy to fall into more passionate kisses and embraces.

There was a moment when she could have stopped it, when she could have stood up and told him it had to end. But it was so divine, lying on the sofa together, feeling the softness of his lips against hers, their bodies moving to a private music – not that they ever went too far. Not a real affair.

One evening, Daphne heard a noise from the doorway. A sharp intake of breath. The light snapped on.

Paddy stood in the doorway, her face a mask of shock. Daphne sat up quickly, pulling her clothes straight. Christopher too shot upright, standing on the carpet, his hair dishevelled.

'It wasn't. . .' he began, hurrying over to Paddy.

Paddy put up her hand, as if shielding herself. She turned the saddest eyes Daphne had ever seen towards her. 'And I thought you were my friend.'

Daphne could hear her muffled sobbing as Paddy ran out and up the stairs.

Casting a horrified look at Daphne, Christopher ran after his wife.

Daphne sank down on the sofa, her face in her hands, feeling as if she had been dipped head to toe in shame. If only she could erase the last few minutes. Not that they had really done anything very wrong. Not a complete affair. She loved

Tommy as much as she ever did, loved him absolutely, for goodness' sake.

But that didn't change the painful truth that Paddy was now heartbroken. Daphne began to feel hot all over. What if Paddy couldn't forgive Christopher? What if she had wrecked the Puxleys' marriage completely?

Her heart gave a lurch. And what if Paddy wrote to Tommy? Daphne spent a sleepless night.

In the morning there was a knock on her door. Paddy came in, her eyes downcast. She looked gaunt and ill. 'I've decided I won't say anything to Tommy,' Paddy told her.

'Paddy, I'm so sorry. Let me explain. You must know it was nothing. And nothing really happened. I never wanted to hurt you. You've been so kind—'

Paddy cut her short. 'I want you to leave Langley End,' she said coldly. 'By the end of the week. I never want to see you again.'

As Daphne was shutting a badly packed case, Bunny telephoned.

'Daphne, *Come Wind Come Weather* is selling like hot cakes. People are finding your stories wonderfully moving and inspiring. Would you have time to do a few more?'

'I'm sorry, Bunny, but I don't think I can. When it comes to listening for that small voice, I think my receiver might be broken.'

CHAPTER 13

FOWEY APRIL 1942

Fowey was unrecognizable, teaming with troops, the harbour bristling with naval boats of all descriptions. Ferryside had been requisitioned by American officers. Mummy, Angela and Jeanne were now living in a small house on the esplanade with no room to take in five more refugees. Daphne managed to find a cottage to rent at the head of Readymoney Cove. The usually lovely view of Polruan across the water now marred by a grid of iron bars eighteen feet high, stretching from one side of the bay to the other.

In spite of the upheaval, Daphne was determined to stick to her routes and immediately began to produce the next new book, a saga set in Ireland, based on the stories Christopher had told her about the Irish mansion his family had lost in the uprisings. She worked in a tiny room that was little more than a corridor next to the kitchen.

'It's certainly marvellous how well you concentrate,' said Margaret, Kits still wet and yelling in his cot, the girls still in their nighties and asking for breakfast.

It was depressing to hear that poor Tommy would not be allowed home for Christmas that year. He was sent to the North African desert, his knowledge of the terrain from his time in Alexandria now vital to the Allies. He had never been in more danger. She prayed each night for his safety, kneeling shivering by the bedside as snow lingered in deep drifts around the cottage and across the beach.

Then in February Tommy's aide-de-camp called with the news she had been dreading.

'Daphne, Tommy's alive but his glider came down. He's got a serious shoulder injury, a blood clot on his knee.'

The few weeks that Tommy was allowed home to convalesce felt like a gift, talking and laughing like old times, snuggling up together in front of the fire – Daphne taking care not to jolt his injuries – while snow lingered on in freezing weather unknown for a Cornish spring. But as soon as he was finally able to walk up and down the small beach with the ugly web of iron bars stretched across it, and just as the children were getting used to having Daddy home, the army called Tommy back.

The worry and the loneliness returned as the days and weeks dragged on. When a call came from Christopher to say he was motoring down and would like to visit her, Daphne hesitated. But he was, after all, the main inspiration for her Irish historical saga, *Hungry Hill*. She badly needed to chat with him to help the novel move forward, she told herself.

It would be impossible, however, to have such conversations with the three children piling into the room, and with Margaret there who had taken a dislike to Christopher. She knew of a secluded cottage overlooking the sea, a mile off the track and no one passing by. It was an abandoned watchman's cottage, one wall made of small-paned windows looking out over the sea and the sky.

As they sat together on a blanket in the sun, Christopher put his arm around her once again. She let herself relax against his side, the familiar smell of his sweet tobacco mix.

'I've so longed to see you again,' he said. 'I can't bear to play the piano any more now that you're gone.' He turned to her, his expression earnest. She had always found that boyish face touchingly unguarded. 'Darling,' tears in his eyes. 'You must know it's all over with Paddy. We're finished.'

She pulled away. 'Whatever do you mean?'

'She wants us to share the house but live apart. Separate rooms. Not really a marriage any more, if it ever was. And I've told her, Daphne. I want to marry you. All I do is drink and cry when you're not there. So you see, you could divorce Tommy now. We can marry.'

She scrambled to her feet, stepped away from him.

'But I would never divorce Tommy. Why would you suggest such a thing?'

He seemed to crumple. 'I thought that's what you wanted. I love you, Daphne. My marriage is over. You're all I have now.' He began to sob.

It was shocking to see him hunched over, shoulders heaving, this man in his country tweeds and well-polished brogues. She managed to calm him down. Talked him into going back to Paddy, see what he could salvage. She could never divorce Tommy. She loved him as much as ever. She was sorry, she was sorry, she was sorry.

Afterwards he seemed like a man pulled from a wreckage,

still not sure if he could get up and walk, stunned, speechless.

In silence, they drove back to the hotel in Fowey where Christopher was staying. She watched him go into the building, walking shakily. Feeling like a criminal she went back to the cottage in Readymoney Cove where the children would be waiting.

She had thought that she was in charge of a harmless game. It had started with dreams of two tiny figures on a secret island and had ended up with a wrecking ball crashing through Paddy and Christopher's marriage.

And somewhere behind her as she walked home, Rebecca cackled and tossed her hair. 'What do you care? Darling, I'm always here, whenever you need me.' By her side, a small figure, Peter Pan, stony-eyed. I told you, I kill people once I'm done with them.

CHAPTER 14

FOWEY 1943

Early one afternoon, the sun showing a little warmth in a pale blue sky, Daphne wrapped up in tweed jacket and cord trousers, a scarf wound around her neck, she set out over the fields to find Menabilly, a walk of less than an hour from Readymoney Cove.

A year earlier, Angela had written to say that the contents of Menabilly were going to be auctioned off and would she like anything. Daphne had written back to say, yes, she would like everything, the Georgian cupboards, the Chippendale chairs, every last stick of Victorian rattan furniture, but since she had no room to store anything she had had to let it all go. What would the house feel like now that it had been cleared of its contents?

Reaching the woods she found branches and entire trees blown down by the gales. But the first tender leaves were coming out of their scaly bud cases on the sycamores, bluebells and green wild garlic leaves carpeting the forest floor. The rhododendrons among the ivy-draped trees had begun to bloom with scarlet lights. With a feeling of optimism and renewal, Daphne came out on to the path that led to the house.

But reaching its front, she stopped, horrified. Since she had last seen it, the house had been battered by years of winter gales, the shutters torn off, windows broken. The building seemed in danger of collapsing beneath the weight of foliage clinging to its walls. Pushing the ivy aside to peer through the grimy windows she could see fungus beginning to sprout from walls and ceilings, damp wallpaper peeling away, piles of debris from falling ceilings scattered across the floor, patches of wet running down the walls where roof tiles had blown away.

Menabilly was dying.

Why did no one care? She strode home along the clifftops, growing more furious with every step, determined to do something. Though what? Each time she asked Dr Rashleigh if she could rent Menabilly, he refused.

Well, it was worth one last try. Without taking off her coat, she hurried to her room and wrote a letter to the Rashleighs' solicitors. Posted it with a feeling of sadness. She knew that it was futile. And once again, she wished that Tommy was there to talk to.

A few days later, a reply came back from the solicitor. She read it with disbelief. Dr Rashleigh would be willing to let her rent Menabilly House if she would agree to pay for all the repairs, though she would not be recompensed in any way when she moved out. It was completely ludicrous as an offer. The costs would be enormous. She would be insane to agree to such terms. It was impossible to get workmen or materials to do renovations in wartime. And she needed permission from the war office to begin, which would be a miracle in itself.

She wrote back immediately to the solicitor to say that she would take the house.

She told no one except Tommy, writing him a letter to confess what she had done.

A few days later, brimming with excitement, she suggested to Angela that they take the children to picnic on the lawns in front of Menabilly, enjoy the lovely weather.

'There's something different about you,' said Angela as she reached for another apple-jam sandwich and lay back comfortably on the picnic rug. Life had dealt Angela wide hips and short legs and a snub nose, and she was still waiting for Mr Right to appear one day, but she was never one to complain or whine, a jaunty silk scarf at her neck, her Pekingese dog nearby, a life filled with friends and fun. 'Something you're not telling me.' Angela considered her sister thoughtfully. 'You've taken a lover.'

'Much more scandalous.' Daphne lowered her voice. 'I'm going to move into Menabilly.'

'Here?!' Angela let out a scream. The children paused in their play, looking over at Daphne with her flushed cheeks, Angela's look of horror.

You can't mean this house?'

Daphne nodded, her face radiant. 'But I don't want to tell the children until it looks ready and, you know, a bit less. . .'

'Like a ruin,' said Angela. ' It's not even habitable unless you're a bat or a fox. It's an utter wreck.'

'So long as I carry out all the repairs, Dr Rashleigh's going to let me to rent Menabilly on a twenty-year lease.'

Angela snorted. 'Well, what's that going to cost? And does he pay you back you when you leave?'

Daphne shook her head. 'I know, I know. But, Piffy, to be honest, he could have asked me anything and I'd have said yes.'

'You may be the richest writer in England now and all that, according to the papers, but this *grande folie*...'

'That's rubbish anyway. It all goes in tax. Do you realize they've taken almost everything I earned from *Frenchman's Creek*? There's barely anything left for us to live on. I ought to wear a sign saying "Paid for an entire spitfire".'

'Well, there you are. This place will bleed you dry of the rest. And you'll still have to move out in twenty years' time.'

Daphne shrugged. 'I'll be old by then, over fifty. Anyway, I've signed the lease. I'm going to bring Menabilly back to life.'

Angela groaned and lay back down on the picnic rug. 'You truly have gone mad this time. This is Rebecca's revenge. You finished her off at Menabilly, or Manderley or whatever, and now she's coming back to finish you off with this mad project.'

Daphne half-closed her eyes as she looked over at her house. 'I sometimes wonder if it's wrong to love a place so much, to love stones almost more than people. Do you think I'm being too silly?'

Angela leaned on one elbow. 'If anyone can do it, it's you. You were always determined to do things your own way, and I admire that.'

'Thanks, Piffy. But remember, not a word to the children yet. Tessa's got a thing about the house, says it's too gloomy.'

Walking back through the lofty trees behind Angela and the children, Daphne paused her step, the oddest impression of someone behind her, a woman standing in the shadows of the trees, stubbing out a cigarette, a faint smell of smoke.

'Hurry up, Mummy,' called Tessa, anxiously.

Scribbled letters came from Tommy, written on the backs of bills, on a torn-out page from a ledger, whatever he could find to hand when he had time, sometimes a phone call, but he seemed so far away. Tommy was now on the front line in Africa, more or less Montgomery's right-hand man. She thought of the peace of the desert dunes, where she and Tommy camped out under silent stars – now the site of fierce battles, the troops suffering heavy casualties.

Tommy understood how much it meant to her to restore Menabilly.

I know it's been your dream, Ducks, he wrote, *but don't be too disappointed if you're still in the Readymoney cottage by Christmas. You've taken on a Herculean task. War here too boring to describe. What do you think of this?* He'd sketched his latest idea for the boat he hoped to build as soon as the war was over. *I think we can afford it, Ducks, since "Rebecca" has done so well.*

But all the money in the world was not going to help Menabilly if she couldn't get permission from the Ministry of Works, which was extremely unlikely in wartime, the architect told her. She submitted her application. To her amazement, and the architect's, a man from the Ministry of Works agreed to come and see Menabilly. She paced around the building with him, sketching out with her arms what needed to be done before the house was lost for ever, recounting the long history of the Rashleigh family. The man from the ministry wrote dispassionately on his clipboard, his face a mask. A feeling of defeat as he drove away without further comment.

A week later she had her reply. She had permission to begin. And more unbelievably, the ministry was going to award her two hundred and fifty pounds towards essential works. She danced around the cottage kitchen with Tessa.

'What is it, Mummy?' asked Tessa, always a little suspicious.

'Oh, Mummy's just happy.'

Kits and Flavia joined in, madly jumping up and down. The grant was enough to replace the roof, install electrics, perhaps even provide hot water.

But there were still so many more battles to wage. And she was determined to have the house ready for Christmas when Tommy came home.

Daphne managed to assemble a team to bring Menabilly back to life: architects, builders, plumbers and electricians. But as they toured the house they found a host of new problems: no water supply, impossible to run electricity to the house, too many rotting windows to get them replaced by Christmas. But each time Daphne would beg, 'Please, please, do try and think of a way.'

All through summer and into autumn, Daphne was longing to tell the children what she was doing as she left them once again with Mummy and Angela and drove off with Margaret to see how her house was progressing, but she was determined to tell them nothing until they could go and see their nursery set up and the house ready to welcome them.

The japonica and ivy were pulled from the walls to reveal beautiful sugar-spun stone in shades of pale verdigris and magenta, from a rare mine on Dartmoor, she was told by the mason who was repairing the water-damaged stone. The roof was mended using the same silvery Cornish slate tiles, the blank modern windows replaced with Georgian sash windows. They found a water supply: a well in the kitchen, and a nearby pond for the bathrooms. Electricity was connected. Fireplaces and chimneys mended and swept.

There was still a breath-taking amount of cleaning to be done, and just at a time when no one could get help, a whole army of maids and charladies arrived carrying buckets and mops and cloths, their hair tied up in scarves, to help scrub and dust alongside Daphne and Margaret.

By the time the November rains came in, Daphne was finally able to stand at the windows of the long room overlooking the gardens, and know that the house was weather-tight. Her furniture had been taken out of storage and brought down in a small convoy of several vans. A deep-orange carpet now covered the floor in the long room, sofas in sprigged linen in the same tones. Framed *Punch* prints by Grandfather George hung from the panelled walls. Gerald's portrait looked down on the grand piano. In the downstairs nursery room, with its large murals of Peter Pan, stood a rocking horse with red nostrils, just like the one she had glimpsed when she had first seen Menabilly.

The Victorian wing leading off the back of the house, however, was still derelict. The doors at the end of the long room that led through to its abandoned rooms were locked and bolted, its rot and the cobwebs put firmly out of mind.

With mounting excitement she took the Christmas decorations from their boxes and brought in a tree.

Two weeks before Christmas, she finally told the children what it was she had been doing for so long. They helped to pack up their things and drove to the house, amazed to see the ivy that had enshrouded it gone. Inside, Kits and Flavia ran from room to room shouting with glee, all the fires lit, the pictures crowned with holly, though Tessa hung back, her arms crossed.

'How am I going to get to school from here?'

'Don't worry about that. We'll have a tutor come in and teach you all. Won't that be nice? And look at all the space to play, your own woodlands and a beach nearby. I would have thought this heaven as a child.'

Tessa threw her plait behind her shoulder, folded her arms firmly once more. When did she grow so tall, her woollen skirt far too short above long bony legs? 'But how am I going to see my friends? I'm not going to miss Agatha's birthday party after Christmas?'

'Of course not. I'll drive you there myself.'

She watched Tessa stomp away and plump down on a chair, refusing to explore the house any further. A memory came back of being at Cannon Hall at that age, the sense of isolation, longing to know what was going on outside in a world where the only people she met were Daddy's theatre people. How she'd quiz the governess and the servants for hours about the lives they lived when they walked away through the gates of Cannon Hall.

But then, she hadn't had the chance to live at Menabilly as a child. Flavia and Kits seemed already entranced. She felt sure that Tessa would soon begin to enjoy it.

When Tommy finally arrived home for Christmas, Daphne was wildly excited to show him what she'd done. She and the children went down to the gate at the bottom of the drive to wait for the first sight of his car.

'Hello, Loons,' he called, getting out of the car, leaving his batman to drive the Packard as they walked arm in arm up the rhododendron drive. Daphne cast sideways glances at this newly created Sir Frederick Browning, tall and distinguished in his khaki uniform.

'Children, did you know that Daddy is a real live knight now?'

'Do you fight dragons?' asked Flavia, holding on to his hand.

'Much worse. I have to deal with army administration.'

'Daddy's been made a Sir by order of the King in recognition of his work in setting up the First Airborne Division,' recited Tessa, glancing towards Tommy for a nod of approval.

'And may I present to you Loons, Lady Browning,' he said with a twinkle. Kissed her on the cheek.

They reached the house, the low sun glinting yellow in the windowpanes. The colours of the stone deepened and glowing in the afternoon light, the noble dark oak doors with their fantastical carved scenes thrown into relief.

'You've been fighting your own battles here, I think, getting old Menabilly into shape. And thank you, darling, for keeping everything going here. You know, I won't mind one bit if it's a little like camping inside the house this Christmas. It's what I'm used to – though in a warmer climate. You did say the fireplaces are functioning.'

Daphne said nothing, biting her lip as they went inside to find a gleaming little mansion, decorated ready for Christmas. 'There's a hot bath as soon as you like. And look, we've a telephone installed. The post office told me there was no hope of getting one in before Christmas but I pleaded with them that you needed one for important war work. I only hope that won't be the case.'

'You have done wonders.'

He was here by her side, with his familiar smell of leather and lavender, a scent of snow-dampened wool from his greatcoat. 'But it wasn't really finished until you came home. Nothing's home without you.'

But as they walked from room to room, she saw how thin he looked, as if his air of military authority had whittled him into a different shape.

He had changed.

He'd brought dates from North Africa, slightly squashed oranges, a bottle of brandy. Goat-skin tambourines and embroidered toy camels for the children.

She took him up to their bedroom and set his little teddy bears, the Boys, next to his side of the bed. He looked round approvingly, took off his shoes and put on his red Moroccan slippers.

'You didn't change the old Victorian wallpaper then?'

'I rather liked the thought of Menabilly's past inhabitants lingering on here.'

He lay back, smiled at her with the familiar old crinkle around his mischievous eyes.

He took her hand, gently pulled her down beside him. Tommy was home, here in Menabilly. Whatever she had done in the past, however stupid she'd been, this was all she wanted. The rest was a mirage, a story in a book. The page was turned, the book closed, and here was her real life. They lay side by side, in this oasis of peace. She heard his breathing slow and deepen. He was sound asleep.

CHAPTER 15

MENABILLY JANUARY 1944

Christmas came to an abrupt end with Tommy's return to North Africa.

Another parting, not knowing if they would see each other again.

She helped pack his case, watched as he repacked it, shoulders seeming more squared by life in the army. He was returning as a major general, in charge of all airborne troops, liaising directly with Eisenhower and Montgomery. She was proud of him. There was a frame of steel in Tommy's character. But only she knew how close the candle burned to the rest of his fabric, worn down and brittle from so much responsibility. He didn't seem recovered at all by the time his batman came to pick him up and she and the children waved goodbye to him in front of the house.

Perhaps things would be better next leave. She felt a now familiar plunge of cold water inside – if there was a next time.

With Tommy gone, she let Menabilly fold itself around her like a blanket, walking in the enchanted snowy woods as she began to think about a new book.

With little help available in wartime, however, keeping the fireplaces of Menabilly going in such weather was a full-time job, chopping wood, rising early to start laying fires in the high-ceilinged rooms that remained icy even when the fires were blazing and too hot to stand near, keeping them stoked. At night, they wore layers and layers of clothes but still felt cold, lay listening to the scampering of tiny claws across the bedroom ceilings. Every dusk, bats swirled from the roof and flittered away through the park.

'They have just as much right to be here as we do,' Daphne told the children. 'Nothing to be afraid of.'

After breakfast on a tray in bed each morning, dressed in layers of cords and jumpers and a sheepskin waistcoat, Daphne sat at the desk in her bedroom. She was now working on a screenplay for her latest book, *Hungry Hill*.

Months passed by, the rhododendrons banks of scarlet candles when Tommy came home for his next leave in late spring. A blissful week with the children, rambling through the Cornish countryside, but all too quickly he was gone, and it was back to the oh-so-unsatisfactory scribbled notes from Tommy, annotated with diagrams of the boat he'd love to build after the war.

Sometimes, she wondered – though she hated herself for such disloyalty – if it wouldn't be easier not to see each other at all until it was over.

Then her heart turned over, because what if that had been his last visit home?

What she did know, and she felt increasingly sure about it, was that it was going to be hard to get back to normal once the war ended – if they could remember what normal was. She wrote about such fears in her letters, couldn't help herself. *So many people, wives and husbands, kept apart by this hateful war. I do worry about how we're going to pick up again when all this is over.*

He wrote back, reassuring, hopeful, *I love you more than ever, darling . Once we're together again it will be like old times, don't worry.*

She wished she could feel as certain.

The weeks continued to go by, Tommy swallowed up inside the belly of the war. At the end of May, he wrote to say not to worry but she might not hear from him for a while. He couldn't say what, but something big was going to happen. She put down the letter, the horrid claws of anxiety sinking into her skin again.

It was clear that some big push was on the cards. Fowey Harbour was crammed with warships and landing craft ready to leave for some unspecified invasion.

A couple of days later, a call from Angela. She and Jeanne had been working on the market garden plot over by Bodinnick, heads down to the weeding, when they had stopped and looked out over Fowey Harbour to realize that every last American and Allied ship had gone, and with them the American major for whom Angela had had such hopes.

'Something's happening, Daphne,' said Angela in a high voice, trembling with excitement. 'It's really begun.'

As the Allied invasion of Normandy rolled out the only way Daphne had of knowing what Tommy might be doing was to listen to the wireless with its unbearable blow-by-blow accounts of planes going down. 'The gliders are going down now. . . there they go. . . into heavy fire.' It was obscene. Narrating as people died. There was a good chance Tommy might be in one of those planes.

Feeling nauseous, she switched the wireless off, although the war was on everyone's lips. The entire country tense with what might happen next.

Tommy wrote as often as he could, on whatever paper came to hand, but the long weeks of summer crept by, an agony of waiting to hear from him and know that he was all right as she tried to keep life as normal as possible for the children.

Then rumours began to mount that something truly dangerous was taking place across on the Continent, but Tommy, maddeningly, was once again not allowed to tell her. A letter came from him on 16 September, then suddenly nothing. Silence for days.

She was woken one morning by the telephone. It was a journalist. Could Lady Browning confirm that General Browning had been killed in France and how did she feel about it?

Daphne slammed down the phone. Picked it up again to begin frantically dialling anyone at the Ministry of Defence who might know something, the phone slipping in her sweat-soaked hands. She had to wait all day, trying to appear cheerfully normal for the children. Finally a call came through from someone in Whitehall. Tommy was alive and well. She went through to the long room, wept, and had two straight gins.

The first reports came through in the newspapers with details of a massive push by Montgomery to speed up the end of the war by advancing into the Rhineland. Tommy's airborne troops had gone ahead in the largest airborne fleet in history, gliders and aircraft landing behind enemy lines to capture bridges over the Rhine and halt the German advance.

But not long afterwards, other reports came in. Tommy's airborne troops had landed in their thousands, but three quarters of them had been lost, cut off by fog and captured by the Germans. Seventeen thousand men dead. Someone had to be blamed. The newspapers decided it was Tommy.

Daphne clutched *The Times* to her chest, crushing the hateful words. There was no one that Tommy cared about more than his troops. He would never willingly send his mean to death. He would send himself first. She rang Chink, his friend from Sandhurst.

'For your ears only. Tommy told Monty that trying to take Arnhem was a bridge too far, but the commander insisted. And you have to remember that the mission was eighty-five per cent successful, which is good odds in a war, but Tommy won't see it like that with so many of his men lost. He thought of them as family. He's going to need your support, Daphs.'

She put down the phone and stared at the blank wall in the hallway. How was Tommy ever going to recover from this?

CHAPTER 16

LONDON OCTOBER 1944

Even with his back to her, Tommy's bearing is unmistakable as he stands in the middle of Claridge's foyer amidst its vast arching doorways, its gilded art deco mirrors. The familiar sharp cut of his long khaki jacket, neatly cinched in at the waist by the gabardine belt, the peaked general's cap under one arm. She's wearing her blue tweed skirt and jacket, Muriel's fur coat with the diamond brooch from Daddy. It's been months since she and Tommy last saw each other. There's always so much expected of their brief times together. Perhaps this time will be more relaxed, now that the worst of the war is over. Soon he will be coming home for good.

She walks up behind him and puts one hand lightly on his shoulder. He turns round, his face breaking into the most wonderful smile. But how tired he looks, a little too gaunt, a hollow look around his eyes. She can see in a moment the terrible toll that the past few weeks have had and her heart goes out to him. She's heard all about the terrible losses suffered by his battalion, but seeing him so physically devastated, she begins to understand what it has meant.

The girl goes ahead to show them to their room, as if

Daphne couldn't walk there in her sleep, so well does she know the layout of Claridge's after all the parties and coming-out balls held here when she was a girl.

'You will be in the Princess Mary Suite,' the girl says as the three of them stand in the lift. 'A courtesy of the hotel,' the girl replies, glancing up at Tommy. 'We wanted to show our appreciation.'

Tommy thanks her, but his charming smile seems mechanical.

Daphne's glad to see it's one of the old Edwardian suites rather than the newer jazz-inspired art deco ones. Tommy will prefer that. The butler has laid out champagne. She shrugs off her fur coat and drops it on the sofa.

The moment the butler leaves, Tommy folds her against his chest, rocks her for a moment, comforting them both. She can hear the rapid beating beneath his breastbone, the too-fast heartbeat of a man living on his nerves.

'Darling, you're exhausted.'

'I'm fighting a beastly cold, old girl. Sorry to be boring. Shall I open the champagne?' He turns the bottle to examine the label. 'Looks like rather a good one.'

'Mm. Yes, please.'

He pours expertly, the bubbles to the brim of the glass but not running over.

They clink glasses. 'I was thinking. We could go to a show. *Salad Days* is on at the Wyndham's.' She knows Tommy adores musicals, although they are not really her thing.

'Would you mind if we just had an early night? I'm not sure I could stay awake long enough to see an entire show out. That's how feeble your husband has become.'

'Well, if you're fighting off a cold, best thing.'

'I'm sorry. Am I hopeless?'

He tops up the glasses, though she's barely had a sip, drains his glass. 'What I could do with is a long soak in the tub.'

She draws his bath. Sprinkles in bath salts. He comes in wearing a white bathrobe but waits until she's left and closes the door before he gets into the hot water. She hears him sinking down, the sound of him blowing his nose. She takes her fur from where she left it on the sofa and hangs it in the wardrobe. Tommy hates untidiness. Checks her hair in the mirror and then wanders around the empty rooms, trying to ignore the horrid feeling of being on the clock for their weekend of leave. Is she making enough effort for it to be special, memorable?

What she'd half-hoped might happen after so long – sharing Claridge's deep and extremely comfortable bed with its satin cotton sheets – looks rather unlikely now with Tommy so under the weather. She's a tiny bit relieved. She unpacks her bag, hangs her dress in the cupboard, lays her nightdress on the double bed. Goes back and tidies it away in a drawer. She's putting her toiletry bag on the dressing table, unpacking her face creams, when she catches sight of a rather hard-faced woman in a side mirror with the sort of overly tidy hair that she dislikes – realizes that it's her. And she thinks for a moment of Christopher Puxley, all the things she can never tell Tommy, how she's coped with the crushing anxiety of the past few years.

The bathroom door opens. Tommy comes out, his face close shaved and shiny, wet hair scraped against his head, the widow's peak receded a little further back. Even now, in his bathrobe, he still hasn't lost that air of authority that he brings back with him, a deep note of masculinity.

'A snifter before supper?' he asks, opening the Chinese cupboard with its array of spirits. Horrendously expensive, she thinks, but doesn't want to be a wet blanket.

She knows that he's drinking more at the moment because of Arnhem, the blame he's given himself for the men surrounded and captured, thousands of deaths. She knows that he advised Monty against pushing as far as Arnhem Bridge, but at the end of the day it was Tommy's men who were lost, so Tommy shoulders the insupportable guilt. But she also knows that Tommy won't even broach the topic, let alone say how he really feels about it. A feeling of helplessness comes over her again, as if she is viewing him from very far away. There's nothing she can do to help him or change anything.

'I was thinking perhaps pheasant and peach melba for supper. We could eat up here in the room,' says Tommy.

'Sounds perfect.' That would be the moment to tell him her good news. She's managed to buy Hunkins' boatyard. Something they've wanted to do for a long time. They'll be able to build the boat he's been dreaming of, and drawing plans for, all through the war. She sees them spending their days together down in Menabilly, sailing out from Fowey Harbour. She isn't sure where he'll be sent by the army once the war is over, but it has to be somewhere near their home. Tommy understands that.

'And how about a little pre-prandial.' He rings for martinis.

When the butler brings coffee and petits fours after the meal,

Daphne springs the news about the boatyard. His delight seems muted.

'You'll be able to pop across all the time, make sure *Iggy Two* is being built exactly as you want. You'll surely get weekends off. Wouldn't be so bad if you were working out of Portsmouth, say.'

His smile is strained, he screws up his napkin into a tight ball, straightens his knife to the right angle on his cheese plate. 'Thing is, Ducks – and don't be upset, darling – but I might be sent to Ceylon for a while. Just until things are settled with Japan.'

Her voice feels tight. 'But how long for?'

'A year, eighteen months. Mountbatten's requested me personally to go as his aide, you see, and it's not really possible to turn him down.'

She nods, but she doesn't see at all, tears clouding her eyes. She blinks. 'But I thought. . . They say the war will be over in a matter of weeks.'

'Not in the Far East.'

She feels exhausted, the boatyard pointless now. 'You know, I'm feeing awfully tired. Perhaps we should turn in. And you with your cold.'

'You carry on. Have a long bath if you like. I'll just read through some papers.' He takes out a briefcase. She hears the cupboard open, a brandy poured.

In the bedroom, Tommy has put his teddy bears on the bedside table. His Boys. He always carries them in his attaché case now, puts new bows on them every year. She picks one up and its rigid button eyes look back at her. A maid had been in to draw the curtains and make sure the blackout drapes are in place. The bed sheets are turned back, the lamps turned on. The room is luxurious, with oil paintings, gold-leaf ormolu on the panelling, a chandelier above the bed, but it feels fusty and airless.

She's forgotten what it's like to share a double bed. She lies rigid, dying to thrash about or spread her arms and legs into the cooler spaces of the sheets, but she doesn't want to disturb Tommy. Not that he seems to have managed to go to sleep. He coughs incessantly, turning over and whipping away the blankets, or sitting up to sip water and catch his breath. He rubs at the leg that was so badly injured when his glider went down. When he does sleep, somewhere in the small hours, he wakes her, calling out in his dreams, anguished and frantic. She puts her hand on his forehead cold with sweat. It's the same old nightmare from Gauche Wood. But now, there are new groans and mutterings. Arnhem.

He wakes with a gasp, sits up against the headboard. Reaches across for his handkerchief. Blows his nose and says thickly, 'Sorry, darling. I'm keeping you awake tossing and turning with this cold. Can't seem to breathe.'

'It is stuffy in here. Just try and get as much rest as you can. Goodness knows you need it.'

He lies down. She keeps a hand on his chest and he stays immobile, though she can tell he's still awake, feels the vibration of his heart, the familiar smell of his skin that conjures up with piercing poignancy the days when they would always lie close together in their double bed before the war. He doesn't move an inch, trying not to disturb her.

'Ducks, I'm going to go through and sleep on the sofa next door. Looks comfy enough,' she offers.

He grasps her hand and holds it tight. 'Please don't go. I've longed to have you here by my side again. My own peace of mind.' She lies in the dark, willing him to sleep. When she hears his breathing change, she gets up and wanders into the next room anyway, switches on a sidelight and smokes a cigarette.

The guilt and the regret creep in like the smoke from her cigarette even though it's all completely in the past and she's determined never to do any such thing again, to make it up to Tommy.

Is it her fault, her punishment, that it's so hard to find one's footing when they are together, the mists of uncertainty and misunderstanding?

When the maid comes in the next morning, Daphne's asleep on the sofa, her feet cold and a crick in her neck. The maid draws back the blackouts and the curtains, the criss-cross lattice of paper strips to stop the glass shattering visible beneath the long net curtains.

The maid helps her unfasten one of the windows to let in some air. The noise of traffic comes in. She can see a gap in the buildings opposite where a bomb must have fallen, the rubble swept up into tidy mounds.

In the bedroom she finds Tommy up and dressed, the blades of his cheekbones and the curve of his nose so sharp, flesh pared away. He's phoning down for breakfast.

'Coffee? Toast? Eggs?' he asks her, the phone on his chest.

'Yes, please, all of it. The full menu and damn the expense. I've always said I don't need fancy things to make me happy, but it is awfully nice, isn't it, to ring a bell and have things like kedgeree for breakfast?'

They walk around Berkeley Square, no hint of the magical nightingale that Vera Lynn sings about. In the afternoon Tommy sleeps and suddenly it's their last dinner together before he has to go back in the morning. For the past four years their marriage has felt like a series of encounters in a busy railway station, life rushing around them, always watching the time on the departures board.

That night she lies and listens to him coughing and blowing his nose again, tossing and groaning in his sleep. If only he would talk to her about what he's been through but she knows that Tommy will never discuss the last few terrible weeks. It will lie coiled up inside him like heavy ropes sodden through with grief and guilt, the noise of the bombs and the rifles ringing through his sleep every night.

At breakfast she notes the nip of whisky he slides into his tea and realizes that Tommy, for all his immaculate dress and his perfectly charming manners, will never be the same again. He is drifting away from her on the current of all that has happened, and she is left on the bank, powerless to help him.

'Forgot to ask,' he says. 'How's your new play doing, up in Manchester?'

'*The Years Between*. Well enough.' She spreads dark-yellow butter on her toast, honey. Amazing how the grand hotels don't seem to run short.

'Remind me what it's about, Ducks.'

'A man who's presumed dead comes back to his wife after the war. Meanwhile she's had to make a new life for herself, a Member of Parliament and about to remarry. The question is how they deal with all that. I think it's something that a lot of people will rather identify with in a way, the problems of being apart for so long, such different experiences.'

'A little far-fetched, though, wouldn't you say, becoming an MP.'

'Women do, though. A lot of women have had to take on very active roles during the war. I think it's going to take quite a lot of adjusting when it's all over and the men come home.'

'Ah yes, the magazine articles you've been sending me. But, Ducks, I do think you don't need to worry so much. Once we are together again for good we'll soon get back into our dear old ways and routines, I'm sure of it. I honestly love you as much now as the day we were married. It's only the thought of coming home to you and the children that has kept me going.'

'Do you really have to go to the wretched Far East now? It just seems so unfair. The war's over for most people but you have to hang on until the Japanese get round to signing their surrender. Can't you say no to Mountbatten?'

He looked betrayed that she should ask such a question.

CHAPTER 17

NORTHOLT JULY 1946

Daphne took her powder compact from her bag and checked her face in the little round mirror as the Humber drove through the dull, flat fields to RAF Northolt. All in all, she didn't look too bad. Her blonde hair, still smelling of setting lotion after a morning at the hairdresser's, fell in soft curls to her shoulders. She'd also had a facial, her lips painted her favourite shade of red. Nothing she could do about the little worry lines on her forehead; she was after all almost forty. She wore a green woollen suit and a silk blouse, Daddy's brooch of little diamonds on the lapel.

Over the past six years all she had seen of Tommy was on the briefest of leaves. They'd each lived lives about which the other knew nothing really and now the war was sending her husband home as a virtual stranger, as with so many other couples. How were they to find their way back to their old contented intimacy? She'd written to Tommy hinting that they shouldn't expect things to be plain sailing. Sent him articles clipped from magazines about the sort of problems couples might face.

Would he mind, she'd written, if they had separate rooms just to begin with, next door to each other? Give him time to recover a bit. She'd felt sure he'd understand that she was referring to his nightmares. He hated to wake her up, full of apologies in the morning. And it wasn't so unusual for people like them to have their own rooms, after all.

She didn't say how much she was dreading having to lose her private space to work and to think, her bedroom being her office. She didn't tell him she had learned to be independent and loved it rather, striding around Menabilly in her favourite Garbo-style suit with elegantly baggy trousers, long blonde hair to her shoulders, the dogs and the children romping through the woods.

There had been that awful week when Tommy had not replied after she'd mentioned the separate rooms. He usually wrote every day. Finally he'd written, *Don't worry about us getting back to our old selves. It will all soon come back to us.*

And what better day for them to meet up after so long than today, their wedding anniversary? Tommy had written her the most marvellous letter saying that he loved her more than ever, how proud he was of the way she had been so steadfast and uncomplaining all through the war – which made her feel like a heel. How he couldn't wait to be home and begin the rest of their lives together.

She found herself longing to breathe in his reassuring scent now, tingling to feel the solid shape of him as they embraced again. It had been years, but in time – she was sure of it – they would learn to be romantic with one another again. They would.

'We'll be there shortly, Lady Browning,' the driver said, his expression cheery in the mirror. 'I expect Sir Frederick will be very glad to be home.'

'I think he's been having rather a good time of it out there, all the parties and dinners. Don't know how he's going to feel about having to eat the sort of rations we've got used to. Beans on toast every night.'

'And you must be very proud of the work he's been doing out there, getting the peace signed with Japan.'

'Oh, very.'

The car drove along a wire-linked fence, a dusty field stretching to the skyline. In the distance she could see concrete buildings, several planes painted khaki and green.

Her stomach felt hollow with excitement – or was it anxiety? So many years of not knowing where Tommy was, whether he would survive the next day.

And still it had not ended. When Kits and Flavia had burst into the drawing room almost a year ago to announce Victory in Europe, she'd barely looked up from her newspaper, already knowing that Tommy was due to be sent straight out to Ceylon.

'Yes, yes. Now get back to bed where you should be.'

No celebrations at Menabilly for VE day. 'VD day more like it,' said Angela, as they looked at the newspaper pictures of people getting drunk in Trafalgar Square and kissing strangers.

The car stopped in front of a collection of tin Nissen huts, a fluttering windsock. No sign of Tommy's plane. Then she heard a faint mechanical whine in the distance. A tiny black line grew into the squat shape of a plane fuselage, wings wide as an albatross, straightening ready for landing. It bounced as it hit the runway and jolted towards them. The blur of the engine propellers resolved into blades and finally stilled. With a loud creaking noise a side section of the plane folded down into a stairway. People started to come out. And there he was, a tall figure at the top of the steps. Tommy. She felt a rush of love, wanted to run over to him as he strode across the tarmac, but she checked herself, didn't want to embarrass him the midst of so many army types. The moment he reached her she was going to fling her arms around him.

Then she noticed a young woman walking by his side, slim and pretty, curly brown hair, twenty years younger than Daphne at least.

Tommy pecked Daphne on the cheek, his manner crisp and curt, still in full general mode.

'Ducks, meet Maureen, my secretary.'

When Tommy had written, praising his wonderful secretary to the skies, Daphne had imagined someone stout and fiftyish, not a pretty twenty-year-old, brown hair in a mass of curls. This woman knew far more about Tommy's life over the past year than she did, part of the endless cocktail parties and dinners that being in Singapore seemed to involve, closeted with Tommy in his office each day. Daphne felt wrong-footed. Instead of throwing her arms around Tommy and kissing him all over his dear face, she stood stiffly, feeling ridiculously jealous.

Was she his mistress?

'And Maureen's rashly agreed to carry on being my secretary when I start at the Ministry of Defence in Whitehall,' he added.

'How very kind,' said Daphne with her usual charming warmth, the words like lead in her mouth.

Maureen beamed.

*

The children were lined up outside Menabilly along with Todd the governess and Hanks the cook – looking for all the world like the staff waiting for the second Mrs de Winter.

Daphne's old governess, Todd, had stepped in when the Nanny left suddenly. Daphne had written endless letters begging Todd to come and save her from the resultant chaos. The only problem was that dear old Todd in her tweeds and lace-up shoes had an opinion on everything – including the best way to win a war. Daphne only hoped that Tommy wouldn't be too irritated by her holding forth.

'Good grief,' said Tommy, looking at the children through the car window as they drove up. 'Can the children really have grown so much?'

'It's still the same three terrors. And according to Todd they've been up since the break of dawn waiting for you.'

She bit her lip. At five years old, Kits only knew Tommy as the man in a soldier's uniform who came and went occasionally. Flavia too would have few memories of him in the role of a father. Tessa at thirteen remembered more of Tommy from before the war; but Daphne knew how anxious Tessa was to feel her father's approval, and the stresses of war had left Tommy with a short fuse, flying off the handle if things were not done properly – just what Tessa didn't need.

Tommy shook the children's hands as if carrying out a troop inspection.

The children clattered up the Queen Anne staircase with Daddy; Flavia, trying to help with his bag then giving up, ran ahead to show him the bedroom that Mummy had got ready for him.

'Here, you can help me set out the Boys,' he said, opening his attaché case. The children took out the small teddy bears and carefully arranged them on top of the chest of drawers.

'They've got new bows,' said Flavia. 'Did they miss us, Daddy?'

'They're pretty tough, as little chaps go, but I think they did. They are very glad to be home.'

Daphne opened the door leading through to her room. 'Isn't this nice. Gives Daddy a bit of peace and quiet, chance for a good old rest, and Mummy's room is right next door, you see.'

'In case he gets scared?' said Flavia.

Kits had found a roll of blueprints in the case and opened them out. 'Is it a boat?' he said, leaning on them so that they crushed into the eiderdown.

'What the bloody hell d'you think you're doing?' yelled Tommy, making them all jump. 'Didn't anyone tell you not to touch other people's things? You need to learn some bloody manners, young man.' Shouting at Kits as if he were a squaddie on parade with unpolished boots.

Kits shot over to Daphne, his hand clinging to hers, his blue eyes wide. Daphne picked him up and stroked his blond hair. Tessa and Flavia had also backed away.

'You mollycoddle that boy too much,' Tommy said, the steam going out of him. 'Oh, look here, I didn't mean to be abrupt. Buck up, Kits.'

'I'll get Todd to make you a goodly cup of coffee and you can have a little rest. Come on, Loons.'

'Doesn't Daddy like me?' asked Kits as they trooped back downstairs to the kitchen.

'Of course he does. It's just that Daddy had to shout at people for his job, you see, get them into shape and make good soldiers of them. It might take him a little while to remember we're not some of his soldiers.'

'I'm a soldier,' said Kits, wriggling out of her arms as they reached the bottom of the stairs. 'Or a pony.' He whinnied and he and Flavia galloped through the hall to the kitchen.

Daphne lay awake that night, waiting for Tommy to open the door and come through. She could hear him moving around behind the wall. She'd half-expected something might happen the night before when they were in the rather severe little flat he had taken on for his work in London. After all, their first night back together had been their wedding anniversary, with distant memories of a boat moored beneath star-filled branches, but they were of course both too exhausted.

It was past midnight. He must be asleep by now. He evidently wasn't coming to her. She turned over and scrunched the pillow up to get comfortable but sleep wouldn't come.

For the next night and all the nights that followed, Tommy gave no sign of wanting to come to her room. They had six weeks together at Menabilly before he had to be up in London for his work at the ministry, only coming home for weekends. Surely they must resolve things before then.

But the days ticked by and still nothing happened. Daphne began to feel hurt, wondering if she had changed that much, or were her clothes too drab? She began to feel positively rejected – abandoned, in fact. Did he not find her attractive any more?

Sometimes, she got up from bed and padded out into the corridor to see if there was still a sliver of light under his door. More than more than once she had seen that his light was on, but found it impossible to go in.

Sitting at her dressing table in her pyjamas one evening as she applied Pond's cold cream to her face, she leaned forward and took a long hard look at herself in the mirror. Her face did look subtly fuller, fine lines around her eyes. Was this what Tommy saw, a woman heading for middle age?

She looked round the room, the desk piled with books, the typewriter in the middle. There was a photograph of Tommy on her bedside table, but otherwise the room was full of her things, her clothes in the closet and chests of drawers, her mementoes and creams and hairbrushes. The pictures in the room were now the ones that she preferred. While Tommy was away, she had become successful, famous and rather well off. Yes, she had longed to have Tommy home, but she had also worried about having to step back into being a wife. Was this why things were going badly wrong now?

At first she had wondered if something had been going on with his secretary, Maureen, until she had realized what a straightforward girl she was, and very much in love with her fiancé.

Or could Tommy somehow have intuited what had happened with Christopher, her muddled flight into an almost affair? She felt that flutter of shame and regret once again for those weeks of living in some kind of dream, as if she were someone other.

She went to the window and looked out over the dark gardens and woods, the trees silhouetted against a sky of opalescent clouds. The sort of moonlit evening when she liked to walk through the woods, down to the sea, past the cottage at Pridmouth that she thought of as Rebecca's cottage, a hint of cigarette smoke in the air. Could one be haunted by a character from a book, a book that one had created?

She felt stalled and disconnected, bleary with lack of sleep. When she did sleep she'd had disturbing dreams of Michael walking towards Sanford Pool. She shook out a sleeping pill and swallowed it with a gulp of water. She had to get some rest or she couldn't write next day.

She woke next morning remembering a dream in which Tommy had come in to see her, but she'd been unable to wake up. He'd left with a look of deep sadness on his face. She wondered, had he really come in?

He didn't mention anything at breakfast, as pleasant and companionable as ever. She couldn't think how to broach the subject. It was becoming more difficult with every passing day.

The six weeks of leave before Tommy started to commute to the War Office in London each week were almost over. And still nothing had happened. Not a hint, not a sign. She found him reading the paper in the long room, tweed waistcoat and jacket, a Gieves & Hawkes cravat. He was still immensely attractive with his aristocratic profile and his gentle manners, hair brushed back in an immaculate widow's peak.

'Morning, Ducks. Would you like some of the papers?'

'Not for me. What would you like to do today?'

He shook the paper out, folded it away. 'Weather's looking good. What if we took a picnic on the boat? I can rustle up a basket in the kitchen. Just the two of us.'

She hurried to get ready, plimsolls, trousers and a sweater, a scarf around her neck. Perhaps, she thought, as she brushed out her hair, when they were out in *Iggy*, with Tommy in such a positive mood, she could talk to him. They had to talk about what was happening between them at some point.

They headed out across the shining water, clear jade depths as they reached the open sea. Behind them, the familiar hillsides, the old cottages heaped up to make the little towns of Fowey and Polruan, a wide sky of milky blue glass, the spray in her face as Tommy pulled out the throttle, the boat jumping the waves. They pulled up in a small cove. She lay down on the long wooden bow of the boat, eyes shut, feeling the rocking motion of the water and the sun on her face. Tommy had seen a stonechat on the rocks. He got out his binoculars. Handed Daphne hers.

'Do look, old thing. Not often you see one of those.' She opened her eyes and saw his silhouette against the light, slim and upright as ever, and her heart jumped. He was so exactly like the young Tommy again. She was shaken once more by how much she loved him still, those vivid memories of their honeymoon on the Helford River, hidden away among the overhanging trees.

She stood up to join him, took a deep breath.

'Ducks, there's something I wanted to talk to you about.

Something I've been putting off, but that's really important in my view.'

He gave her a stricken look. The bright sun showed up the deep lines on his face, all the worry of the past years etched into his forehead. He nodded, frowning. 'I'm quite relieved you should say that. I've been wanting to talk about things too.'

'Have you?' She felt a load lightening.

'Yes, but I wasn't sure how to broach the matter. Wait.' He went to his bag and came back with a handful of papers and put them in her hands. She looked at them with confusion. Mess bills, bills for his tailor, bills for the boat he was having built and shipped over from Singapore.

'I do seem to have accrued rather a lot. I'm so embarrassed about it. Not sure how I'm going to pay them off. So I was wondering, with the books selling so well and the film rights coming in, if you might possibly be able to do something about them.'

She was lost for words for a moment. 'Bills. Oh, I see.' She shuffled through them, not really looking. 'Oh yes, of course. Let me take these and I'll make sure they're settled.'

'Thank you, dearest. You don't know what a relief that is. I'm such a silly old fool. Been worrying myself sick, to be honest. Now, what was it you wanted to talk about?'

'Oh, nothing. It was nothing really.'

'If you're sure? How about I get on and cook us up the best bacon and eggs. Food always tastes best out on the water.'

In fact she had no appetite at all for greasy bacon with a swell rising in the sea. But she picked her way through the plate as best she could with a feeling of panic. Were they drifting into something that seemed more like friendship than a marriage?

Could you be good friends in a marriage and nothing more? She still absolutely adored Tommy, as much as ever. Couldn't imagine life without him.

A prickle of something like shame across her skin. Was it her fault?

She closed her eyes. She'd ruined Christopher's marriage. Was this her punishment now?

That winter, the snow piled up three feet deep outside the house. The electricity went off. They had to dig out the wartime supply of candles, eating nothing but plain stew cooked over a Primus. They ran along unheated corridors, hands and noses frozen, or burnt from sitting too close to the open fires.

Menabilly had never been so beautiful, however, the bastion of rhododendrons around the lawn glittering with blankets of snow, the sun setting yellow and agate behind the black fingers of the trees. At dusk, a deep-blue light and silence settled over the woods, time hushed and waiting.

She had always loved the long room with its burnt-orange carpet, its white panelling and comfortable chintz sofas, its ancient Chippendale furniture and family pictures hung around the room. Tommy, however, seemed to think it shabby.

It was probably as well that winter that Tommy was away most of the week staying in the poky flat in London, avoiding the worst of the cold which he hated so much.

*

'I have to tell you some news,' Tommy began as they sat in the long room companionably one spring evening, she reading, he poring over plans for a boat. 'Good news, I think. A new post.'

She looked up. Had he managed to find something nearer to Menabilly? She'd asked him to try.

'I've been asked by Prince Philip to be Comptroller for Princess Elizabeth in Clarence House. One can hardly say no. I'll still be down on the sleeper most weekends as usual.'

Her heart sank. 'Oh well, yes, that's wonderful news.'

So what was the future going to hold now? she wondered, as she lay alone in her room, Tommy on the other side of the wall. He'd be away in London most of the time, Tessa and Kits due to begin boarding school. She had always loved her secret world at Menabilly, putting off visitors, wanting to be alone. But now another feeling was beginning to creep in. She was feeling lonely.

Stubby coltsfoot daisies began pushing through the sodden leaves of the undergrowth, snowdrops appearing in their secret places beneath the trees. But inside, the house still felt cold, all life suspended.

The weeks went by, a strange and restless feeling of something approaching, some crisis. Walking along the upper path through the tangled woods of Menabilly one cold afternoon, she felt ambushed by grief, vivid memories of Tommy's warmth next to her in bed, their ease with each other, their strong and youthful bodies in a secret harmony.

Was that gone for ever now? She had to stop, the surge of pain overwhelming.

She was on a path that led through the highest point of the wooded hillside, a row of overgrown beeches standing guard along the edge of the steep drop. It had once been a driveway for carriages to the house, now a mere green ghost of itself carpeted with wild garlic leaves. But one could easily imagine the carriages passing by. A place where time was never quite stable. A rustling in the trees, a mocking sigh from deep in the shadows. Always a price to pay.

Daphne walked back to Menabilly in the gathering twilight and found the hallway in darkness. Groping for the light switch, she longed to pick up the phone and talk to someone about what was happening, but there was no one she felt she could tell.

A failed marriage. How shameful.

CHAPTER 18

LONDON SEPTEMBER 1946

Tommy's flat in London was on the seventh floor of a modern red-brick ziggurat, little square windows looking out over the back of King's Road. It was sparsely furnished from bits and pieces on loan from his sister. A few rugs covered the bare floorboards. Always a lingering whiff of gas and cologne. Walking around the spartan place, Daphne felt guilty. She tried to come up at least once a month, but a real wife would leave Cornwall and be with her husband all the time. They'd buy a family home and she'd live in London – and write nothing. Then who would pay the bills?

'Good of you to come, Ducks. I know how much you hate to be away from Menabilly. Thing is, it seems I'm booked to go to the ballet at Covent Garden this evening with Prince Philip and some of his people. He's frightfully keen, often goes to opening nights. I'm awfully sorry. I'm sure I can get you a ticket.'

'Don't worry,' she said brightly, feeling a little taken aback. 'You know I find ballet a bit of a bore anyway. I thought I might catch up with Peter Davies. It's been an age since I saw him. He's still trying to sort through the masses of papers that came out of Jim's flat. Wants to talk about them.'

*

Peter had booked a table for them at the Café Royale. The mirror-covered walls gave the room a greenish light, an underwater hall held up by marble pillars twisted around with gilt foliage. Peter was seated at a corner table. She caught sight of herself in the glass, a tight perm, best coat with wide shoulders, a woman nearing middle age indeed, hurrying towards Peter as he rose to greet her.

Even in his Savile Row suit and bow tie, his hair neatly parted and oiled, Peter had the air of someone who knows he is down on his luck. His high forehead was more etched with worry lines than she remembered, red veins on the prominent nostrils at the end of a long nose. She saw with a sinking heart that Peter was suffering from the old depression again, a bane of his since the war. But always the perfect gentleman, he rose to greet her now with a smile, clearly determined to carry on with what passed for cheerful until a better mood returned.

He was drinking a martini. Signalled the waiter. 'A cocktail?' he asked her.

She nodded. 'The same.'

'Thank you so much for coming, Daphne. It's been too long.'

'It certainly has. How are you?'

'Well enough. Peggy's been under the weather, but with three boys to think about, it's always tiring. The thing is, I have felt a little overwhelmed myself recently, reading through all the boxes of family letters that came to light when we were clearing out Jim's flat. Two thousand letters from Jim to Michael alone. So I've come up with a plan to make a book of the most pertinent letters, just for the family, and jettison the rest.'

'Oh, Peter. Reading through the old letters can't be easy. Not when you've had so many losses as a family. Your parents. George in the war. And Michael. . . It must bring back sad memories.'

Peter offered Daphne a cigarette. She shook her head. Daphne noted a slight tremor to his hand as he lit his. 'Yes, it has been difficult, but not always in ways I expected.'

The waiter appeared, a long white apron around his middle. Daphne ordered plaice, Peter a shepherd's pie. He also ordered a bottle of white for the fish, red for the meat. Daphne looked down at the cloth and said nothing. She would never drink a whole bottle but Peter would probably finish both.

'Difficult in ways you hadn't expected?'

Peter blew out some smoke, seemed to be searching for what to say. 'Let me say, there's certain things I've found out about Mother and Uncle Jim that have left me feeling rather unsettled.'

Daphne felt a prickle of apprehension.

He pulled a briefcase on to his lap, rummaged inside, brought out a thin cardboard folder.

'Here we are, letters between Jim and Mother. Do you know, when Mother and we boys holidayed with Jim in Black Lake Cottage, he paid for her to take four maids with her? Same when she went with Jim and some of us boys on holidays to France, always in top hotels. I mean, what on earth would that have cost? A fabulous amount, and well beyond anything Father could have afforded.'

'Well, Uncle Jim was the richest writer in England, even before *Peter Pan*. And dear old Jim, he liked to help people by sharing what he had, making them happy.'

'That's one way of looking at it. But, you see, I knew Jim rather well.' Peter looked pained, hesitated. 'Jim always had to be the one who called the tune. And the more I think about it the more I realise that there's something very off about lavishing so much money on Mother like that. Expensive holidays in Paris with a bevvy of staff. Things that I know were hugely beyond Father money-wise.'

Daphne frowned. The waiters arrived, put down the plates and removed the silver covers. Poured a little of the wine, waiting for Peter to approve it before the glasses were filled. Once they were gone, Daphne leaned forward.

'You're not saying something was going on between your mother and Uncle Jim? An affair?'

'Goodness, no. Nothing like that. Like Nico said, Jim just wasn't someone who ever had any stirrings in the undergrowth. You know, Mary Barrie said that their marriage was unconsummated when they divorced. Certainly, he never touched us, despite the gossip that went around.' Daphne nodded, feeling relieved. She had never believed any such gossip. 'And I'm sure he never touched Mother. And absolutely certain that Mother remained in love with Father until the day he died, and yet, somehow, Jim managed to weave his way in between them.'

'But how exactly?'

'That's the thing. I'm not sure, but these holidays that Sylvia took with Jim, to Switzerland and Paris and Normandy with various of us boys, where Father never went along, I'd assumed Father couldn't have minded. But then I found this.' Peter took a slug of the wine and pulled out a letter from the back of the file. He handed it to Daphne. 'It's from Father, writing to his father in the Lake District. Look there.'

Daphne took it, reading it quickly.

Dear Father,
I am writing to ask if I might come to visit you for Christmas with probably just Peter, Jack and Nico. Sylvia is planning to go to France for Christmas with Mr Barrie and taking George and Michael with her so I don't think I will be able to persuade her to come with me. Mr Barrie has been very generous to us all.

Daphne stopped, looked up at Peter. 'Well, that is a bit strange, that you weren't together as a family at Christmas.'

'Exactly, and don't you think Father would have been terribly hurt? I can see it must have been tempting for Sylvia, the best hotels, terribly grand. But to go and leave Father feeling so sad when he was clearly longing for them to spend Christmas together, that just doesn't seem true to her character. I remember how utterly felled she was after Father died, a picture of grief in her black veil. I know how much she loved Father, profoundly and completely, and it simply doesn't add up that she'd behave like that. So you see, my question is, just what was the nature of the influence that Jim had on Mother?'

'You shouldn't be so hard on her. People do all sorts of silly things they might regret later for the sake of a little fun. Who wouldn't want to swan off to a hotel in Paris and be waited on hand and foot, especially a mother of five boisterous boys?'

'At Christmas? On the sort of holidays that everyone knew Arthur could never have afforded for her?' Peter leaned back in his chair, eyed Daphne balefully in a way that made her uncomfortable.

'But then you've always been very close to Uncle Jim.'

'Of course. He was part of the family, Angela's godfather. And Jim was always someone one could talk to when Daddy or Mummy were being impossible. He was a genius at getting the best out of Daddy on stage, a sort of magic. Daddy would almost become the character he'd written, *Dear Brutus*, for example.'

'Yes, *Dear Brutus*.' Again, that feeling that there was something Peter wasn't saying.

He sighed. 'Gerald was the most marvellous actor,' he continued. 'I was so sad when he died so early. But if you don't mind me asking, he was rather depressed at the end, wasn't he, not really himself?'

'He did get awfully gloomy, yes, at times. Fearful almost. It was heartbreaking really, the way Daddy would cling to one.' She had an impression of Gerald holding on to her arm, and with it a flood of memories. Saw herself on the lawn as a child, laughing as he swung her round. What wouldn't she give to be able to spend a couple of hours with him again?

She turned her focus back to what Peter was saying.

'As I said – and I don't want to be ungrateful when I am aware of how much Jim did for us boys – but don't you see a pattern there, the effect he had on other people, and on this family in particular? There's Jim, good old Jim, at everyone's service, then somehow he's pulling all the strings. And it's only when it's too late, when too much has been lost, that there's that clouding over, the depression and the regret. Sylvia, Gerald, and for us Barrie boys still alive, two of us with depression on and off, Jack and me. Happens to everyone he gets close to. And as for Michael...'

'Michael was an accident. You can't blame Jim for that. And look at Nico, the youngest of you five boys. He's known Jim all his life. Nobody is more cheerful than Nico.'

'Perhaps you're right. Perhaps there are people like you and Nico who can spend years alongside Jim and shrug him off like water from a cabbage leaf. Nico was certainly the only one who thought it was fun to be a *Peter Pan* boy.'

The waiter appeared. They decided against dessert. 'A *digestif* with coffee?' Peter asked.

'I shouldn't stay too long,' said Daphne. 'I don't want Tommy to come back to an empty flat. He does seem to be out a lot with his London life.'

'How is Tommy getting on, by the way? Comptroller to Princess Elizabeth. Sounds very grand.'

'It's mostly quite boring stuff. Worst thing is I get dragged along to do's at the Palace, which I hate, having to get dressed up.'

'You must enjoy it a little, Daph, dusting off your tiara.'

'It is fascinating to see the royals up close. But not as fascinating as meeting up with you and jawing on about the tribe. You've so many memories from before my time. How I'd have loved to be there at the beginning, when you were little boys, inventing Peter Pan with Uncle Jim.'

'Which reminds me, there's a couple of letters here from Gerald to Grandmother Emma, about a weekend he spent at Black Lake with Jim and my parents. Gerald has some interesting insights about Jim, and Sylvia. Read them and tell me what you think. And I came across this.' He took out a red book, golden lettering on the front, *The Castaways*, below a golden silhouette of three small boys in berets.

'It's photos Jim took of that holiday at Black Lake Cottage, George, Jack and I playing pirates in the woods. Michael would have been only a baby at the time, but he was there somewhere with Nanny Hodges.'

They passed the next half-hour looking at the photographs, Peter reminiscing about a sunny afternoon at the cottage when Gerald had come to visit.

'By the way,' added Peter, 'I've written to Mother's old friend Dolly Ponsonby. Asked her if she can shed any light on the effect Jim had on Mother. She was often there and she must have seen what was going on between Mother and Jim, if anything.'

'She's still alive?'

'Indeed. I think she would have insights.'

'Let's hope she will put your mind at rest.'

By the time Daphne left, it was dark, lights on in the shop windows and buses.

She paused at the edge of the traffic, waiting to cross in a cloud of exhaust fumes. In front of her, one of the many bombed-out sites that still scarred London.

She thought again of what Peter had said about some maudlin influence that Jim might have had on him and his brothers. Poor Peter, he'd come back from the Great War deeply shaken, unable to talk about it. It had taken him a long time to get back to himself, and he was still prone to bouts of low spirits. Uncle Jim was hardly the cause of such depressions. Uncle Jim had never wished harm on anyone. Certainly not on her.

And yet she couldn't ignore a nagging feeling of something out of balance as she turned towards Whitelands.

Inside, the flat felt very empty and pointless without Tommy. It was a relief to hear the key in the door. She got up, kissed his cold cheek. He seemed so solid and sure of himself, carrying some of the glamour of his evening into the flat.

'Hello, Ducks. You still up?'

'Thought we could have a nightcap. You can tell me all about your evening.'

'It certainly was the most perfect production of *Coppélia*. You really must come next time. You'd like it more than you think.'

He seemed animated, moving about the room, handsome in his tall guardsman's way, his voice mellow and calming.

'After midnight, Ducks,' he said, stretching. 'Better get some sleep. Early start tomorrow.' He headed off to the bedroom with its twin beds. No hint that she should follow.

It was odd to be sharing a room again, like strangers thrown together in some hotel room, over-cheerful and formal.

She might as well stay up a little longer. She sat on the sofa, leafing through the *Castaways* book that Peter had given her, photos of George, Jack and Peter in floppy berets and linen tunics. Jim had posed the boys in montages of pirate activities, his St Bernard, Porthos, playing the part of a tiger in a paper mask. Or in a boat on the lake. There were captions underneath. *We made the pirate Swarthy walk the plank.* She examined the pictures closely as if looking for clues among the forests and the ferns.

She remembered the letters from Gerald to his mother, ones she'd never seen before. It was both difficult and sweet to read his words now, a young man, recounting a far-off summer's day.

And as she read she wondered what Gerald could have noticed going on between Sylvia and Jim – enough to make Sylvia forget how much she loved her tall and handsome Arthur.

CHAPTER 19

BLACK LAKE COTTAGE SURREY 1901

Twenty-eight-year-old Gerald du Maurier was the leading man in Mrs Patrick Campbell's theatre company. Easy-going and affable, Gerald took stage directions well, Mrs Patrick Campbell's soft arms welcoming him into the warmth of her bed each night. Their love was a secret, if a badly kept one. To have a favourite, she'd told him, would only cause jealousy among the troupe.

Favourite no more. She had sailed away to America with the rest of her players – without Gerald.

The invitation to spend a few days away at Black Lake Cottage with Sylvia and her boys came as a godsend. They were staying there for the summer as guests of James Barrie and his wife Mary. *I mentioned to Jim that you're between jobs at the moment*, Sylvia had written. *Jim would love to see you again. He's always had a soft spot for you as an actor.* Her husband, Arthur, would also be coming out to join them for the weekend if his work permitted. Gerald could travel up with him on the train from Victoria.

Of all the five du Maurier siblings, Gerald had always felt closest to his sister Sylvia, both of them known as a little wayward in the family lore, he the indulged baby, she the secretive middle child, hidden thoughts lingering in her grey eyes, a crooked little smile. Sylvia had inherited that elusive quality of something held back that her father, George, had possessed, the teasing empathy that had won him so many friends as a young artist in both Paris and London.

Too many friends, was Mother's opinion. She'd always disliked any talk about Father's bohemian days in Paris, with too much wine and smoking, drawing classes where little laundresses modelled in a state of undress. But that was before he married and settled on becoming an English gentleman, a hard-working illustrator who turned out several gently satirical cartoons for *Punch* each week, often using his family as models. The five little du Mauriers had been quite famous as children.

Father's late-blooming career as a writer had come as a surprise to everyone, his books a wild success on both sides of the Atlantic.

What Gerald wouldn't give to be able to talk to Father now. Father would appreciate the difficulties of a young man making his way in the world.

At Victoria Gerald found an empty railway carriage where a fellow might smoke in peace. He wore his new cream linen suit. By his side newspapers and magazines, a bar of Fry's chocolate. Before him lay the prospect of a long, agreeable weekend in the Surrey countryside. He saw himself chatting with Jim. His plays were always smashes. 'Thought of a part for you, Gerald.'

The compartment door slid open and Sylvia's husband, Arthur, appeared. A tall man with a long face that was so handsome one couldn't but stare, classically proportioned, a ruddy tone in his cheeks. Arthur was still wearing his sober black frock coat, coming straight from the law courts.

'Sylvia told me to look out for you,' he said, stowing his top hat and leather case in the netting above the seats. 'Just managed to jump on before it pulled out. Hate to miss seeing the boys at the weekend.'

'How are the little scamps?' Gerald leaned back comfortably. Once you'd set Arthur off on the subject of his boys there was little need for any further effort. Gerald believed too much effort – in acting as in life – was bad form. An idea whose time had come, since he had won quite a bit of praise for his naturalistic style on the stage, hands in his pockets. He wasn't traditionally handsome as actors went – and this did worry him – his brow too square and boyish. But his large expressive eyes and mouth managed to convey emotion in a way that captivated audiences. Mrs Patrick Campbell had told him so – but she had told him many things.

A pony and trap was waiting for them at the station, the Barries' disgruntled gardener at the reins. 'Not really my job, this ferrying of people,' he said as Arthur handed up the bags. 'Mrs Barrie don't appreciate the dangers of greenfly this time of year.'

They drove through narrow lanes sunk deep between banks of ancient hedges, cool green tunnels where beech trees joined overhead, glimpses of fields of sun-brightened grass. A set of gables appeared above a thick laurel hedge. 'Here we are,' said Arthur. 'Black Lake Cottage.' Gerald peered up at the house. More gables than one would expect for a cottage.

Sylvia was in the garden, dozing on a steamer chair. Next to her, a table covered in a white cloth, a vase of frothy cow parsley and peonies. She wore a dress of white muslin, a straw hat with an amusingly tiny crown and large brim. A book lay face down on the table. Arthur strode across the lawn. She put her arms up to greet him, a brilliant smile. He kissed her on the brow. Gerald envied them. No one was more in love than Sylvia and Arthur.

'Boys not here?' said Arthur.

'Off in the woods with Jim somewhere. I hardly see them these days. I do believe they love Jim's dog far more than they love me.'

Arthur scanned the dark woods that came right up to the back of the house. 'No doubt they'll be back soon.' Politely cheerful. Failing to conceal his disappointment.

'And Michael?'

'Nanny took Baby in for a nap. She thinks he might be developing another of his colds.'

'Nothing too serious, I hope?'

'Michael is proving to be a little delicate, a weak chest.'

Arthur looked stricken 'He must see a doctor when he gets home.'

Sylvia turned her attention to Gerald.

'Do go and let Mary know you are here. You must be desperate for some tea in this weather. We all are.'

Mary Barrie was already hurrying down the steps, a pretty woman in her forties. 'You're here. Marvellous.' A strangely engineered accent, unctuous, but with stubborn East End vowels here and there. In another life, Mary would not have mixed with people like the du Mauriers, but that was the theatre for you and Gerald was all for it.

'Oh dear, I don't understand why the maid hasn't brought tea yet.' She called for the maid, her voice surprisingly loud.

A girl came out, carrying a tray loaded with silver pots and jugs. When a cup fell off on to the terrace, Mary hurried over to remonstrate. 'Two safe trips are better than one big trip, Ivy.' Sylvia looked away across the lawns. Arthur went and helped the maid pick up the pieces.

'Shall I be mother?' Mary sat down at the table and began pouring tea. 'Now, you mustn't worry about getting that next role, Gerald,' she said as she handed him a cup. 'I remember how that feels. One of the reasons I set up my own little company, before I met Jim.'

Gerald's shoulders twitched. Had they all been discussing his plight, then? Well, it was a good thing if it meant Jim was going to help him.

After three rounds of tea, glancing over to the woods that had swallowed his boys, Arthur suggested he go and find them.

'I'll come with you,' Gerald said, rising out of his deckchair.

'Look for the adorable red berets,' Mary told them. 'Sylvia is such a marvel with a needle and thread.'

'But nothing compared to you, Mary dear,' said Sylvia, mildly. 'The designs you created for the stage.'

'One does try.'

The sounds of china teacups and the women's voices faded as Gerald and Arthur entered the forest with its humid smell of hot resin and bracken. Dim corridors of tree trunks led away into deeper shadows, the thick carpet of pine needles softening their footfall. A thrumming of woodpigeons. The hollow ricochet of a woodpecker.

'We should head towards the lake,' said Arthur, with the confidence of a man who sets out to retrieve his sons every day. After a while, they heard barking.

'Porthos. Jim's dog,' he said.

'Named like the dog in Father's book? It's not a St Bernard?'

'Oh yes. Jim's quite the fan of your father's novels, it seems.'

'I see. Well, good for him.'

They came out on to the lake's edge, surprised by its brightness after the gloom of the forest. Arthur gasped. A swaying body was strung up from the branch of a tree. On the ground three small boys in red berets were pulling at the rope and arguing about who should have control, a dog as big as a sheep jumping around and barking madly. Seated on a log, a small man in a wrinkled linen suit a size too big, a canvas fishing hat pulled down over his eyes, was writing in a notebook. As soon as the boys saw Arthur they let the stuffed dummy drop and ran to him. Jim put his notebook away, rose to greet them.

'You're just in time to witness the end of the terrible pirate Captain Swarthy. I let George, Jack and Peter decide his fate and you know how heartless boys are.'

'It does seem rather dramatic,' said Arthur.

'And so glad you've come to join us, Gerald,' said Jim. Jim had a surprisingly strong handshake for a small man. Gerald felt the deep-set eyes sizing him up.

The boys had forgotten the dummy, left sprawled in the bracken, straw spilling out of its stuffed jumper and trousers. Gerald was a far better Captain Swarthy. They made him walk the plank, cheering as he plunged from the end of the jetty and came up, shirt sodden, weeds round his shoulders, cursing them with satisfying oaths.

'My other du Maurier boy,' Jim said.

'My boys are Llewelyn Davies boys, in fact,' murmured Arthur.

'Always a great mistake to grow up,' said Gerald, smiling broadly at the boys as he picked weed off his shirt. But I say, I am shivering rather.'

Gerald ran back to find dry clothes. The others followed more slowly. The sun was beginning to go down, hiding and dazzling between the trees. A cool smell of earth rising. Eight-year-old George and Uncle Jim led the way, deep in a discussion, embellishing each other's suggestions for the next day's castaway adventures. Jack walked with Arthur, his rapt face turned up to his father's mild voice. Peter trailed after them, glancing behind every so often with a worried look. Something Jim had told them, no doubt. Arthur stopped, waited for Peter, took his hand also.

They found Sylvia dozing in her chair, her book face down on the grass, a shawl around her shoulders, long shadows stretching across the lawn. Nanny and a nursery maid hurried out to take the boys for tea and baths. Gerald heard Peter tell her, 'Nanny, you know you mustn't let Baby Michael fall out of his pram.' Did she know that babies who fell out of their prams died and went away to the island of birds?

Nanny looked over at Uncle Jim crossly. 'Such nonsense to tell children.' A glance over at Sylvia, who must surely have heard, but no response.

Gerald wondered if Jim would broach the subject of finding a part for him that evening but he remained silent through supper. Once or twice during the meal he took out his notebook to write in it. Afterwards, Jim went through to the conservatory to work at his desk.

The others played cards in the sitting room. Arthur and Sylvia went up early to bed, Sylvia saying how exhausted she was. The two of them arm in arm.

Gerald played cards with Mary until she also said she really ought to go to bed. She went through and kissed Jim on the top of his head. 'Don't work too hard, dear.' Gerald caught a tiny flick of Jim's head, pulling away from her, before he stood and gave her a valiant peck on the cheek. 'Goodnight, dear.'

Gerald took his courage in his hands, picked up a bottle of whisky and two tumblers from a side table and went through to the conservatory.

'What are you working on?'

Jim considered, lighting up a new pipe. 'I never know. It's a rather odd story, some would say, about a baby who gets taken away to the island of birds. Learns to fly. There may be some pirates in it and castaways in there. And there's an odd little man, childless, who kidnaps a boy, right from beneath his mother's nose without anyone noticing. Oh yes, and a wild boy who can fly but never grows up.'

'Does sound rum,' said Gerald.

Jim fetched out a cup of tiddlywinks counters. They played for pennies. Jim won.

Did Jim realize, Gerald wondered, how desperate he was to talk about a possible new play, find out if there was a part for him in it?

Apparently not. Gerald went up to bed feeling deflated. Sylvia must have been mistaken. His was a small room at the back of the house that had kept the day's warmth. He opened the casement window, the pine trees creaking in the dark breeze. Perhaps it wouldn't be so bad to join one of those lesser companies, endlessly trudging around the provinces, damp sheets and unsatisfactory boarding-house breakfasts.

He came down rather late next morning. Sylvia and Jim were talking on the terrace, she enthroned in a high-backed rattan chair, Jim on a stool nearby. Gerald helped himself from the silver covers on the sideboard, took his plate out to join them.

'Anything interesting to report?' Gerald said, breezily. 'You two seem rather deep in conversation.'

'Only silly things,' smiled Sylvia, turning her pretty face towards him. Everyone said the baby, Michael, took after her, the same delicate features and large grey eyes. 'Nothing earnest is allowed when the weather is so lovely.'

'You might well have found our discussion interesting, in fact,' said Jim. 'Your late father's ideas about the mind's ability to travel to other places, into the past even – given the right sort of concentration, the right sort of mind.'

Sylvia looked down at her lap, a little smile.

'Gosh,' said Gerald, cutting up bacon. 'I've never been be able to sit still long enough to try anything like that. Sylvia perhaps. She's the one who got into all father's secrets. She tried to mesmerise me once, all that hand-waving and stuff.'

Hush. Don't be silly, Gerald,' said Sylvia. She waved her hands now as if shooing him away.

Jim clasped his hands around his knees, gazed at Sylvia who lowered her grey eyes. 'There's always a secret at the heart of Sylvia. A hidden life that she shares with no one but the select few.'

'Such nonsense. I spend all my time darning holes in socks and running after small boys.'

'Certainly, no one could be a more perfect mother to boys,' said Jim with a sigh. 'Since Sylvia was almost born a boy herself.'

Sylvia shook her head, looked rather pleased.

Gerald chewed on his toast. Some tosh going on here, surely. Sylvia mysterious? He recalled her epic tantrums ringing through the house in Hampstead when they were small. Anyway, Sylvia seemed to be lapping it up.

All the same, Gerald felt uncomfortable. This was not a conversation Arthur would have liked. Sylvia's husband came from a family of strict Christians who did not care for anything with a whiff of the occult.

'Arthur around?' asked Gerald.

'He's taken the boys for a walk,' said Sylvia. 'Under protest, I'm afraid. They were hoping to use the Swiss army knives that Jim gave them. But Arthur confiscated them at breakfast.'

Gerald noted the small pile of beautiful clasp knives with red cases.

'And very sensible too,' said Jim. 'But still, thirteen attachments, including a bottle opener. A boy's dream.' He passed one to Gerald. 'For you.'

Sunday they played cricket, Sylvia joining them to bat, Jim in his slightly too large canvas hat acting as umpire. More friends turned up, Conan Doyle and Jerome among them. No chance for Gerald to chat with Jim as the hot afternoon slipped by.

The next morning, as he and Arthur were heading back to London on the Victoria train, Gerald had the dissatisfying feeling of having been played.

The train pulled out. Arthur sat, a frown on his face, leafing through a book that Jim had given him, *The Boy Castaways*. 'Only three copies in existence,' Jim had said, 'and this one is for you, Arthur.' On the red cover, three golden silhouettes of small boys in berets carrying picks and hoes. Inside, twenty large photographs. George, Jack and Peter sailing on the lake in the rickety dinghy or fleeing from Porthos in his lopsided tiger mask. Beneath each photograph Jim's wry comments. *We set out to be wrecked. We drank all the grog. We made Swarthy walk the plank.*

Arthur closed the book, his expression sad, a little pained.

In the rush of the train pulling in at Victoria, gathering the bags, he must have left it on the seat, he said, for his copy was never seen again.

*

Gerald returned to his mother's house once more, feeling depressed. Then a note came from Jim. Would Gerald do him the honour of reading for a new play, nothing much, *The Admirable Crichton*.

The old snake, thought Gerald. So he had been stringing him along.

A few months later Gerald had found himself shipwrecked on a desert island, night after night plus matinees, with a young actress named Muriel Bowman, a mass of fair curls, blue eyes, petite and gamine.

Just as in Jim's script, they fell in love. Later, as he signed the register at the back of the church, it did occur to him for a moment that perhaps his life was being written by Jim. Gerald's career soared as the star of Jim's plays, with parts written just for him, colluding and sliding into the fabric of his character. Uncle Jim became a regular visitor at the grand stucco house overlooking Regent's Park – Gerald could now afford such luxury. Jim was godfather to their first baby, Angela.

Sylvia is mother to five boys now, little Nico the youngest. The perfect family. One afternoon Gerald arrives home to find Sylvia in the drawing room, in tears. Arthur is dying of cancer. Jim is the rock she can rely on, sitting by Arthur's bedside, paying the medical bills, helping them send George to Eton when they can't afford it. 'Don't worry about the expense. I've far too much money and money is nothing except where it can help.'

Three years later, the family reels in shock again when Sylvia dies from the same disease while holidaying with Jim and the boys in a remote Dartmoor cottage. Jim already pays for the boys' education, spending as much time as he can with them each day, pays for the house Sylvia has lived in with the boys. No one is surprised when Jim becomes their guardian. There's barely a comment. His boys. The five boys whom Jim fused into a mercurial amalgam to make Peter Pan when they were small had now become his family.

But one by one they have grown too old for tales of Peter Pan. Now Uncle Jim can also be found sitting with Daphne and Angela in the nursery, perched like a crumpled bird on the fender, mesmerizing them with secret islands, prompting them as they swoop from chair to chair or swim like mermaids across the carpet. All night long Daphne continues to swim and fly through the night in her sleep. And it becomes clear to her that she has a secret only Jim knows: she may look like her sisters but really she is one of the boy cousins whom she has long idolised, longed to be there with them when the stories were first told in Black Lake Woods. She is part of Jim's little gang, living on the edge of magic and adventure. She is really a wild boy, dancing at the edge of Neverland, thumbing her nose at the rest of the dull old world.

How annoying to have to go down to the world of grown-ups after tea and have to shake hands and be kissed by people with prickly whiskers and smelly perfume. Daphne seems quite shy, they say, when Daphne glowers at Mummy's guests and longs to get back to the nursery where she can get on with her adventures, a trusty stick for a sword.

CHAPTER 20

MENABILLY 1947

Daphne travelled back to Menabilly, her head still full of Jim and Sylvia and the little boys. She thought once again how much she would have liked to be there at the beginning, playing castaways in the woods of Black Lake Cottage in the days before the world had known war. But she could see now that there had evidently been some psychological game going on, some flattering of Sylvia by Jim.

Back at home a fine rain had come in, settling over the woods. The rooms inside felt chilly, an east wind making the fires smoke. Once again, she found herself unable to settle to work. And she still slept badly, worrying about what was going to happen between her and Tommy, plagued with disturbing dreams, Jim leading the children into the woods, Michael sinking under the water.

Waking one night from another such dream, she realized something odd. She had always believed that Michael's drowning was accidental. But in her dreams, it was no such thing.

*

'Telephone call for you, Daphne,' said Esther, the new housekeeper, knocking on her door one afternoon. 'I think it's your publisher in New York.'

Daphne hurried down to the hall and picked up the receiver from where Esther had left it lying on the table.

'Hello, Nelson. Lovely to hear from you.'

'Bad news, I'm afraid, Daphne. That confounded plagiarism claim about *Rebecca*, it's back. This time we'll have to answer it once and for all. I'm afraid we're going to need you to come over and take the stand here in New York.'

'Oh, Nelson, no. But I thought it had gone away.'

'It's the woman's family stirring things up now, trying to cash in. I know it's all completely trumped up and a hell of a nuisance but we're going to have to answer it in court. Look, why don't you try and make a bit of a holiday of it. Bring the children and stay with us in Oyster Bay. My wife, Ellen, would love to have you. I realize you hate to fly so I'll get you all booked on the *Queen Mary*. Good news is Ellen will be on the ship too.'

Daphne's heart sank. She thought it had all been settled, but now it was going to court. There was absolutely no case to answer, but what if she couldn't clear her name? She'd be ruined, both in reputation and her finances, as would the publisher. There was a film of perspiration on her hands as she put the receiver back into its cradle.

And how could they travel on the *Queen Mary* when all they had were the old jam-along clothes they wore every day? Tessa would be at boarding school, but Kits and Flavia would be coming with her. She looked in at the two youngest playing in the nursery. Square-faced little Flavia with her cropped hair was wearing boy's shorts and a holey jumper. Kits was wearing a too-small playsuit. She glanced down at her old trousers, a darned Fair Isle sweater and a sheepskin waistcoat. Americans were always elegant and dressy, no clothes coupons to navigate there. Her head starting to pound, Daphne put a call through to the seamstress in Par. They were all going to need a whole new wardrobe if she were to survive this trip.

As she listened to the phone ring out, she pictured herself standing in the dock. What might she be asked under oath? She might not have committed plagiarism, but there were other sins she was guilty of.

CHAPTER 21

THE QUEEN MARY 1947

The *Queen Mary* rose above the quayside like a jutting lump of mountain ready to set sail, the tallest of the three black funnels already belching out black smoke. Kits and Flavia clung to Todd when the ship let out a sonorous boom.

'And you're sure all the bags are on board.'

'Maureen's seen to it,' said Tommy. 'Now stop fretting, Ducks. You are going to have a grand time, lap of luxury and all that.'

Daphne touched her newly permed hair. It was shorter than she'd expected, the curls too tight. Did it make her look middle-aged? Her new silk jacquard suit from Harrods felt stiff, her high heels pinched.

'I feel doomed. Apparently the Doubledays have glamorous parties every weekend. You know I like supper on a tray in the library best of all, a little time alone to think.'

'You'll charm the socks off them, Ducks.'

'And then Ellen Doubleday says she's going to be on board. We're bound to bump into her, one of those ghastly, stick-thin American women like Wallis Simpson, no doubt, too much make-up and jewellery. I'll be spending the whole voyage trying to avoid her. And that's before we get to New York and the court case.'

Another blast of the horn.

Standing on deck, she and Todd and the children waved as the ship began to pull away and Tommy became no more than a tiny speck among the crowds.

She still felt annoyed by his dismissal of her concerns but there was no conceivable way she could have told him that her worst fear was not money: it was having to stand up in court and explain how she came up with her novels. She could barely explain it to herself. All she knew was that it was deeply personal, from a place deep down in her soul. How could she explain that Rebecca was not so much a character in a novel as a dark being that had possessed her as she wrote, that the second Mrs de Winter was also herself?

And she could never bear to reveal to the court and the inevitable journalists how she had found the love letters in Tommy's desk from Jan Ricardo, become spellbound by the bold curling letter R. She couldn't bear to be seen as some silly, jealous wife.

Worst of all, she was leaving for America with nothing resolved between her and Tommy. They were still the best of friends, Tommy as dear and as charming as ever, but she missed the physicality of him near her in her bed. She'd never expected this complete rejection, an old coin taken out of circulation, left at the back of the drawer.

*

The two adjoining staterooms booked for their passage were every bit as luxurious as promised.

'I must say, this is splendid,' said Todd. 'And so many flowers for you, Daphne.'

'I'd be quite happy just travelling with a cake of soap and a toothbrush.'

'Hmm. I seem to recall a rather large vanity case of lotions and potions went into someone's packing,' said Todd with one eyebrow raised.

'I do think it's nice to make an effort with the old face, not frighten the horses. And at least you have the chance to live as you should for once, Todd dear. I know you could be staying in all sorts of fancy houses instead of ramshackle old Menabilly. You deserve a little luxury after putting up with me for so long.'

'You were a rather delightful little girl. Head in the clouds, as I recall, but never dull.'

'Well, I'm certainly not planning on leaving this cabin much. And I'm hoping to put off meeting the no-doubt ghastly Mrs Doubleday as long as possible.'

The children ran about, examining the mahogany bunks and little cupboards. Daphne opened Kits' case, began unpacking his clothes, a red suit and a blue suit with short trousers. There were identical clothes in Flavia's case but in a larger size.

Daphne was placing clothes into the drawers when there was a knock on the door. Expecting it to be a cabin boy, Daphne called out, 'Come in.'

She turned to see a slender woman in a white dress, dark hair falling to her shoulders, a pale oval face and the warmest smile. She held a basket filled with white roses.

It was Rebecca.

In shock, Daphne sank down on her bunk, pulling Kits to her side as if needing something to hold on to. She knew she was being ridiculous, but there was Rebecca, standing in the doorway, bringing with her a tumult of feelings that Daphne had long tried to shut away.

'Hello. I just wanted to introduce myself and make sure you have everything you need. I'm Ellen Doubleday.' Her voice was soft and gracious, a lilting American accent. But Daphne sat staring at her, hardly understanding what the woman was saying.

Ellen's large brown eyes showed puzzled concern. She could see that there was something wrong with Daphne, but Daphne still sat speechless. Ellen placed the flowers on a side table. She told the steward standing in the corridor to bring in a second basket. It was filled with wrapped presents for the children, Daphne and Todd.

And all the while Daphne's heart was beating fast, a pounding noise in her ears. The shock of encountering Ellen was like a sledgehammer. 'Thank you,' was all she managed to say.

'I expect you're exhausted,' said Ellen with the sweetest smile. 'I'll leave you now, but perhaps tomorrow we can dine together?'

Daphne nodded, resolving to avoid Ellen like the plague, and pierced through with an anguished longing that she barely understood.

For Ellen.

Kits had slipped away, opening his presents with Flavia, the children crying out happily at their new toys. Daphne remained stock-still on the bed, her heart still hammering.

Or was it, she thought, the hammering of that boy whom she had shut away, years ago, drumming on the lid of the box and shouting to get out?

All through childhood, she'd often thought of herself as a boy at times: playing cricket in the garden with her dress tucked into her knicker bottoms; the boy who had crushes on her schoolmistress in Paris; the suave young man who fell for Molly Kerr. But then she'd grown up, locked that boy up firmly and thrown away the key. She was a girl, and with plenty of admirers. She had fallen in love with Tommy and married and had a family. She loved her husband and her children above all else.

But now, like a stroke of lightning, that boy had been let loose again, flying around the cabin like Peter Pan, laughing at poor old Wendy, back in full force, and longing to take everything she had and throw it down at Ellen's feet.

It was impossible to avoid Ellen. The next day she popped in to ask if Daphne would care to join her on deck. She was wearing a slim dress with a linen swing jacket, a small hat that cradled her head like a bird's wing, white gloves and tiny diamond earrings. Her eyes, Daphne saw, were velvet brown, filled with empathy and kindness.

Each day they sat together on deck, both stretched out on sunloungers with rugs over their knees. The waiter brought them steaming bowls of chicken soup at mid-morning.

'I won't hear of you not eating, Daphne.' Ellen was one of the most intelligent people whom Daphne had met: educated, well read, a terrific conversationalist but also a vastly sympathetic listener. They discussed children, husbands who worked too much, books, plays. Daphne could hardly wait to carry on chatting with her each day.

Ellen changed three or four times a day. Daphne caught glimpses of rows of silk and velvet dresses in Ellen's closet, longed to bury her arms and face in them. Seeing Daphne touching the fur and chiffon, Ellen insisted that she borrow one of her dresses for dinner. Daphne slid a green silk ankle-length ballgown over her legs and body, fastening the hooks and eyes at the side. The dress fitted beautifully. The scent of Ellen's perfume still in the fabric, Coty's L'Aimant.

This must be how women like Ellen and Rebecca walked into a room, she thought as she joined Ellen at the captain's table wearing the dress. Ellen was everything that Daphne longed to be as a woman, and yet at the same time, in her presence Daphne felt like a trembling young man wanting to throw himself at the feet of the woman he adored.

A longing so intense that Daphne felt bereft if Ellen gave her attention to anyone else. To Daphne's distress, it seemed there was nothing she could do could stop this ridiculous deluge of feeling towards Ellen.

She could only hope that Ellen thought her strange behaviour due to nerves about the upcoming trial.

*

Nelson and Ellen's house at Oyster Bay was a wide, modern mansion overlooking the sea. Inside, polished marble floors, a sweeping staircase at the end of a long hallway, a huge drawing room filled with Louis XV furniture, Aubusson carpets and spotless chandeliers.

And warm. It was a far cry from the rats and freezing corridors of Menabilly. Daphne could feel Todd's approval rising by the minute as a butler showed them up to their rooms. The children had yellow and blue chintz beds, their own bathroom, Todd's room and bathroom next door. Daphne's room overlooked the sea. A maid appeared and began to unpack the luggage. It was clear that Ellen ran Barberrys as perfectly as Rebecca had Manderley.

A light knock on the door and Ellen entered. She had changed into a simple brown dress that emphasized her slim figure, a white ruffle at the neck. With her hair in dark coils, she looked like a painting of Mary Stuart. Once again, Daphne wanted to gather up every flower in the house and thrust them in Ellen's arms.

'I expect you are tired after such a long voyage, so we're not expecting you to come down for any formal dinner. Would you like me to send supper up on a tray?'

'That would be very kind. Yes, I'll stay up here, thank you.' Daphne closed the door, feeling shaken. How was she going to manage weeks like this, so close to Ellen?

After supper, the maid ran her a deep bath in the marble-lined bathroom – no greenish water pumped from a nearby pond into a freezing bathroom here. Then she lay awake in bed, trying to regain some control over her feelings. She could not understand where this thunderclap of longing for Ellen had come from. Was it simply because Ellen was so uncannily like Rebecca with her dark hair and her effortless command of the house and servants – though with none of the dark manipulations with which Daphne had imbued that character? But then why should that stir up such a strong reaction? It made no sense.

In the end she took a sleeping pill. Woke the next morning to a maid bringing in the sort of lavish breakfast that had long disappeared in wartime Britain except for hotels like Claridge's where money was no object. Eggs and crisp bacon, pots of honey and marmalade, fresh orange juice and the most heavenly coffee. The maid opened the curtains on to a beautiful autumn day.

'Mrs Doubleday says the car will be here to take you into New York to see the lawyer at ten, ma'am.'

Daphne's stomach turned over. She left the rest of the breakfast untouched.

In the gloomy marble halls of the New York District Court on Foley Square, Daphne was the only woman among gangs of men in expensive suits. She wore a grey coat dress with the new style of fuller skirt, a row of small buttons down the front. A hat and white gloves, new court shoes. Her uniform for the fight. She held up her small chin as she walked into court. Was this how Daddy felt walking on to the stage?

The first session was to hear the expert witness, Harrison Smith. He was clearly on Daphne's side. He'd gone to the trouble of reading almost every novel he could find on second wives.

'There are many common themes,' he told the court. 'A mysterious house, a painting of the first wife with eyes that seem to follow one, there's haunting and madness, but only in *Rebecca* does one find a murder and only in *Rebecca* does one find such a clearly original text. After all that I have read, I find no evidence of plagiarism.'

The two prosecuting lawyers, however, were relentless. 'Isn't it the case that Miss du Maurier has stated in her own writings that her father Gerald and her grandfather George were only loosely acquainted with the truth, that her great-grandmother was a mistress of King George who took bribes for recommendations for naval appointments? How can one trust a woman who comes from a family with such a poor moral compass? Plagiarism would be a small stretch after such antics.'

Daphne willed herself to show no emotion as she listened to them pulling her apart, reporters on hand to write down the juiciest titbits.

She couldn't shake the feeling that she was really on trial for every secret sin she'd committed. More than that, she felt on trial for the evils of the world, because when you peeled back the surface, wasn't all mankind selfish and rotten at the core?

Each evening she was driven back to Long Island in the Buick feeling exhausted, a small, figure slumped against the leather seat, a pounding headache, rain sleeting down as the autumn weather turned cold. Ellen would take her through to the drawing room and sit her down on the sofa next to her. 'And you do not say a word until you have got something warm inside you, my dear.' Daphne sipped milky Earl Grey tea and nibbled on cinnamon toast, a child's tea, while Ellen listened to what had happened in court, eyes shining with concern, her empathy a balm for the day's bruises.

The weekend brought the first of the dreaded dinner parties. The house was to be filled with glittering people from New York.

The children came through to her bedroom in their pyjamas to say goodnight and found Mummy still in her under-slip, looking distraught. She lit another cigarette.

'Can you believe it, Loons?' She gave a snort of laughter. 'Look, Tilly the maid thinks my evening dress is a nightie.' She pointed to the bed where the children saw Mummy's white snakeskin evening dress, laid out neatly next to her bed jacket.

'What on earth am I going to wear tonight now? And if she thinks my best frock is a nightie, what the hell does the maid think my nightie is?'

Seeing the children's horrified faces, Daphne burst into laughter. Soon they were all collapsed on the floor, holding on to each other and laughing until tears ran down their faces.

Daphne sat up, wiping her face. 'Only one thing for it.' She pulled on the dress, a glimmering white sheath with narrow shoulder straps. Stood in front of the mirror, pulling the fabric straight. 'If only I could wear a pair of velvet trousers and a nice boyish belt.'

'But, Mummy, you look beautiful,' said Flavia earnestly. Kits nodded.

*

Standing at the top of the stairs she saw women in dresses in the new style, closely fitted waists, full skirts in bright chiffons and silks, *décolleté* necklines, evening gloves and hair decorations. Daphne hesitated, her heart beating fast. She smoothed down her iridescent white dress. Then she heard Nelson's booming voice. 'Well, here she is, our famous author.'

There was applause as she walked down the curving staircase. Ellen, in pale blue tulle, a hairpiece made of feathers, took her hand. 'Now, just about everyone here wants to meet you. Where do we start?'

She watched Ellen moving about the room, in awe of how this Rebecca of Barberrys could conjure up such a perfect evening, the food, the flowers, the constantly flowing cocktails and wine. She watched Ellen say little words to her guests, top up Nelson's water glass with a hand on his shoulder, a smile. Ellen was the complete woman, immaculate and lovely. Her beauty impossible to resist.

Everything about Ellen left Daphne utterly defeated.

Ellen insisted on taking Daphne shopping in New York. 'We have to get the best for our star. You are representing the company, after all.'

Daphne returned, feeling spun round and exhilarated. She spread the linens and silks and satins out on the bed. She'd almost forgotten what it felt like to dress up again after years of Make-do and Mend. And what exactly did one wear once one reached forty, in that no man's land between the ease of flowered youth and the staidness of middle age? A problem she had dodged with trousers and jumpers.

There was even a new dress for Flavia, a red flowered confection with starched netting petticoats. 'Daphne, you're raising a tomboy. The poor child has no idea she's a girl. How is she ever going to learn how to dress?'

Flavia fought her way into the frock through the layers of netting, looked in the full-length mirror in awe. 'But I can keep it, can't I, when we get back to Menabilly?' The children had once been invited to a party at one of the county homes nearby. Having no dresses, Tessa and Flavia had worn pinned-up skirts of Daphne's. Opening the door the grand hostess had thought they were common children from the village and told them they were not allowed in the grounds. An hour or so later someone had come out to ask what Lady Browning's children were doing sitting on the steps in the garden.

'So can I keep it, Mummy?' Flavia asked anxiously.

Daphne eyed the lace collar sticking up around Flavia's square chin, the folds of red fabric around the child's legs. 'But, darling, however could one climb a tree in that? I think you look so much nicer in cords.'

'Well, I think it's jolly, Mummy.'

'Oh dear. Here we go,' said Daphne with a sigh.

Later, when they returned to Menabilly, the dress did indeed disappear. Flavia knew not to ask about it. She almost hanged herself accidentally that year playing, as ever, the sort of boyish games in the trees that might impress Mummy.

The court sessions continued relentlessly. Each morning the Buick drove Daphne to New York, her face white and tense.

The time had come for her to testify in person. It was like being asked to stand naked in public and tell the world her darkest secrets, the secret passions that circled the soul like pecking birds. People thought she had based the mousy second Mrs de Winter on herself. What would they say if they knew Rebecca had also sprung from her, ripped a hole in the fabric of her life, falling for Christopher, deluging her with longing for Ellen?

Only the knowledge that Ellen would be there, waiting for her, kept Daphne sane as she dragged herself back to court each day. When she got back, Ellen would join her in her bedroom where they ate supper on trays. They talked endlessly, confidences pouring from Daphne. She adored how Ellen leaned in close and stroked her arm, how her serious brown eyes reflected Daphne's painful day. She felt soothed by her perfume, falling deeper and deeper under Ellen's spell.

And Ellen seemed not to have the first idea that this was happening.

Or did she?

Sometimes Daphne wondered if Ellen was flirting with her, taking her face in her hands, kissing her forehead. But it hardly mattered. There was nothing about Ellen that Daphne did not adore. Watching Ellen move around her room dressed in expensively tailored frocks, jewels sparkling like a Victorian marchioness, her dark hair coiffed and shining, she was not sure at times if she wanted to love Ellen or to be Ellen. It was Ellen in her dreams, Ellen to whom she wanted to tell everything, to give everything to. She stopped off on the way home at Saks or Bloomingdale's to buy her gifts, not caring how much she spent.

It was only later that Daphne would realize that nearly all the confidences went from Daphne to Ellen. The truth was, Daphne still knew almost nothing about the real woman.

The court dismissed the plagiarism case. Newspaper bulbs flashing around Daphne as she left courtroom for the last time, Nelson helping her into the car. She was so thin and exhausted that she collapsed into bed. She ran a fever, slept through the day for a week. Each time she woke, she would see Ellen sitting by the bed.

'Daphne dear, if it's too much to travel back to England, you know we would love to have you stay for Christmas.'

Tommy telephoned, his voice sounding far away and crackly, the line bad. She could picture him in the cold hallway, the telephone receiver in his hand, in front of the stained-glass window that some past inhabitant had installed to welcome a bride. He sounded lonely. It was time to go home.

CHAPTER 22

MENABILLY CHRISTMAS 1947

The children were besides themselves, jumping up and down wildly and making the gloomy hallway seemed cramped as Daphne, Mummy, her sisters and Todd waited for Tommy to open the double doors into the long room. Ever since they moved into Menabilly it had been the height of Daphne's year to have the whole family gathered together there for Christmas.

And the high point of each Christmas was Tommy's unveiling of the Christmas tree.

'Tommy does like to make a thing of it,' said Daphne's mother, pulling her woollen jacket tighter around her shoulders.

'And it is never less than splendid,' said Todd stoutly, casting a supportive glance at Daphne.

'Are you ready yet, Daddy?' Flavia and Kits took it in turns to yell through the narrow gap at the edges of the doors.

Finally Tommy threw the doors open. The light had gone out of the day making the tower of candles burn brighter, creating a magic that made even Tessa pause and clap her hands. With a swelling heart, Daphne looked at the faces of her three blonde children gazing at the lights. Tommy with a bucket of water on hand in case of emergencies patrolled the candles as they burned precariously close to the fir branches. But the twinkling tinsel and silver balls made even the risk of burning down the house seem worth it for a moment. He dashed forward as a candle at the side flared up, snuffed it out.

Behind the tree were the firmly locked double doors that led through to the condemned Victorian wing, whiffs of musty air and rot seeping through.

As master of ceremonies Tommy made the children wait until everyone was seated with a glass of sherry or ginger beer. They toasted the tree, toasted each other, and then Tommy began handing out the presents.

While the children played with their toys and books and her mother and Todd began to nod off – and as Tommy's tally of festive drinks began to mount, along with his irritability – Daphne crept upstairs into the cool quietness of her room.

On the bedside table, Ellen's photograph smiled at her. She picked it up, planted a kiss on the glass. 'Happy Christmas darling.'

She sat down at her desk, imagining a different Christmas, sitting with Ellen in the drawing room at Barberrys, the tree no doubt magnificent. She'd been sorely tempted to take up Ellen's invitation to stay on for Christmas when she was so unwell, but not to return home to Tommy for their family festivities would have been unthinkable and so she had struggled home.

'Of course. If you are strong enough to manage the journey, your place is beside Tommy,' Ellen had said with that soothing voice that so undid Daphne.

She took a sheet of notepaper and began yet another letter to Ellen. Far more letters went across the Atlantic to Ellen than came back the other way, but Daphne could not stop writing. Things she had never spoken of before, told no one but Ellen, poured from her pen.

Dearest Ellen,

I sent for some of your perfume from Harrods. Coty L'Aimant. I spray it in the air and close my eyes when I am alone. If only I could be with you now and kiss your eyes. Not in any way that might make you feel that you had to respond, and damn you it makes me so ashamed to feel I am always the supplicant and probably bothering you horribly – though you are too kind to ever say so – but Ellen I have never been able to open my heart out and be so myself with anyone else. I don't want a thing in return. In fact all I want to do is to give you things, like a child giving gifts to its mother, or like a young man with nervous hands, wanting to pile gifts in the arms of his beloved.

The thing is, darling Ellen, and I've never told anyone this before, but I've always had the feeling that I'm a strange half breed who may look like a girl – and a quite attractive and successful one at that, who fell in love and married and had children – but inside me there's always been another self, a boy or some sort of free disembodied spirit who likes to dance alone at midnight. I was always being someone else as a child, never myself, but always Peter Pan and never Wendy. For years now I've locked that boy away, thrown away the key, but the minute you walked into my cabin on

> the 'Queen Mary', he was back, and stronger than ever. It floored me completely. And ever since, he's wanted to give you everything he could, flowers, jewels, love.

When the letter was finished, Daphne took the diamond brooch that Daddy had given her as a girl, wrapped it in tissue paper and parcelled it up with the letter.

A couple of weeks later, Ellen wrote back, in her usual calm manner.

> It's good that you've kept him a secret, otherwise think what you would have lost. All that you hold dear as a family and for your children could have been lost chasing after this fancy. And though I respect how you feel, you must know that I could never imagine responding to your feelings. I am so sorry. Perhaps if my hormones were different I could be someone who could love other women, but I know that I will never feel that way, dearest Daphne. And thank you for the brooch. I know how much you treasure it. But it is too much. I will wear it but I will return it to give to Tessa or Flavia next time we meet.

Daphne went for long walks in the cold rain, trying to see the sense in what Ellen had written, but it was no good. Her feelings for Ellen were overpowering, like being blown forward in a gale. The truth was, she felt wounded to the core by Ellen's insistence that she could never return her feelings. And the sting of humiliation.

Please keep the brooch [Daphne wrote back]. *But don't ever lump me with that L word. What I am, is something I have invented myself, neither boy nor girl, but some disembodied spirit that wants to dance free of all the constraints of this narrow life. And it is this boy, this spirit, that is at the heart of all that I create. Before I met you, I had begun to think he had left me, that all around me was dead and static, but you, Ellen darling, brought him to life again. And now I may be in torment, but don't feel sad. I was so lonely and hopeless before, and now I have hope again. I have you.*

I haven't been able to write a word for so long, but at last, I'm working again. I've an idea for a play. A young man who falls for his fiancée's mother – not that the woman in question, let's call her Stella, will reciprocate. Stella will be based on you. And you can guess who the young man will be based on. Our secret.

Ellen did write back, friendly chatty letters. Nothing like the stream of heartfelt confessions that flowed from Daphne's pen. In the quiet surrounding the house, the days short and lit with a low winter light, Daphne went about the house, talking with the children and Tommy, but always waiting to get away to write her letters to Ellen, or to work on her new play with the Ellen/Stella character.

Not that it was possible to get much done. The house was bedlam with workmen repairing the damage caused by winter storms, tiles missing and rain pouring down the chimney in the long room.

She had a wooden hut built, hidden away at the end of the rhododendrons. As soon as it was ready, she set off there each morning, wearing two jumpers and a jacket, a woollen cravat around her throat, lighting a little oil stove to keep off the chill. She sat alone in her hut, overlooking the back lawns, summoning up Stella and the son-in-law who had fallen in love with a woman who could never be his. Sometimes she carried her characters back with her, sat at the supper table dreaming of Stella and Evans. It was important that the actress capture the essence of Ellen; perhaps she could wear a red and black dress like the one that made Ellen look so perfectly like Mary Stuart.

'So what do you think about it, Ducks?' she heard Tommy ask her as they finished another tough mutton stew cooked by Hanks.

Tommy and the three children looked at her, an expectant silence. They seemed to want her opinion. Whatever had Tommy been lecturing them on? Boats? A political lecture?

'Couldn't honestly say, Ducks,' she replied, as if her mind wasn't made up either way.

Tommy started at her. He looked hurt. 'You didn't hear a word, did you?' He threw down his napkin. 'Good God, woman, you live in a dream.' He scraped back his chair and stalked out. He'd be in a bad mood all evening. Listening to his ballet music and sipping whisky.

Why couldn't she take Ellen's advice and be more supportive of Tommy? Whatever it was that was happening to her, and she could barely understand it, she knew that she still loved Tommy. She longed for them to find a way back from the impasse between them – just as in her play, where Evans and his wife Cherry, stuck as they are with sleeping in separate rooms, eventually find a way to love each other once again.

But how could things change when she and Tommy never talked about anything that mattered these days? It was all so hopeless, with him being away in London so much. But at least she would be up in London more for the rehearsals of the new play. She would try and be a better wife, focus on Tommy, she promised herself. Somehow find a way back to each other again.

CHAPTER 23

LONDON 1948

It was strange to be sitting in the plush stalls of a London theatre again, the musty smell of scenery along with its attendant whiff of excitement bringing back poignant memories of being backstage with Daddy at the Wyndham's.

If only she didn't feel nauseous with worry. It was so important to pick the right person to play the Ellen/Stella role or *September Tide* would be ruined. But to her horror the director was suggesting one of Daddy's old girlfriends – his last, in fact, Gertrude Lawrence. And yes, she was a tremendous hit on Broadway. But she was also, in Daphne's opinion, far too brassy to play her ethereal Stella.

But the director was adamant. The play needed a big star.

As Daphne sat at the back of the theatre watching rehearsals, day after day, the oddest thing happened. Gertrude began to take on the demeanour of Ellen without ever having met her. It was uncanny. One afternoon, as Gertrude crossed the stage to pick up the lilies that the son-in-law had left on a table – the same flowers that Ellen so loved – it was Ellen whom Daphne saw, walking across the stage in all her dark-haired grace and her beauty. She blinked hard. A trick of the light? Some trick of the brain?

Gertrude came down from the stage, clutching her throat. 'A bit croaky but a few seasons singing in the *King and I* will do that to one.'

'We'll have to be careful about that, Gertrude,' said Daphne, frowning.

'Don't fret. I have my medication, dear.' She produced a hip flask. 'Now, I'm due to meet Noël for supper at the Savoy. What do you say? Care to join me?'

'I think I should be going back to the flat,' said Daphne, picking up her coat and bag. 'Early night.'

'Oh, come on, Daphne. You look as though you need a bit of cheering up. Far too pale and serious for a daughter of Gerald. I've got my car outside.'

Gertie had had her enormous Buick brought over from the US. She drove fast and erratically through the London traffic, a cigarette in the corner of her mouth.

'So come on, spit it out. What's troubling you, little Daphne? Not like a du Maurier to be so glum.'

'I'm just wondering if anyone will come and see this rather strange play.'

'What on earth do you mean? They'll adore it.'

A taxi blared at them, the driver gesticulating angrily. Gertie wound down the window.

'Oh, fuck off. We're in a hit,' she yelled at him.

Daphne stared at her. Then they both burst out laughing, the two of them still in giggles as they entered the Savoy.

'Oh no, darling,' Gertie told the waiter, tipping her wide hat in front of the mirror for better effect. 'That table's far too stuck away in the corner. Do find one where everyone can see us.' She gave him the most charming smile. He changed their table.

Gertie insisted on saying hello to everyone who passed by. She seemed to have the same need as Gerald to make people fall in love with her, signing autographs with a flourish and a radiant smile, making everyone feel that they were the special focus of her attention. So like Daddy – if Daddy were a brassy blonde who swore like a trooper.

They were a party of six, including Noël Coward, who was almost as outrageous as Gertie as the banter and gossip flowed with the sparkling champagne, Gertie directing proceedings with her long cigarette holder. Daphne had forgotten how much fun it was to be around theatre people.

'Oh wait, wait,' Gertie called out, 'I heard the most marvellous thing the other day.' She paused for a beat until she held her audience captive. 'Now what was it? A woman before her twenties is like Africa, part virgin, part explored. In her twenties she's like Asia, hot and mysterious. In her thirties she's like the USA, high-toned and technical. In her forties to fifties she's like Europe, quite devastated but interesting in places. And in her sixties she's like Australia – everyone knows where it is but no one wants to go there.' Gertie basked in the laughter, drew on her cigarette holder elegantly and winked at Daphne.

Daphne got back to the flat in Whitelands House smiling and humming the tune the orchestra had been playing, 'I've Got a Crush on You'.

Tommy was still out. Dinner with Prince Philip, or was it another ballet?

Perhaps they might have a nightcap together when he came in. She took a book to read, tried to make herself comfortable on the hard little sofa. After a while she gave up, went to bed feeling cross and depressed that Tommy appeared to have no need of her in his London life. Did he resent leaving it and having to come down to Menabilly each weekend – in spite of his protestations that he loved the place?

Ellen would never abandon Nelson for days and weeks at a time. Really, the way Daphne was going on was all wrong, working like a man, leaving Tommy to get on with things on his own.

She got into the chilly single bed. She thought of those first days when they had thrown their lot in together, feeling a pang of loss in her chest for their honeymoon on the Helford River, that sweet, heady turbulent time as newlyweds when they were part of each other's lives. It all felt like a dream you could never summon back.

She heard the sound of Tommy's key in the lock, the thump, thump of him taking off his shoes, padding into the bedroom in his socks, taking his pyjamas to get changed in the bathroom. She listened to the sound of teeth-cleaning, water running. He came back in and settled down in his bed.

'Night, night,' he whispered.

'Night, night,' she whispered back.

She had to try harder, she resolved, as she fell back to sleep, but it was as if a devilish Rebecca lingered in the room. Yes, do try to be good, but we all know how that goes.

As the play went into production and began to tour the provinces, Daphne found herself travelling to join Gertie as much as possible, claiming that she needed to make sure her star was well looked after, no sore throats or chills that might stall the production. But really, she began to realize, she was beginning to crave Gertie's company, almost as much as she had Ellen's, and Gertie was happy to play along, supplying the affection and warmth that Daphne so longed for. Gertie was funny and cheeky and dangerous in her large hats and dressy clothes. Gertie was the drug that Daphne mixed for herself to cope with Ellen's distance.

The autumn was glorious. Daphne was still hoping that there might be a breakthrough with Tommy, a crack in the surface of the dry soil that might let the old sweetness well up.

They had never got on better, in fact. When Tommy was home at the weekend, they spent as much time as possible out on the boat, rocked on the calm, mesmeric waters, Tommy by her side as she steered the boat as far as the Fal. She had not for one minute stopped finding Tommy attractive, the scent of his cologne, his elegant and athletic limbs, his sensitive face and air of sureness. She missed him so much at nights. She began to wonder if they could still have another baby. It wasn't too late. Another boy, perhaps? But how on earth was that going to happen when it was impossible even to broach the subject?

Perhaps it was time to face the fact that she and Tommy might never return to the closeness they had once had.

*

Then a letter came that left Daphne so thrilled that the children wanted to know what had happened.

'Mummy's going on holiday, Loons,' she told Kits and Flavia, her face beaming.

She had all but given up trying to convince Ellen to spend a couple of weeks away with her in Italy. But now Ellen had written out of the blue to say that she would like to go after all.

Daphne, Ellen wrote. *You have persuaded me. Perhaps a trip to Italy is what I need. You sing the praises of Florence and Italy so beautifully that I feel I must see them for myself – and to see them with you would be perfect.*

Two weeks alone with Ellen. She could barely admit to herself what she was hoping for as she booked a room with twin beds.

For months she had thought about Ellen, dreamed about her, written letters and even spoken on the phone, but what would it be like to be with her in person again?

The real Ellen was every bit as entrancing as Daphne remembered – and far more irritating.

'I was thinking we could explore the Duomo tomorrow,' Daphne suggested as they sat over supper. 'Then we could eat in this marvellously authentic place down a little back street that the doorman was telling me about.'

Ellen had changed her outfit from an afternoon coat dress to an exquisitely cut blue silk gown for dinner. Diamond combs sparkled in her dark hair.

Ellen pulled a wry face. 'Daphne, I was so hoping to do a little shopping tomorrow. The gloves and shoes in Italy are to die for. And we must have seen just about every artwork there is to see in Florence.'

'Gosh, yes, of course, though it seems a little odd to want to come to Florence and go shopping.'

Ellen sighed. 'Then if you don't mind too horribly, I would love to find somewhere for supper where one doesn't come away with indigestion, where the floor is clean. I know how you love these out-of-the-way places, finding ideas for your books, but my stomach would thank you for a little fine dining in a good restaurant.'

'I thought you liked the café we ate in yesterday.'

Ellen raised an eyebrow, put a hand on her stomach. 'It was a little rough.'

'Well, if you do want to waste a day going round shops. . .'

'Daphne, I do.'

'Very well.' Daphne looked at the empty plates, the meal finished. 'Shall we go up to our room?'

'I think I might stay and smoke a cigarette with my coffee. If you don't mind.'

Up in their room, Daphne put on her silk pyjamas, a midnight-blue silk dressing gown. Outside, the evening had a rich apricot glow, a turquoise sheen behind the Florence skyline. She brushed out her hair in front of the mirror, the soft bristles touching her cheek. She shivered.

Why had she been so brusque? As soon as Ellen came up she would apologise. She hadn't realized how difficult it was going to be. So close to Ellen – and yet so far. She settled down in bed with a book and waited. An hour went by. By midnight, Daphne was ready to pull on some clothes and go down and see what had happened. The door opened, Ellen, blithely humming a tune.

'What on earth kept you?'

'I'm so sorry. I started talking to the couple behind us, people from Wisconsin, and you know how it is, the time just went by.'

'No, I don't know how it is. And the people behind us were so dull. How could you possibly waste so much time with them when all the while you knew I was waiting for you up here?'

Ellen sat down on the stool by the dressing table. Looked at Daphne ruefully. 'I like talking to people, even people you might find dull. I'm sorry, Daphne, but I think that you expect too much of me. I don't really understand why you get so angry.'

'You don't understand why I feel angry, after you ignore me and leave me alone for so long? Don't understand how much I love you? How I can't bear to be apart from you. You must know. Or else you are being so disingenuous that it takes my breath away.'

'Daphne, what do you want from me? I've told you, I simply can't respond in the way you would like me to. I've said before, perhaps if my hormones were different, then I could be what you want, give you what you want. Please don't be angry. One has to have a sense of proportion sometimes, a sense of humour.'

'Oh, I think you'll find I have a sense of humour. I'm simply shaking with secret laughter about how you carry on all the time. And now I think I'd like to go to sleep.'

Daphne snapped off her bedside light and turned away. Lay down in abject misery, tears in her eyes.

'Oh, Daphne. Please don't be like that. You are my dearest friend.'

'I never know if you do care for me, or if you are just stringing me along – your best-paying author. You realize I haven't even been paid by Doubleday yet. Nothing. You and Nelson still hold all the money I've earned for you.'

'How can you think like that? You know how these things take time.' Ellen moved to the bed and sat down by Daphne. 'I'm sorry you're so angry. Daphne, I care for you very deeply, as a friend, but just not in the way you want. I'm not made like that.'

Daphne blew her nose, her voice thick with tears. 'You must think I'm ridiculous, laugh about me when you get home.'

'Daphne, never.'

Daphne sat up, dabbed at her eyes. 'I'm being ridiculous. I know it. I'm sorry. But I simply don't know how to stop.'

The next day was miserable as they walked around Florence. Watching the slight figure of Ellen framed in the Tuscan sunlight, unsure whether Ellen was her angel or her demon, the seed of an idea began to form in Daphne's mind. A young man living at Menabilly, infatuated by a beautiful Italian woman he barely knows – and never for a moment will he be sure if she is his saviour or his poisoner.

Daphne returned to Menabilly to find a particular kind of misty Cornish rain had settled over the peninsula, casting a gloomy greyness over the landscape, the trees dripping with a cold pattering of rain when she walked the sodden paths, the grey sea roiling as if under a grubby tarpaulin. She felt deeply dissatisfied with how events had turned out in Florence, regretting how selfishly she had behaved with Ellen, spoiling the last few days of their holiday together – though Ellen had told her that friends can weather each other's little foibles. She wished that she could go back and relive the week, control her emotions towards Ellen, but the truth was, Daphne realized, that if she were to relive the week she would most probably do the same again.

She walked down to the shore, stood letting the tide wash over her rubber boots until the sand under her heels was dragged away by the tide and she felt she might stagger backwards.

Her feelings were wildly beyond her control, something internal pulling her to do things that were stupid and distressing, even harassing Ellen like a tipsy old gentleman leering over someone's wife at a cocktail party. Was that really how she was behaving? How sickeningly embarrassing if so.

And worse still, she seemed completely unable to stop herself. Even though she knew it was dangerous to her marriage and her family. If Tommy ever knew. . .

Filled with the need to somehow lessen Ellen's power over her, Daphne rose early next morning and set out for her writing hut tucked away at the back of the rhododendron banks. She put a sheet of paper into the typewriter and tapped out the title of her new book. *My Cousin Rachel.*

The only way to be free of the strange power that Ellen had over her would be to write her out of her life. She would kill her. She had not yet decided if it would be an accident or a murder but the elusive, inscrutable Rachel would perish.

It would be her fantasy version of Ellen that she would be killing, the dream of Ellen superimposed on top of the perfectly nice and ordinary real Ellen. But it still felt as though she were committing a crime.

CHAPTER 24

CAFÉ ROYALE LONDON 1949

Though Daphne thought often about her last conversation with Peter, it would be a while before she saw him again. Hidden away in her hut at Menabilly, she worked each day on *My Cousin Rachel*, wrapped up in jumpers and a coat, the oil heater as close as possible without scorching her side. She had never felt so deeply involved with a book. She became Phillip, watching as the beautiful Rachel poured a cup of mysterious tisane for him to drink, wondering if it would kill him even as he took it from her hands to drink.

With *My Cousin Rachel* finally at the publishers, Daphne arranged to meet Peter at their usual haunt, the Café Royale. Peter had decided to publish a book of George du Maurier's letters and had called to ask if she would write an introduction to them.

She found Peter at his usual table in the corner. She kissed him on the cheek. Noted that he seemed in better spirits than last time.

'Thank you so much, Daphne, for agreeing to do the

introduction for Grandpa's letters. I'm compiling a collection of letters from Mother and Father and their generation for the family only, but when it came to Grandfather George's letters, they are so jolly and interesting, I thought they would make a very agreeable collection that people might like to read. With him being so very famous in his day.'

'It's lovely to have a chance to read his letters again. I've always wished I could meet him. He sounded like the most intriguing person.'

'He was indeed, a man of secrets. By the way, I heard back from mother's old friend Dolly the other day. Very interesting. I think her letter may well shed some light on what went on between Sylvia and Jim.'

'Whatever did she say?'

'Nothing overtly scandalous. But Dolly seems to believe that Jim somehow played on Mother's secret of knowing Grandfather's trick of hypnotism.'

'Sylvia knew how to hypnotise people?'

'Yes, here we are, listen.' He began to read from Dolly's letter.

Sylvia came and we talked for hours about her inner life, her family, especially her grandfather. That afternoon she told me how one goes about hypnotizing someone. Something she shares with few people. I believe her father may have carried out such an effect upon her, and she on other people, though this was a tremendous secret, and I doubt that Arthur ever knew, his family being so rigorously church minded. I suspect however that Jim did know, and that this was a secret they shared.

'There it is,' said Peter. 'Jim wormed his way into that secret part of Mother her knowledge of mesmerism, and made her feel special and mysterious. She was no longer just the mother of five boys – though he was very open about idolizing her as that too – she was the inheritor of the du Maurier secret. I think she felt she was a different Sylvia entirely when she was with Jim. She must have been flattered by such attention. You know, he even wrote her into his book *Tommy and Grizel*. Described Mother exactly, the tilted nose, the crooked smile and grey eyes, the dark wavy hair and teasing manner.'

'I do remember hearing Daddy saying Grizel was partly based on Sylvia, but isn't that just how writers work, basing a character on a real person?'

'Yes, but it was somehow more than that for Jim. It was as if he painted a fantasy portrait of Mother, and she adored it so much that she began to almost live it. As if he rewrote Mother. And I think it was only after Father died that she came to her senses. She felt racked with guilt in fact, but by then it was too late.'

'But really, Peter, this idea of Jim creating a secret Sylvia, by playing on the family fables – I can't believe Uncle Jim would be so cynical.'

Peter shrugged. 'Jim was a great game player. His substitute for a relationship with a real person, I do believe. And I found this.'

He took out a dark blue photograph album with a tooled leather cover and passed it to Daphne. 'Jim took most of the pictures in here with that little camera he used to wander around with. He made up this album for her. His portrait of Sylvia. I find it quite disturbing.'

Daphne began to turn the pages, thick brown card with one or two portraits per page. A shot of Sylvia and Arthur's first house, although only Sylvia's name was written beneath, *Sylvia du Maurier*, as if she had never married. This was the first sign that something was off kilter. No mention of Arthur at all. Page after page of photographs of Sylvia, posing for the camera with little George and Jack, the boys wistful and cheeky, Sylvia the ideal mother gazing adoringly at her children. A turn of the page, and here is Sylvia, burdened with a great bundle of blankets, hair falling in wisps, passing the child to Arthur who makes a brief appearance. Then just Sylvia again with her children, wearing the darling little coats and berets she's sewn herself. Or with Baby Michael in his lace bonnet. In some pictures she looks a little frayed at the edges, not smiling, having to pose for Jim's camera yet again – a mother with so much to do. But in other pictures she's more prepared, as if playing up to expectations, serenely framed in a doorway in an elaborate little straw hat decked with flowers and feathers, embroidering a small garment for one of the boys. Charming. Several pictures follow of her on the beach with the wind catching the wing of a towel that she throws around a small naked child. The overexposed printing makes her look washed away, the towel ethereal, the child a wisp. She wears a wide-brimmed hat that must have taken a great many pins to keep in place in the wind, a silk sash round her waist, not so slim now tied firmly in a bow. How nice to be photographed and seen as worthy of worship after five boys. Baby Nico in the pram now, Michael a wistful toddler.

And here's an idyllic summer tea in the gardens of the cottage. A white tablecloth and mismatched chairs from the dining room set out beneath the tree. Berets for the boys, a boater for her. A lace-trimmed blouse with pearls. Sylvia looks tired. She leans in to a serious little Peter who frowns at the camera and holds up a cherished stick.

So many charming poses of Mother and her little boys,' Peter said as she turned the pages. 'After we became famous as the Peter Pan boys, it was as if Mother wore her children the way other women wore pearls or furs.'

Daphne kept turning the pages. Sylvia with Michael, on a trip to France with Jim, Sylvia on the balcony of a Normandy chateau, Michael below, acting out *Romeo and Juliet* for the camera. Another of Jim sitting on a bench with Michael, showing him some trick, the child entranced – Sylvia away to the side.

And suddenly, the boys are in Scotland, dressed in full fig of breeches and glengarries on a fly-fishing holiday. Black armbands. A holiday to help them forget the death of their father. Sylvia in widow's black, sitting crumpled by grief, her face behind a veil, aged by misery.

Peter leaned closer to look over at the picture of his mother in mourning and sighed. 'I didn't see it then, of course, children don't, but I believe the regret she felt when Father died all but killed her. She'd left him on his own so much while she danced to Jim's tune in Neverland.'

'If that was really the case, it does sound terribly sad. Poor Sylvia.' Daphne flicked back through the pictures again.

There was something about this photographic capture of Sylvia that felt disturbing, familiar – that made her feel most uncomfortable.

Suddenly, the penny dropped. She put the album down. 'But of course, he pinned her. Jim pinned his fantasy of Sylvia on to the real Sylvia. That was always how he created the characters in his stories, pinning his imaginary version of a person on to a real person. Goodness, I do the same thing myself when I write. There's no harm in it really. Unless you start to get real people mixed up with a fantasy version. . .' Her voice trailed off.

'Well, I would say that harm was done. Inveigling Mother to put a shard of ice in her marriage. I think she regretted what she did tremendously when Father became sick. She was very cool to Jim for a while. But looking back, I can see now that she couldn't do without his help while Arthur was passing away. Jim paid all the hospital bills. And after Father died, Jim was there at the house all the time, helping Mother, paying the bills for schools and the house – until she also died and Jim adopted the five of us.'

'I still think you are being a little harsh. Uncle Jim wasn't perfect, but he was doing his best. He loved your parents. Both of them, in his own way. And he loved you boys like a father.'

'And I'm grateful. But that doesn't alter the fact that love sees the real person, their faults, cares for who they really are. What Jim did to Mother, inventing a persona for her, all this –' he swept his hand across the photo album of Sylvia – 'it was a form of soul murder. And as for what happened to Michael. . .'

'What do you think happened to Michael? Do you think it could have been suicide? It's been bothering me lately.'

Peter sighed and shook his head. 'Nico and I have talked about it often and we have come to accept that one can never know either way. There's been some talk of Michael being very close to Rupert, too close, not being able to accept that people might know. But then, you see, they took towels with them. They must have intended to use them, and then perhaps one of them got into difficulty.'

'Or made a decision at the last moment. . .'

Peter's shoulders sagged. 'How can one know? Peggy wants me to stop going through the family letters. Says it's too much, all this reliving the past. In fact, I'm thinking of calling my collection of family letters *The Morgue*.'

Daphne travelled back on the *Riviera* sleeper to Cornwall, still feeling shaken. Could it really be that Jim had used Sylvia as if she were a mere hook upon which he could hang his fantasy of her? Sylvia then caught up in the magic of the illusion to the extent that it had had a damaging effect on her marriage and her family – leaving Sylvia riven with regrets after Arthur died?

She didn't want to make the connection, but there it was in front of her.

Hadn't she done just the same, pinned her fantasy Christopher on to the living man? Damaged his marriage. Her marriage. How could it be that she had replicated Jim's habits so well, without even realizing it until now? Leaving a wake of chaos behind her, her friend Paddy heartbroken, Christopher pining for her and drinking heavily. She might as well have dropped a bomb on their marriage. Worst of all, she'd betrayed Tommy when all the while he had believed she was doing all she could to keep their home together, waiting for him to return.

It wasn't just the war that had put a distance between her and Tommy, she saw now, it was also the secrets that she had begun to keep.

Jim, it seemed, had taught her well.

And what of Ellen?

She'd always been the one leading when Christopher, to some extent aware of the game she was playing. But her feelings for Ellen were so powerful that they had run wildly beyond her control from the moment she had first seen her. What if her feelings for Ellen were nothing more than some muddled fantasy, where she was using the real Ellen as a peg from which she could hang her own version of her – but this time without even realizing what she was doing? Some sort of breakdown that was going on inside her head?

And what if, God forbid – because she had never meant to be such a cynical person – what if she was harming Ellen by acting out her muddles? How must it have felt for Ellen, a kind but straightforward person, to find herself at the centre of Daphne's urgent daydreams when Ellen would have been much happier chatting over tea about the children, or going out shopping for new gloves?

Her brain whirring, Daphne decided to get up and go to the restaurant car where the bar might still be open. Perhaps she could get some coffee. She pulled on her clothes, slipped on her shoes. She walked along the rocking train holding on to the sides of the corridor. Dawn was coming up along the skyline, a deep crimson behind the trees, the flat fields of Somerset slipping by, grey and sleepy. Here and there, a stretch of water sparking red.

'We're not really open to serve breakfast yet, madam,' the attendant told her. 'But we can bring you coffee.' She sat by the window, clinging on to her cup, sipping at the hot, bitter liquid.

Was Jim so mixed up with his fantasies that he had had no idea of the harm he was doing?

Surely he had done the best he could, tried to care for his boys. She had always been able to rely on him when no one else understood her need for stories, both as a child and as an author.

Then she thought of his book, *The Little White Bird*, where the old major blatantly crows to himself about how he steals a child from beneath his mother's nose. There it was, hidden in plain sight, how Jim had wormed his way into Sylvia's life, even becoming the boys' legal guardian without opposition from the rest of the family.

How could she have seen it and yet not seen it? And hadn't Jim also written a book about a man with a maimed soul who can't love anyone, who can only conjure up a fantasy love, kills the real person in front of him and replaces them with a fantasy version, until the poor actual girl in front of him cries out in pain, 'Oh, but you can't do that to me. Kill me like that.'

Daphne sat feeling as though she had just woken up. Jim knew what he was doing, taking real people and holding them hostage to the doll-like fantasy he created from them.

The coffee on an empty stomach and little sleep was making her feel on edge. They were beginning to serve breakfast and she signalled to the waiter for rolls and butter. She tried to focus. Could it be that Jim had got so far inside her head that, without even realizing it, she too had created fantasies of people and tried to dance with them like puppets? She felt duped, and dizzy. Was anything she had done genuine, any relationship real?

She fumbled for her bag and took out her wallet. Found the pictures she always carried of Tommy and the three children. This was real. These were whom she loved and would give her life for. Her family. When it came to Tommy it had always been him that she loved, with all his irritations and faults and weaknesses. And as for the children, she had never played games. She prided herself on treating them as people in their own right.

But around her were the corpses of relationships that she had turned into dreams, secrets that had poisoned her marriage. Wasted years running after illusions. An anger began to bubble up. What would her life have been like – and the life of Michael and her cousins, of their parents and Daddy even – if Jim had never inserted himself among them?

Over the following days, feeling unsettled by what she had come to understand about Jim, Daphne found the door was now open to other questions that had lain at the back of her mind.

For some reason, as she lay in bed waiting for sleep, she thought of Daddy on the opening night of one of Jim's plays, *Dear Brutus*. His finest role. She's ten years old, sitting with Mother and Angela watching an eerie tale of people lost in a wood, who are given the chance to become for a little while the people they might have been – the sort of betwixt-and-between world that Jim specialised in. Suddenly, it comes back to her, as clearly as if she were there again, leaning out into the darkness of the theatre to see her Daddy better. It was quite confusing because the character on stage seemed just like Daddy, and with him was a daughter who looked exactly like her. The girl had her short, fair hair, even the same dimple in her chin. But in the play the girl behaved so oddly, winding herself around Daddy until he grew angry and accused her of being too knowing. Knowing what? If that wasn't confusing enough, the daughter turned out to be nothing but an illusion, a figment of his imagination, fading away into the woods as the sun came up with heart-rending cries of 'Daddy, don't leave me.'

Daphne couldn't imagine a worse grief than losing her father. She had run sobbing out of the theatre.

Daphne snapped on the bedside light, sat up in bed, angry and indignant. Had no one thought to warn her? But there was worse. For some reason, a comment overheard at one of the Sunday parties at Cannon Hall came back to her. She's seventeen again. It's high summer, a tennis match on the lawn, Daddy as ever insisting on new racquets for every set. She's above on the terrace by the conservatory with a book. She can hear the people in deckchairs below talking.

'But don't you think it's embarrassing, the way Gerald can't keep his hands off her?'

She'd wondered which actress they meant.

'I'm surprised Muriel doesn't have more to say about it, her own daughter.'

Daphne had felt the colour flood to her cheeks. Surely they weren't talking about her? And Daddy? She'd been furious. Of course Daddy held her hand a lot, kissed her, an arm around her all the time. He loved her. How dare they.

Now, as she lay awake in the small hours, forty years later, she wondered how she would feel if Tommy acted like that with her daughters, Tessa or Flavia.

She had never liked it when Daddy was so clingy. A silly need of Daddy's always to be the one. No wonder Mother had been so furious with her at times.

Daphne turned over her pillow. What had Jim been thinking when he wrote that play with the Daddy and Daphne characters? Could it be that Jim had seen something in Daddy to make him write a play so off kilter about Daddy and her? Or perhaps it was the play that had somehow set it all in motion, acted out night after night by Gerald and his imaginary child, until Jim's words sculpted a template of how the real relationship was to be between them, placing on to them a twisted version of who they were and who they might become. Which they had played out. She had been Daddy's girl. Kisses from Daddy that she saw now were rather suspect.

And all the while Mummy had become colder and colder, leaving Daphne stranded in a hall of fantastical mirrors, Jim's images of her and Daddy thrown back and forth.

For a girl to have no mother she can talk to as she grows into a woman, the world is a lonely place.

But then hadn't she always been aware, even as a small child, that there was a side to Uncle Jim that was tricky, the dark side to the fairy tale? She'd always wondered, watching *Peter Pan* on the stage, how Peter Pan was allowed to stand, hands on hips, and crow about how he killed people – wondered why none of the grown-ups objected, as if in the world of fantasy one may do and say as one likes.

And she had understood too that as a writer the dark side was necessary, for without a trickster who is willing to step beyond the taboos and speak the truths there can be no true stories.

She'd followed Uncle Jim, determined to tell truths that no one else would.

But now she felt duped by Jim. He was not a whole man. Beneath the whimsy and the jokes and games, he was cynical and dry as a husk, ready to use those around him as puppets in his fantastical versions of the world. And she had willingly followed him into those sterile and deathly shadows.

CHAPTER 25

LONDON 1951

Walking along the upstairs corridor one Sunday afternoon, she saw Tommy through the open door of his room, gloomily packing the last of the Boys into his case.

Tommy spiralled down into a low mood every Sunday evening as the time came for him to get the night train back to London, but recently he'd seemed even more anxious about going back to his life there than usual. Was there some problem at the Palace? Was he lonely?

But it was no good asking since he would never confess to finding things difficult. She felt a pang of that old guilt. A real wife would go with him.

'Tommy, you know I'll be at the flat with you at the end of the week. I need to see my publisher and I want to meet up with Peter again.'

'Wonderful.'

'Look, why don't you and I go out for dinner? That place you used to like so much in Covent Garden.'

He looked almost alarmed for a moment. Then smiled. 'Why not the Savoy?'

'Even better.' She went downstairs with him to the taxi,

something still jarring about his momentary expression of fear, as she waved him goodbye.

Peter was waiting outside the theatre in Camden, sheltering beneath a large black brolly. He was studying a poster for the performance, a dark figure with crooked fingers and hypnotic eyes who was casting a long shadow over a sleeping young woman.

She had to call his name twice before Peter turned round. He really did need shaking out of the moods he had fallen into of late, poor Peter. She pecked him on both cheeks.

'You should have gone in, not waited in the rain.'

'I was wet already. I rather like to wander around the area and think of Grandfather when he used to live here as a boy. That's how I came across this. I don't expect it'll be a very good production, I'm afraid.'

'It's just lovely to have a chance to see *Trilby* again.' Daphne felt her cheerfulness increasing in order to counteract Peter's gloom as they went into the lobby and bought tickets.

The curtains rose on a student's art studio in Paris, three young men at their easels drawing portraits of a girl in a white shift. It was a delightfully amateurish performance, the accent of the innocent Irish model, Trilby O'Farrell, so hopeless that Daphne had to bite her fist to stop herself from laughing. But the camaraderie of the students was poignant to see, evoking their grandfather as the idealistic young student in search of beauty and truth, filled with jokes and songs. And in love with Trilby – until the mesmerist Svengali lures her away with his hypnotic seances and destroys her, breaking the young student's heart.

Outside, a thick fog shrouded the street. They crossed the road to where the windows of a pub shone out against the night, the glass engraved with swags of flowers and running with condensation. Inside it was crowded, smelling of damp coats, beer and grease.

Daphne found two stools at a rickety table in the corner as Peter pushed his way through the crowd and came back with two glasses of whisky. Daphne tipped the whisky round in the bottom of her glass.

'One wonders where Grandpa found a character as dark and sinister as Svengali.'

Peter nodded thoughtfully. 'Have you ever read Felix Moscheles's diary?'

'Isn't he the student friend Grandfather lived with, the one who actually taught him how to hypnotise people?'

Peter nodded. 'According to Felix, he and grandfather used to practise mesmerism regularly on a servant girl called Caddy. All quite tame by today's standards, but I think Grandfather felt a lot of guilt about it later. By the way, I've been discovering some strangely specific connections between Jim and Grandfather. Did you know that Jim wrote a light opera for the D'Oyly Carte company?'

'I had no idea.'

'You wouldn't. It was a complete flop. But listen to this – it was about a servant girl called Caddy who knew how to mesmerise people. Isn't that odd. Exactly the same name as the servant girl in Paris who Felix and Grandpa used to mesmerise as students.'

Daphne put her chin on her hands, frowning. 'That is a bit odd.'

'Jim must have read Grandfather's books. And I wonder if he also read the diary or met Felix perhaps. Anyway, I think Jim became fascinated by Grandfather du Maurier and I suspect he tried to meet him before he died, but failed to. So then he became fixated on the du Maurier children and grandchildren, stalked us as being the next best thing until he finally got access to the family.'

Daphne was taken aback but Peter was the kindest of people and not the sort to make dark accusations – unless they were founded.

'So you're saying that Uncle Jim set out to get an entry into George's family? But surely Jim met you and your parents by chance, when you were children playing in Kensington Park.'

'So the story goes. But you see, Jim had form when it came to stalking the great and the good. If he wanted to get to know someone he'd find a way, invitations to dinner, writing intriguing letters. I've seen him do it. Jim collected people. And I think he wanted to collect Grandpa. Tell me again how Uncle Jim got to meet us.'

'But you know the story as well as I do. Uncle Jim came across you boys playing in Kensington Gardens, began telling you captivating stories of fairies and such. Then one day Jim found himself sitting next to Sylvia at a party, realized she was the mother of the little boys in the park, and she realized he was the man the boys talked about so much, and it went on from there.'

'A happy coincidence. But you see, I think Jim knew perfectly well that we were George du Maurier's grandsons even before he began telling us his stories of fairies. Then he set himself up to meet Sylvia, getting himself invited to the society party of the year where he knew she'd be'

'But how could he possibly do that?'

'I asked Dolly about it. She says he invited the hostess's children to read for some fundraising play he'd written, and of course he was invited to the party as a thank you. Jim worked pretty hard to get inside the du Maurier family, I reckon.'

'But if Jim was so very keen to be a part of the family, are you saying there was something sinister in that?'

'All I know is that Jim's world of ghosts and gloom was no place for a child. I do think our lives would have been very different otherwise if we'd not been left with him.'

'But Sylvia wanted him to take care of you, surely. It was in her will.'

'That's the shocker, Daphne.' Peter took a long sip of his whisky. 'Going through Jim's things in his flat, I've found two versions of Sylvia's will. One written in her hand, and one copied out by him – with a significant change in Jim's. In Sylvia's it says she wants Nanny Hodges and Jenny, her sister, to look after us boys. In Jim's version, it says she wants Nanny and Jimmy to look after us. He changed Jenny to Jimmy. Jim changed Sylvia's will. He didn't so much adopt us as kidnap us.'

'Because he cared for you.'

'Look I'm going on too much. I know it feels like a bit of a shock, thinking like this. And I'm the first to admit that Jim did so much for us boys, but when you begin to see things in a different light, one can't help feeling a little fooled. Angry even.'

'Have you spoken to Nico and Jack about this?'

'Yes. Jack is fuming but then he fell out with Jim long ago. Nico says it changes nothing. He says we should remember how much fun Jim was, how he would go out of his way to help us with school work, finding the perfect birthday present, the wonderful holidays. I would like to be like Nico, but there are questions I want answered.'

She left Peter at the Tube station. Watching him as he disappeared down the escalator, his shoulders drooping, she felt concerned. Perhaps Peter was right, stirring up the ghosts of the past was unwise.

That night she took out her copy of Peter's newly printed *Letters of George du Maurier*. Reading Grandpa's books, she had always loved how he was able to transport her back to his past so vividly. Grandpa had talked about being able to enter a trance-like state as he wrote, to live out other lives on the page. She'd always felt with some pride that she too had that same ability to imagine vividly. But now she was beginning to wonder whether it was a blessing or a curse to be able to leave the world so easily and step into a fantasy.

She closed the book, images of Paris a century ago still playing in her mind. One section in particular had struck a worrying note.

CHAPTER 26

PARIS 1860

In Gleyre's atelier in the rue Notre-Dame des Potirons, twenty students crowd round a girl wearing nothing but a length of silk draped over one shoulder. White unblemished skin, elegant lines that cry out for a pencil to worship them, Virginie is one of the many *grisettes* in the student quartier, laundresses or shop girls, who can be persuaded to pose for a few sous. The problem is to keep them in place long enough for the capture on paper. Most begin to complain and fidget after five minutes. So, standing before her now is Felix Moscheles, long dark hair, a paint-spattered smock, a grubby necktie, talking to her in a low voice. Slowly, he moves his hands in circles in front of her face, commanding her to keep her eyes on him. His hands circle wider, down to her stomach and out to her elbows as if describing wings, over and over, until the girl's gaze softens and she drifts into a trance.

They lean in, twenty men concentrated on one body. A forest of easels bristle around her; beyond them, cracked plaster walls spattered with dabs of oil paint in every colour. The room smells of the rum punch the students have chipped in to buy, of coal smoke from the drum stove, of sweat and pipe tobacco from twenty giddy young men set free from their mothers' advice.

'Tell her to touch her face,' says one. She slowly follows the order, as if in her sleep. A tightening of breath in the room.

'Her throat,' says another.

'Enough,' says George du Maurier. 'This is not a circus.'

Felix tells Virginie that she will remain exactly as she is posed, seated on the wooden bench, legs to the side, one arm propping her up, her face looking back over her shoulder – a nymph at the well about to flee – until she is released. The hours pass to the sound of pencils scratching on paper, the smell of paint and turpentine. The room grows colder but no one stops to bank up the coals in the drum stove. The light begins to go. The students talk of supper, twenty sous at Chez Anton.

The mesmeriser performs his hand movements in reverse in front of the girl and issues a command. She wakes from her trance, blinking, surprised to find herself where she is.

She tries to stand. Immediately crumples to the floor, crying out in pain. They lift her on to the couch where she passes out entirely, her blueish skin cold as marble as George pulls a cloak over her nakedness. He tries to revive her with warm wine but it runs out of her mouth. Someone goes for a doctor.

Later, George walks home, horrified by the doctor's warning. Any longer and the girl might not have survived.

Never again, he vows with his room-mate Felix.

And yet there is so much to learn. A few months later, under the tutelage of Felix, George has also become proficient in the mysteries of mesmerism. Both of them practise on Caddy, the pretty daughter of the tobacconist who says she loves them both. As they love her.

One night, a loud banging at the door. Holding up a candle, George opens it. In the narrow stairwell a man has a boy on a string, the child barking and whining like a dog.

The man explains that after seeing one of Felix's demonstrations he managed to hypnotise the child into believing he was a dog, but he has no clue how to bring him back. It takes Felix hours to restore the child to sanity.

When they are gone, as a thin dawn comes up over Paris, and George and Felix breakfast on black coffee and hard bread, the last of the wine, Felix shakes his head. 'That's the trouble with amateurs. They see one demonstration and assume mesmerism is easy to copy. But it's one thing to put an idea into someone's head, another entirely to take it out again – the essential thing. But if you don't remove that fancy, then it will lodge in their soul like a cuckoo and your poor subject will have no idea from whence the idea came – may even think it a part of their very self.'

CHAPTER 27

MENABILLY 1951

The next morning Daphne sat over breakfast for a long time, brewing an extra pot of coffee, still thinking about her conversation with Peter and about Grandfather's letters. Perhaps she had inherited Grandfather's intense ability to imagine. There had even been a critic who'd commented on just that in a review of *Rebecca*: 'No one has the ability to imagine on the page like Daphne du Maurier.' She'd thought it a strange thing to say at the time; surely all writers did just that. But had the reviewer pinpointed something particular to the du Mauriers?

And she was beginning to suspect that Michael had the same gift. He certainly had Grandfather's sensibility for music and poetry. He even looked like George, slim and delicate with elfin features. Perhaps too a mind that could imagine intensely, with dreams and nightmares so vivid that he would leave his bed and act them out – as with his dreams of drowning.

She refilled her coffee cup and took it to the window, looking out across the gardens. She could feel a connection waiting to be made at the back of her mind.

*

She's at Slyfield, holding Jim's hand as they walk into the woods to her lake, the pond in a clearing between the pine trees and the sycamores. He's talking to her in a sleepy, sing-song voice as he tells her to choose a point on the water and imagine an island, watching it slowly rise from the water and the little figure appear on it. Her own little world that she can fly away to any time she wants, until she must come back, blinking, to the real world. Or she's in the nursery, listening intently as Uncle Jim tells her his stories in his gently lilting Scottish voice, stories of Peter Pan as she flies away above night-time London, free to have all the adventures she wants.

The pieces click into place. Yes, she's always had the ability to imagine intensely, but Jim had led her deeper, showing her how to more or less mesmerise her own mind, how to take a piece of it and throw it on to a distant island where she could dance and play in a new version of Daphne, no longer sure if she was pretending.

Then her heart twisted.

Michael.

Had something similar happed with Michael and Jim, something to do with Michael's dreams of water?

She rang Peter in his office, relieved when he answered the phone.

'Have you got a minute, Peter?'

'Not exactly snowed under at the moment,' he said.

'Peter, did Jim ever talk to Michael about islands? Some sort of trick Jim would do, taking a child to the edge of water and conjuring up a story between them?'

'I don't know. There's the lagoon chapter in *Peter Pan*, of course. Michael would have been about five. Jim asked Mother and Michael down to Black Lake Cottage because he said he needed Michael to help him write a new scene for the play. We thought it a bit rich that only Michael should go. Jim had a way of telling a story with Michael in that quiet voice he had, passing the story back and forth, telling it together. Mother says they went for a walk to the lake to think up the new scene.'

Daphne was silent for a moment. 'So Michael helped Jim imagine the scene where Peter Pan almost drowns?'

'Yes. They went down to Black Lake and stood on the shore of the lake, more or less pictured it happening, I understand.'

'Then the nightmares started.'

'Yes, they did in fact. It was after that.' Now Peter was silent. Then he said, 'You're thinking of Sanford Pool.'

She walked to her writing hut, clutching her elbows. Sat staring out at the lawn through the window, playing the same scenario over and over in her head. Michael, five years old, the same beauty as Sylvia. A tilted nose, grey eyes with dark pupils, a distant gaze over the world of mortals.

At an age where what is real and what is imagined is all the same thing.

Hand in hand, Jim in his baggy suit, the little boy in blue linen knickerbockers and a Russian peasant top, as they go deep and deeper into the woods. There's a soporific buzzing of bees, Uncle Jim's voice has a light, lilting burr that makes one feel drowsy.

On the shore of Black Lake they stop, still hand in hand. The water is deep green, still as steel, reflecting the dark trees.

'Do you see it there, the island where Peter Pan was stranded?' he asks Michael.

Michael examines the glassy surface, looks up at Uncle Jim.

'I don't see an island.'

So Jim teaches Michael, the most susceptible of them all, how to play the island game. 'Close your eyes, or almost close them, so that all you see is blurry, and concentrate very hard.'

Michael screws up his eyes, stares at the water.

'Can you see it, a tiny island, rising from the lake?'

Michael's eyes twitch with the effort of keeping them half-closed.

'Just in front of you, across the water,' intones Jim quietly. Do you see it now?'

'Yes, yes, I do.'

'Keep looking. And there is someone there.'

'I see him.'

'Peter Pan?'

'It's him. It's Peter Pan.'

Slowly, the story unfolds, until the waters finally rise and Peter almost drowns. Michael can hear the mermaids calling out to Peter, trying to pull him under. But he's fighting them off.

Is he fighting them off?'

'But see how brave Peter is,' says Uncle Jim. 'Nothing scares Peter. He says that death will be an adventure.'

'Yes, I rather like that,' Jim says to himself. 'The idea of him being so carefree in the face of death.' Jim gets out a notebook and writes down the phrase.

Michael is still staring at the water. His face is white. He screams out. 'Uncle Jim, he's gone. Peter's drowned.'

'No, I think the water's started to go down again. I think he's going to be all right after all,' he tells Michael cheerfully. He squeezes Michael's hand and they walk back, Michael turning every so often to look at the water.

That night, the seekers come in through Michael's window for the first time, calling to him as he stands alone on a tiny island with the water rising around him. Seeking to snatch him down into the deeps as he tries to beat them away with his hands.

The first time the child's screams echo through the house.

Once the mesmerist has put an idea into the sleeping mind, it will lodge there for ever, unless the mesmerist knows to take it out.

She sees Michael in Sanford Pool, striking out with his newly learned swimming skills towards Rupert who is sitting on the edge of the weir across the pond. But they call to him suddenly. Panicking, he can't think, can't remember how to swim as they pull him down. Rupert dives in, tries to hold him up, but it's too late. The seekers have come, and one way or another, Michael knows they will have him.

Daphne sat wiping away tears, nursing a rising anger to think the man she had so idolised could cause so much damage. Be it unwitting or not.

She pressed her hands against her temples. This trying to sort out what was real and what was not was starting to make her feel as though she was going mad.

Not long afterwards, Daphne was hit by a thunderbolt from the blue. A telegram came to say that Gertie was dead.

Gertie had been the one person she could turn to for affection. Lying on the bed together, Gertie was happy to take Daphne in her arms and hold her. Gertie was her Ellen.

Now Gertie was gone.

'I had no idea Daphne was so close to Gertie,' she heard Todd saying to Tommy as she took away another untouched tray of food. Daphne sat in her room, unable to speak. Devastated. Unable to explain that she was mourning not only a dear friend but also the fantasy life she had built around Gertie, the comfort it had given her. A realization that left her shocked and floored.

'You know,' she had told Gertie as they lay together, 'I can't remember my mother ever holding me on her lap or cuddling me. Isn't that strange.'

What if Gertie had been some psychological quirk – something the psycho boys would have a field day with?

Was she, in fact, losing her mind?

Feeling desperate, she searched out the Foyles catalogue. Ordered several books. *How People Go Mad. The Complete Works of Jung.*

*

Over the following weeks, Daphne read all she could find of Jung with a sense of urgency, staying up late as the fire crumbled away, sitting up in a cold bedroom to continue reading.

The self and the shadow self. Could it be there was some unconscious trickster part of herself, hidden away in her unconscious, that wanted to take risks, be daring and have lovers, and yet was also that part of her that wanted to create and to write? A disembodied sprite, always wanting to dance away beyond the boundaries, for good or for bad.

What if she were to do what Jung was suggesting, to make peace with this shadow part of herself, to recognize it and to somehow train it to be less chaotic? A friend and not a foe, one that might come to understand and cherish the things she truly wanted in life. Her life with Tommy and the children. And kindness and goodness, loyalty and truth.

There were times, going down into the depths of the heart's darkness, trying to grasp hold of her mind and understand who she was, that she felt overwhelmed and scattered in pieces. But as the weeks went by, she began to feel herself surfacing, stabilizing.

She was also writing some of the darkest stories she had ever penned: *The Birds, Monte Verità, Kiss Me Again Stranger*. Working out her obsessions and mapping her tangled personality on the page, slowly finding a way to the light.

Or the hope of finding light.

CHAPTER 28

MENABILLY CHRISTMAS 1956

Christmas that year was as happy as it had ever been. The whole family came to stay. Tessa and Flavia dressed in heels, hair pinned up and lacquered, had taken charge of cooking Christmas dinner, keen to impress their men. Flavia had got married at just nineteen that summer, but Daphne was determined to let her children make their own choices. 'All I ask,' Daphne had told Flavia, 'is that you make sure your feelings are real. One has to be careful that one isn't falling in love with some fantasy version of a person, or that they aren't falling for some fantasy version of you.'

Kits acted as kitchen boy, Tommy as the butler and the house shone with candles and firelight. Gathered together around the tree in the long room, Daphne reached across and took Tommy's hand. If only she had understood herself sooner. What a fool she'd been to risk her marriage to Tommy, the only man she had truly loved, for her phantom crushes on Christopher and Ellen. It had taken hours of puzzling over books by Jung and Adler to realize that she needed to bring together the two conflicting sides of herself into a more mature and contented whole. She felt proud of that.

Like the protagonist of her new book, *The Scapegoat*, Daphne had decided to put family and Tommy first, the only things that were real and that mattered. She felt proud of this new book, but she had a feeling that the critics wouldn't understand it.

Later, the presents given out and opened, paper everywhere, she noticed how Tommy stumbled over a book left on the rug. Kits steadied him, raised his eyebrows at Daphne. Should she say something about how much he'd had to drink? He'd never really stopped the heavy tippling since he came home from the Far East, worse if anything.

'Daddy, what on earth are you wearing?' asked Tessa, narrowing her eyes at a silk cravat tied around his neck and tucked into his shirt. 'Who on earth thought you'd wear something purple and lime? Is anyone here losing their eyesight?'

Tommy put his hand to his throat. 'Present from someone in London. I quite like it.'

After New Year, Nico and his wife were motoring through Cornwall to visit Jack in St Endellion and decided to call in at Menabilly for a couple of nights.

Nico made himself comfortable in a chintz armchair, tall and well built, pink cheeks and charming manners, the endearing buck teeth and unflappable good humour. His wife, Jane, by his side, stout and companionable.

Nico was unfailingly good company. As they chatted around the fire, the conversation turned to the discussions she had been having with Peter, Nico nodding as she outlined the effect she felt that Jim had had on Michael. How he had tipped a delicate, imaginative child into a crisis of nightmares, fears of drowning sewn deep into Michael's subconscious.

How Jim had all but tricked his way into the family, duped Sylvia and damaged her marriage, forged Sylvia's will.

'It leaves me feeling so angry with Jim,' said Daphne. 'Furious, in fact. I honestly think I'm beginning to hate Jim.'

Nico crossed his long legs. 'Well, yes, I can see what you are saying, and I don't disagree that Jim was an odd one. I know Jack's wife Gerrie wouldn't let her children spend time with Jim because she thought he was such a bad influence. Jack never did accept Jim as a father figure. Left for naval college at thirteen, which again he never forgave Jim for.

'But you see, I always found Jim wonderfully good company, always ready to help if you needed something. I don't know if it's because I was such an ordinary sort of boy, very straightforward, but I had a happy childhood. I remember a lot of laughter. If I had a cold, Jim would come and sit on the end of my bed. He had a rubber tooth he'd pop in, pretend to sneeze. Said if his tooth hit the rail at the end of the bed it was going to be a mild cold, but if it hit the wall when he sneezed it was going to be a bad one. Or the time a very grand duchess came to tea and Jim was telling her about his humble childhood in Scotland. Had her spellbound. He told her they were so poor they had one sugar lump on a string that they had to dip in their tea in turn. She was enchanted while we were all stuffing napkins in our mouths, trying not to laugh.

'And the cricket weeks for all my Eton friends that Jim used to organize, so many wonderful holidays in Scotland when we boys were younger. I still go back to the Scottish island where we stayed in a castle overlooking the sea. Though I will admit that what Peter said was probably right, we did spend too long in Jim's world of shadows. Trouble was, no one could see that at the time. Least of all, I believe, Jim. And yes, it wasn't good for people like Michael, or for Peter.'

For the next couple of hours Nico recounted a summer spent in a castle on a remote Hebridean Island. Daphne listened, entranced. But as the story developed, she also felt an undercurrent of apprehension.

CHAPTER 29

SCOTLAND 1912

The ferry was coming in to Kyle of Lochalsh, Michael standing at the front rail wearing his fishing hat, creel on his back, his fly rod to hand, although they had two more boats to take before they arrived at the remote Hebridean castle that Jim had rented for the summer. Their second summer without Sylvia. Fishing had proved just the thing to take the boys' minds off their loss and keep them happily occupied, Michael especially.

He was on the cusp of losing Michael. Jim knew it more than Michael did. In September Michael would be thirteen and would follow George and Peter up to Eton. He'd already joined them in being gruffly dismissive of Uncle Jim's fairy-tale tosh. He too would become embarrassed by the odd little man with the too-big head who stood as his guardian, laughing with the boys in his study. Oh yes, Jim, he's a rum old cove but he does bring an awfully good box of tuck with him.

Soon that afternoon would come – he could see it already, as if remembering a day long gone – late summer, Michael going in with the boys after cricket, talking about tea and not looking back.

Is this how a parent felt, mourning for a child as it moved away? Jim had become guardian to George, Jack and Peter as boys on the verge of becoming young men. Michael, however, had still been a child, had known Jim since he was a baby. He had the child's acceptance that Uncle Jim would always be there, a presence to lean against. Even when Sylvia was alive Jim had visited the boys almost every day. Arthur had moved the family away to the countryside, but Jim had followed, once taking the whole Peter Pan troupe to put on a performance in Michael's bedroom when Michael was too ill to attend the opening night.

After Arthur and Sylvia were gone, it was Michael he had had to watch the most, long nights as Michael wandered the house in nightmares. Being there by the bedside when Michael woke up, doing something ordinary like reading the newspaper to show that all was well with the world. Uncle Jim would be there.

That was one of the hopes for this holiday – that with so much fishing and fresh air and trekking along the hillside paths, Michael would be too tired to dream, let alone sleepwalk.

Nanny Hodgson blamed Jim for Michael's nightmares. 'There's some things that aren't healthy for a child,' she'd say. 'People shouldn't fill a child's head with nonsense.'

As if he would do anything willingly to harm a child like Michael. He would have given anything to stop the boy's bad dreams.

The ferry was pulling up to the wooden pier. Jim walked over to Michael, stood as if admiring the view of Skye, hillsides of grass with patches of stunted rowans and birch. Looking straight ahead. 'So, Michael, if you could have one wish, what would it be?'

'That's tosh, though, isn't it. Wishes don't come true.'

Nico, by his side, looked up. Still undecided about wishes and fairies.

Jim drew on his pipe, held it out to study it. 'I concede that now you are twelve, you are aware of cold hard facts in a way that a foolish old man of fifty cannot grasp, but if you did still believe, what would you wish for?'

'Uncle Jim,' groaned Michael.

'Go on. Humour me.'

'You know what I'd wish for. It won't be any fun without the ghillie from last summer. Alasdair knew everything about fishing. If he could come with us this year. . . '

'Just to humour this old fool, close your eyes and wish.'

'This is tosh,' Michael said, huffing. 'You do know I'm too old for wishes.'

'Humour an old fool. And you too, Nico, close your eyes and make a wish.'

Nico shut his eyes, concentrating hard. Michael shrugged, and closed his eyes begrudgingly.

The boat drifted slowly to the wooden pier. Ropes thrown to the ferrymen. Women in shawls and men in caps and tweed jackets stood waiting for the boat in a cloud of midges, a couple of sheep and a dog.

'Open your eyes, Michael.'

Michael's mouth fell open. Standing at the far end of the jetty was a tall wiry man in ghillie's tweeds, a craggy face and well-worn cap, a jacket sagging with pockets full of feathers and twine to make exactly the fly that the fish needed on any stretch of the river. Alasdair the ghillie.

Michael turned to Jim. For a moment, a flicker of the old belief.

'Fairies come in all shapes and sizes.'

Michael hurried off the boat as soon as they docked. At the last moment he paused, looked back at Jim. It was his particular charm, that feeling he had for others.

'Thanks, Uncle Jim,' he called out. And he was gone. He'd be gone all summer, fishing in the burns and on the lochs with his brothers and Alasdair.

In the dull hotel in Tarbert where they had to spend the night, there wasn't much for the boys to do. Jim kept them entertained by etching his name into the corner of a window. Michael and Nico kept lookout, delighted and shocked, as this imp of a grown-up committed a brazen an act of vandalism. It was down in the corner by the window seat, so only the children would see it, he said, a message from the father of Peter Pan.

The next morning, they sailed along the coast of North Harris, mountainsides steep as a fjords, pink hilltops of ancient gneiss worn smooth by weather, the sea a half-circle of cobalt blue and silver under a blue sky. The castle stood at the foot of hills, the sea before it. A burn in full spate tumbled over smooth rocks where salmon jumped in spring. The castle was in fact a baronial mansion with crenellations and turrets, but it did the job, inside a dark-panelled hall, a heavy oak staircase. Jim took out a penny and a stamp. The boys crowded round as he licked the stamp, placed it on a penny on the back of his hand and tossed it up to the ceiling with a flick. A clink and the penny came down. The stamp stayed stuck to the ceiling.

The boys cheered. Uncle Jim left the same mischievous calling card on the ceiling of every grand house he visited. They'd never seen him miss. It was always fun to see how long it was before their hosts noticed it.

Next morning, he's up early, but the boys are nowhere to be seen. Outside the castle, a summer mist covers the sea, bright as sun through a wet sheet. White fingers of mist are moving down the dark green hillsides, the tops covered in white.

'Peter, Michael and Nico are gone off on the ponies with that Alasdair,' Nanny Hodges tells him. 'Gone to Loch Voshimid. I told that Alasdair to bring the boys back in one piece, out on the loch like that in a little boat.'

'And George?'

'He's still in bed, Mr Barrie. Not had his breakfast yet. Your guests aren't up yet either, Mr Hope and his lady wife the actress.'

Jim asks one of the castle ghillies to take him along the track to Loch Voshimid. It's a couple of miles there through a grey cloud, the world closed in with ethereal walls, layers of mist deepening or melting. Loch Voshimid is another mile along a silent valley between hills like cliffs. They leave the pony and buggy and carry on by foot. As they look down, the mist seems no more than a dulling of the light; but as one tries to see ahead, the layers close one in to a few yards of rock and moss.

They reach the loch, the water as grey as the mist, the hills around flat, cut-out shapes, broken and odd. He can't see the boys.

'They'll be out on the boat.'

He scans the water. Puts his hands to his mouth, cries out, 'Helloooo.'

No answer.

'They must be at the top of the lake where the fishing is best, Mr Barrie. Unless they've gone to the island.' He calls it by a Gaelic name.

'What does that mean? The name of the island?'

'The island that likes to be visited, sir. They say sometimes a person will go there and not come back. The island likes to keep them for company. Then out of the blue, they will reappear again one day, young as the day they left while all the rest of the world has moved on and grown older.'

'Alasdair will have taken the boys there, you say?' says Jim, frowning.

'Rowed near it. The island's barely big enough to stand on really. No room except for the ghosts. We can go and wait in the bothy, sir, until the boys come back.

Finally he can hear them, shouts and hallooing across the lake as they materialise from the mist. They've caught four enormous salmon.

The boys want to return to Loch Voshimid the next day. Jim goes with them, following along the track on one of the sturdy little ponies. The mist has cleared, golden grasses like fur pelts, the tips burnished red, deep springy carpets of magenta heather. The loch this morning is gentian blue. They row out in two boats, the water rippled by a breeze.

The ghillie rows them over to Voshimid Island. Jim wants to see it up close. It's a tiny lump of rock, white gneiss ringed with a tidemark of black lichen, a gnarled and shrubby rowan with red berries, cushions of fresh pink heather, honeysuckle and ferns. The island is a little garden. He sits at the front of the boat and takes out the notebook from his pocket. He sees a young woman, her baby left back at the castle with the nanny. She steps on to the island, her husband turns round, and she vanishes. Never seen again. Years later, she comes back as a ghost, searches everywhere for her baby, but can't believe that the man before her is her own child grown up. She doesn't want him. She wants her baby. There'll not be a dry eye in the house.

He often thinks of what Sylvia would think if she came back, her two eldest almost men, the others changed too. He writes her a letter each year to tell her how the boys are. For a moment he can hear the cry of the woman, searching for her baby, but it's a bird flying up from the island. He shivers.

'Shall we row over to Crocodile Island?' asks the ghillie, pointing to a long ridge of rock in the water. 'It's a good place to fish.' The oars dip and melt in the green water, leaving a wake of circles. The sun has gone in, the loch suddenly black, polished like oil. Jim tells the boys the story of the ghost on Voshimid Island. He calls her Mary Rose.

Michael begins to disappear each day, taking himself off on long walks where he stops to write poems on hilltops overlooking the ocean. As evening falls, Jim wanders in the gloom, fretting, shouting out Michael's name like an eerie banshee, the ghost of Mary Rose crying for her baby. Michael comes back unharmed each time, a visitor from another world, his head full of his poems.

Jim does not write poems. He does not enjoy going for a walk to admire the view. He does not hold with romantic feelings for nature. He does, however, like to dwell in the crepuscular space between evening and night, the slip between magic and reality, the liminal space between life and death. His plays explore magic and ghosts, that forbidden land that he had made his own.

Audiences love his shivery plays, his might-have-been stories.

CHAPTER 30

MENABILLY JUNE 1957

The weather was glorious as summer came in, the rhododendrons still banks of scarlet, the blue flowers of the hydrangeas beginning to appear. Daphne decided to walk to her secret beach near Menabilly where she was able to sunbathe and swim naked away from the eyes of passing holidaymakers, growing browner as the summer went by. But as she was going out of the battered Jacobean door, her canvas bag over her shoulder, the hallway telephone rang. She sighed and went back in, picked up the receiver. It was Tommy's secretary, Maureen, sounding distraught.

'Daphne, is that you? You must get a train here as soon as you can. Tommy's collapsed. They've taken him to hospital.'

The moment the taxi stopped, she thrust some money into the driver's hand and hurried up the hospital steps. For hours she'd been imagining the worst as she sat on the train, damp patches under her arms. A lump came into her throat each time she pictured a life without Tommy. She'd never loved him so much.

Tommy lay in a side room, white as the sheets, his eyes closed.

'Tommy darling, I'm here.'

There was no response. The nurse hurried away to fetch his doctor, Lord Evans. The Queen had sent her own physician to take care of Tommy.

Daphne waited on the chair next to Tommy's bed. His mouth was wide open, his breathing laboured. A tube led from his hand to a drip by his bedside. She stroked his cheek but there was no flicker of recognition. Her heart felt squeezed. If she should lose him. . .

Lord Evans entered with all the authority of a white coat, silver hair and a title.

'I'm so sorry, Lady Browning. We are doing all we can for your husband.'

'What happened?'

'It appears there's been failure of the nervous system. One sees it in men who have given so much through the past years, especially for a man like Sir Frederick with such high standards. Then there's a tendency to rely on drink for Dutch courage, with the resultant damage to the arteries and nerves. He will need considerable care to get better.'

'He has always had quite a lot to drink, but I had no idea things were so bad.'

'I don't think anybody realized. He certainly fulfilled his duties immaculately at the Palace, I'm given to understand. He's a proud man who keeps his struggles to himself, and is thus prone to depression. I'm asking a psychiatrist to have a look at your husband when he regains consciousness.'

'But you think he will?'

'Every reason to think so. Stay as long as you wish, but I would encourage you to go home and get as much rest as you can. It will be a long haul for both you and Sir Frederick. We will let you know if there's any change.'

Daphne returned to the flat feeling shaken and drained. She took an eiderdown through to the sitting room, wanting to be closer to the phone in the hall. She took off her dress and peeled off her stockings, but didn't fully undress in case a call came from the hospital.

She was just falling off into an anxious dream of misdirected taxi rides when the phone rang out. She was immediately bolt upright. She stumbled into the hallway and grabbed the receiver.

The phone was silent.

'Hello, who is this?'

'You don't know me,' said a woman's voice, cultured and icy, 'but I'm Tommy's mistress.'

Daphne felt the floor give way, sank down on a chair. 'I beg your pardon.'

'His mistress of almost two years now.'

'Who is this?'

'I'd rather not give you my name.'

'Is this some kind of joke?'

'And you do know that it is entirely your fault that Tommy is so ill now. It's the strain of trying to keep our relationship a secret, to spare your feelings, that's made him so ill.'

Daphne pressed the receiver against her ear.

'Tell me who you are.'

'I can tell you that I met Tommy through a shared love of the ballet. I don't think you understand how terribly lonely the poor man was. He wasn't even eating properly. So you see, I do blame you.'

She rang off, leaving a blank dialling tone.

Daphne looked around the hallway as though she'd never been there before. Nothing made sense. There was the photograph of Tommy in uniform on the wall opposite. His face looked unrecognizable, a lupine cast to his eyes. And who was she now? A dupe.

Had there been signs that she'd missed? She had never, in a million years, thought that Tommy was the sort of person who would cheat. She'd always been in awe of Tommy's morals. But he'd betrayed her like some fool.

She felt a prickle of guilt. Was this somehow payback for Christopher? For Ellen? She recalled Tommy picking up one of her effusive letters to Ellen from her desk in Menabilly. Stupid of her to leave it lying around. He'd been unusually quiet for the next few days. She'd thought nothing of it at the time, but is that when it began?

She leaned her head against the cool solidness of the wall. Her eyes gritty from lack of sleep. In just a few hours she'd need to go back to the hospital where Tommy was lying so ill.

Tommy was a fool and a coward. He was not who she thought he was. But she couldn't spend her energy on blame and hysterics, much as she wanted to sit here and scream. What mattered now was to get Tommy back to full health. To stay by his side and do all she could to help him.

But when he came round, would it be this ballet person, Miss Covent Garden, who he'd want by his side? Was he in love with her?

When she arrived in the sharp antiseptic air of the hospital the following morning, she was relieved to find Tommy awake. He was sitting up against the pillows, his face the colour of candle wax, dirty grey shadows under his eyes and cheekbones. Older suddenly. A shadow of a man had replaced Tommy.

She'd brought clean pyjamas, and the favourite hairbrushes that she knew he would want. She set one of his teddies on the bedside table.

'Thought you might like some company.'

He turned his head away, tears in his eyes. 'Oh, Ducks, I've been such a fool.'

'Well, no need to worry about all that now. All you need to worry about is getting better.'

'I have to tell you something.'

She straightened the edge of his blanket.

'Well, I did in fact get a phone call last night from someone you'd met at the ballet. Said she knew you very well. Very well indeed.'

'She called you. I'm so sorry.'

So it was true then. She was about to ask more, but Lord Evans swept in, a second doctor in tow.

'Glad to see the patient's awake. May I introduce Mr Shawcross, our attending psychiatrist.'

Mr Shawcross stepped forward, a small man with receding red hair and an eager look. 'It is my opinion that Sir Frederick may be suffering from a chronic depression, contributing to the reliance on alcohol and the resultant damage to his heart. In such cases, we have found electrical treatment to be very effective.'

'What sort of electrical treatment do you mean?' said Daphne, looking at Tommy.

'It would involve a series of mild shocks to the brain.'

'But is that safe?'

'Absolutely. However, you may find Sir Frederick very tired following the treatments.'

'I don't know,' said Daphne, frowning. 'And my husband won't experience any harmful side effects?'

'Not at all. Just a little tiredness.'

After they were gone, Daphne sat by Tommy's bedside, holding his hand.

'Do you think it sounds safe?' she asked.

'I'm sure they know best. But listen, darling. You must know, I did want to end it with her. I just didn't know how to. Bit of a coward, it turns out.'

She felt a wave of relief. He wasn't in love with her then. 'I shouldn't have left you alone so much in that wretched flat. It was selfish.'

He shook his head. 'I've always known I couldn't ask you to leave Menabilly. I should have been stronger. It's only ever been you, Ducks. You and the children.' His voice cracked, his eyes pleading.

'Then we'll get through this together.'

A nurse appeared. 'We need to get Sir Frederick ready for his treatment now.'

She kissed his forehead, cold and clammy to the touch, and left as the nurses wheeled Tommy out to another part of the hospital

Three days went by before Daphne was given permission to see Tommy again. She arrived to find him sitting up in bed but as she walked in he looked at her blankly.

'Darling? It's Daphne.'

'Have I been here very long?' He looked anxiously around the room.

'Three days, dear.'

'What the hell are they keeping me here for? I'd like to go home.'

'You were awfully poorly. Don't you remember? You collapsed at work. They brought you here to recover.'

'Of course,' he huffed. She could see he didn't. What on earth had they being doing to him?

Mr Shawcross came in. No sign of Lord Evans. 'How is the patient doing?'

'Extremely badly. He's entirely disorientated. He can barely remember the past three days. There are to be no more of these electrical shocks.'

'We can't stop them I'm afraid. The treatments must be followed to schedule if they are to work correctly, which is what we want, isn't it, Lady Browning?'

'I'm telling you I refuse,' she could hear her voice growing louder. 'You will stop these treatments now.'

'Please don't get upset with the doctor,' the nurse chipped in.

'It is understandable that Lady Browning may find it difficult at the moment. If you feel that the strain is becoming too much and affecting your ability to make the best decision for your husband, then we can offer you a recuperative stay on the women's ward. It may be for the best. On a voluntary basis, at this point.'

He stared at her, pointedly, as if to say checkmate.

She took a step back. Was he really threatening her? The wretched man didn't want his trick-cyclist methods questioned and so he was threatening her with a stay at the hospital, as if she was in need of mental treatment from him. She could feel her palms getting sweaty, her heart beating too fast.

'That won't be necessary,' she said, as calmly as she could, overwhelmed by a rush of rage towards this charlatan – and by a desire to run. 'I am sure we can see if the treatment is progressing more satisfactorily when I return tomorrow.'

She left the hospital as if escaping a prison. Half-expecting to see nurses running out to drag her back.

She had to get Tommy out of that hospital and home to Menabilly, put him under the care of her own doctor, before the dreadful Dr Shawcross could do any more harm.

The hospital, however, refused to release Tommy until he was well enough to travel. Three weeks went by before they deemed him fit enough to leave – which she put down to rest and Tommy finally unburdening himself to her.

Peter helped to drive Tommy down to Menabilly. Both men were sixty now, and she had always considered Peter to be the frail one. But now it was Tommy who looked older, leaning on a cane as Peter helped him shuffle to the front door.

As soon as he was in bed, Tommy fell asleep, a nurse whom Daphne had hired locally and trusted now keeping watch over him. Daphne went down to find Peter. He was outside, watching the swallows swooping to and fro across the lawns, an apricot glow to the evening sky.

'I'd forgotten how beautiful it is here,' he said.

She nodded. 'And now Tommy's home we can start to get him back to full health.'

'I'm sorry it's been so difficult for you. You've been marvellous, supporting Tommy, bearing up.'

'The truth is, I haven't been marvellous at all, Peter. I've been so muddled up with my own troubles, especially during the war. . . I've rather left Tommy to fend for himself.'

Peter rocked on his heels. 'These wars have a lot to answer for.'

'Well, it's all going to change. I'm going to be like a soldier now, with a battle plan, nothing but operation Get Tommy Better. He has to get better.' She gave a shiver, the damp rising from the grass. 'Come on. Let's go in. I'll open a tin of soup.'

That night she woke from a frightening dream. She had been in a hospital bed, her eyes bandaged. When the bandages came off, the nurse gave her glasses with blue lenses to wear to protect her eyes. But looking through the blue glasses she realized that she was able to see people's true natures: the doctor, the nurses, even her husband, had the heads of predatory animals, all seeking to destroy and betray her. It was the pain of the realization that had woken her. She couldn't shake off a feeling of being surrounded and duped.

She went over to her desk and snapped on the lamp. Sat down and wrote the dream as a story. She wasn't sure what it all meant but writing the story made her feel better. It wasn't a cure, and it wasn't pretty in any way, but at least she now understood the truth of how things were.

Now that he was home, Tommy began to make good progress. Well enough to come downstairs for part of the day, and then to walk along the cedar path.

Daphne felt that she could put it off no longer. She had to tell Tommy about Christopher Puxley. It wasn't fair let him go on thinking he'd been the only one to stray.

It was too much to explain everything to him face to face. Better to write it in a letter. That way it would give him time to think.

She found it searingly painful to put it all down on paper, but she spared herself nothing, told him not only about Christopher but also about Ellen. Explaining that there was nothing real to any of her crushes and affairs, they had simply been part of a mental muddle inside herself, her way of coping with her problems.

That evening, she put the letter on his bedside table with his glass of milk and the sleeping tablets.

'Darling, read it when you have a quiet moment. Things you should know.'

She thought that they would talk the next day. It would be horrid but there would be a clearing of the air and then they could start over together, two equally flawed people beginning from a clean slate, trying to rebuild a life.

But Tommy said nothing. He carried on as if the letter didn't exist – though she knew he must have read it.

'What did you think, about what I wrote to you?' Daphne finally asked as they sat in the long room after supper the next day, the window open on to the evening garden, the first stars visible above the trees.

He was silent for a while. She felt her heart beating in her throat.

'I don't entirely blame you, about Puxley. I know how difficult it was. It's just, I never imagined, all that time I was away, that you might have. . .' His voice sounded choked. He swivelled round to face her. 'Kits is mine?'

'Of course Kits is your son. I told you. It never went that far with Christopher.'

He nodded, went over to his record collection and leafed through the discs. Came back without putting one on. 'It's just going to take some time for me to get used to the idea.'

She felt a surge of anger and hopelessness. She'd forgiven him. 'So I suppose you think I'm to blame for everything really with Covent Garden, not coming to support you in London more, being such a hopeless wife.'

He turned his face to her, a look of surprise. 'Never. It's me who's no good, Ducks. I'm not surprised that you fell for someone else.'

'But it wasn't like that at all. I never really fell for him, just some phantom that looked like him. You see, I think I was just acting things out, because of my own muddled troubles. I've only ever loved you.'

'I'm very tired now. I can't talk about this any more. Not for a while.'

'Let me help you up the stairs.'

'I'd prefer you didn't. I'm perfectly able.'

She sat alone watching the fire die down then also went upstairs, holding on to the oak banister, feeling as though things were imploding once more. How could she make Tommy believe that she did still love him, always had? It seemed as though he was like Kay under the spell of the Snow Queen in the fairy tale, unable to see clearly; she, Gerda, trying to take the sliver of ice from his eye. The staircase turned. She felt dizzy for a moment. The portrait of a woman in a silk dress looked down at her. Or was it that she was like Rebecca, with so many sins of unfaithfulness that one morning Tommy would get up and shoot her?

She honestly didn't know who she was any more.

Someone had snatched away the map of her life. Each morning she had to get up and start re-navigating her way. She developed a debilitating anxiety around anyone but closest family, not sure who could be trusted. Often, she had had the feeling that someone was following her each time she walked in the woods.

She remembered Bunny and his friends talking about fifth columnist groups in the war, the nihilists and communists who might pose as respectable businessmen or politicians but who were really bent on bringing down the government and destroying all the values that the country held dear.

It didn't help that the papers that week were full of criticisms of the Queen, saying she was too priggish and out of touch. They accused her of surrounding herself with out-of-date and snobbish courtiers. Like Tommy, she supposed.

They had no idea how hard men like Tommy worked for the country.

But she knew that if the newspapers ever found out about his affair, they'd use it to undermine the royals and all they stood for even further.

Sometimes she felt sure people were following her if she went into Fowey or Par, journalists probably, posing as tourists, but she was on to them.

A faint voice in the back of her head said she was being ridiculous, but she couldn't stop herself. Alone in the long room one night, Tommy sleeping, she became obsessed by a thought. What if they tried to get at the rest of her family? In a panic, Daphne phoned the apartment in Paris where Flavia was staying with Daphne's friend Oriel.

'Darling. It's me.'

'Daphne, why are you calling so late? Has something happened?'

'Is Flavia with you?'

'Do you want me to get her?'

'No, no. But listen. This is important. You have to be on

your guard because there could be someone following you and Flavia. I really don't think you should leave the flat tomorrow.'

'Who on earth would bother following me or Flavia?'

Daphne dropped her voice to a whisper, shielding the mouthpiece with her hand. 'I can't say but we have to protect the Queen.'

'The Queen? Darling, is anyone there with you? You sound as though you might not have been sleeping well. Perhaps you might call the doctor? You see, one does imagine things when one is so tired.'

'Doctors here can't be trusted one bit.'

'Well, I might call Angela, just so she knows you're a little, um, under the weather.'

A beat of silence from Daphne.

'Oh God. You think I'm cracked, don't you?'

'No, no, dearest, just very, very tired. It's been such a strain, with Tommy being so ill and everything.'

The next morning the phone rang. Angela didn't beat about the bush.

'Oriel seems to think you are having a nervous breakdown. I'm coming straight over.'

With Angela's good sense and laughter, and with hot cups of sugary tea, the paranoia needle began to move down on the dial.

Somehow, she had to get her feet on stable ground again, put an end to the debilitatingly anxious imaginings in her head.

She began to write. Angry stories of murder and betrayal, delving down into the dark side of the human psyche. It felt as though she were feeling a way through the darkness with her hands, locating the hidden shapes that waited to trip her up and finding a way past them, one by one. As she wrote, the obsessions and the conspiracy fantasies began to recede.

'Some days,' she told Angela, 'I feel as though I have been to hell and back, but I'm coming out of it now.'

Early in November, she and Tommy dined in a small restaurant in Fowey.

'There's something I want to ask you,' said Tommy. 'Thing is, Ducks, the Queen has decided that the newspapers may have a point about her appearing remote to people. So she's going to do her Christmas broadcast on the telly, let people see her at home. And she wants someone new to help her write her speech. Did you know Rudyard Kipling helped her father when he did his first speech on the wireless as King?'

'If only we could get someone like that.'

Tommy's eyes crinkled with a smile. 'Indeed. Well, it seems Prince Philip very much liked the stories you did for the MRA in the war, *Come Wind Come Weather*. So he wondered if you might help write the Christmas speech for the Queen's first television broadcast. If you'd like to.'

'They think I might encourage the nation to behave well and cherish their families and have hope and faith. Me?'

'Well, yes, Ducks.'

Daphne put her hand over her mouth and began to cry.

*

At three o'clock on Christmas afternoon, Tommy, Daphne and all the family gathered together in front of the television in Menabilly's long room to listen to the Queen's speech. Only Daphne and Tommy knew of her involvement in it.

Prince Philip had spent considerable time editing draft after draft, adding and taking out various sections until he and the Queen were happy, but Daphne was proud to see that her words still made up a considerable part of the speech.

The National Anthem played to a long view of Sandringham.

'Someone take that damn dog out,' Tommy yelled as Bingo began barking at the screen. 'No, don't start handing sherry round now, Angela. Sit down.'

'Goodness, we're very keen on the Queen's speech,' said Angela, sounding hurt.

The Queen appeared at her desk, a welcoming smile, a pretty dress with a patterned sheen, photos of her children by her side. She looked relaxed and welcoming as she bid everyone a Happy Christmas, saying how glad she was to be able to imagine people gathered to watch the television, just as she and her family sometimes did. It was, she said, another example of how quickly things were changing in the world around them, bringing many new innovations to improve life but also sometimes making people unsure of what to hold on to.

She called for everyone to stand up for everything that they knew to be right, morality and justice, selflessness and courage, to cherish and take care of the many different people that made up the nation, serving and caring for one another, family, friends, and country.

Daphne felt Tommy squeezing her hand tightly, too filled with emotion to speak, as they listened to excerpts from her own pen calling people to stand up for what was right, to build a better world together and to hold on to what mattered.

CHAPTER 31

MENABILLY 1959

When Tommy retired, Daphne cherished having him back at home with her again all the time, although they still kept their separate rooms. It would have felt embarrassing to suggest anything else.

Tommy remained frailer than he used to be, catching colds easily, pains in his leg. And he still struggled not to drink. One evening she noticed the sherry was missing from the sideboard, found Tommy out in the car holding an empty bottle.

Tommy being ill had stripped away anything that didn't matter. She woke each morning knowing her purpose. But at times, the burden left her overwhelmed. She had had little time to put herself back together after the shocks of the past year or so. She still had to fight to stop herself fragmenting into fantasies in the way she might once have done.

And she was still bitter about Jim's role in it all, the trickster in the background with a careless knack for throwing lives off course.

Writing was her saviour at these times. Each morning, if Tommy was well enough, she would head to her writing hut in the garden to carry on with short stories, tales from the edges of consciousness, of murder and deceit, of betrayal and cynicism. Her bitterest stories carried echoes of Jim. A man who kidnaps a woman and her son and steals her essence by painting her portrait in oils over and over. A man with a maimed soul who tries to steal the secret of mystical happiness from a divine family.

She added her heartfelt story about betrayal, 'The Blue Lenses', and packaged up the collection ready to send to Victor. Its title, *The Breaking Point*.

Writing the stories, she realized, had helped her to return to sanity. She put her pencil down and stared out over the lawn where she and Peter had recently stood and watched the swallows.

The last time she'd spoken to Peter he'd been worried about his publishing house falling into debt. 'I should never have let Nico join. After we lost the rights to Jim's work, the firm never really recovered,' he told her. 'And I've stopped trying to make the family letters into a book. It was too sad, reliving all the deaths one by one.'

Resolving to meet him the next time she went up to London, she rang his flat, then remembered that he and Peggy had moved out. They were staying in the Royale Hotel before moving to Majorca to begin retirement. She tried to get him at the hotel, but failed.

A couple of days later, as she was working on edits, there was a knock on the door of her writing hut. It was Tommy. He never disturbed her. His face looked stricken.

'I'm sorry, darling. I think you should see this.' He held out the afternoon newspaper.

She balked at the headlines.

Peter Pan commits suicide

She read the account with disbelief. Peter Davies had spent the morning drinking in the bar at the Royale Hotel. He had then disappeared all afternoon and no one had been able to find him. At six o'clock he had gone down into the Tube station at Sloane Square, waited on the platform and as the train came out of the tunnel had stepped off the platform directly in front of it. It was, without question, suicide.

With a cry of shock, Daphne hurried outside. She looked around unable to take it in, standing on the lawn where they had watched the swallows together.

The newspaper said that no one knew why Peter Davies had taken his life, stepping towards the darkness of the tunnel at the very moment the train emerged from it.

But she knew.

It wasn't just Michael who had been lost when Jim led the boys into his world of shadows. She felt a shard of bitterness lodge in her heart, painful and permanent. She would never forgive Jim.

CHAPTER 32

MENABILLY 1962

That summer, Tommy seemed to be almost back to full health. They settled into a comfortable routine, enjoying each other's company once more, sharing jokes and walks through the woods.

'What do you think about walking up to Castle Dore tomorrow?' Daphne asked as they sat in front of the television in the sitting room. It had become their habit to sit together on the sofa, supper on trays, watching the news and perhaps a BBC play or a documentary on the little black-and-white set. 'I'm delving into ancient Cornish history for the next book. Just the sort of thing you love.'

'Well, let's get the map out and see where you want to explore.'

The following morning Daphne and Tommy set out to walk over the cliffs to Castle Dore, the remains of a fort that been the stronghold of King Mark over a thousand years ago. Tommy in elegantly tailored plus fours and a jacket, boots and a walking stick, binoculars around his neck. She in her flannel trousers and a belted jumper, a knapsack with maps and sandwiches.

A pale blue sky, a breeze blowing, blossom still out on the blackthorn, bluebells hazing the ground beneath. The site of Castle Dore was a mere ghost of the ancient stronghold it had once been, nothing more than grass-covered raised circles on a flat hilltop, brambles and hazels sprouting around a circle of grass. Tommy paced around, outlining where there would once have been a stockade of thick logs atop the inner rampart, a dwelling house for the men. Then they sat together on a stretch of bank between two rowans and ate Esther's ham-and-mustard sandwiches.

'See over there,' said Tommy, pointing to Lantyan Farm at the head of Fowey River. 'That would have been the site of King Mark's palace.'

Daphne took the binoculars, spying over the land where Tristan and Yseult would have kept their midnight trysts in Lantyan Woods. She shivered, handed the binoculars back.

'One can almost feel King Mark and his men moving around with their horses, on the lookout for them. So much that must have happened here.'

They returned to walk the sites of the old story several times, down to the lake that King Mark had made for Yseult, white swans still sailing on the silent waters as they had in the legend. Through the deep and mossy Lantyan Woods where the lovers once met, or pacing the sites of battles, Tommy explaining exactly where would have been the most likely spot.

At times, as they walked along the river it seemed as if they might be walking along the secluded banks of the Helford where they had moored *Iggy* so long ago, the green trees curtaining them, no sound but the river birds and the wind in the trees.

The next few years were a time of contentment, Daphne and Tommy enjoying the peace of Menabilly, the children returning for the summer with their growing families; or travelling to France to research a book on Daphne's French ancestors, set in the time of the French Revolution, *The Glass Blowers*.

But gradually Tommy's health deteriorated again. He became bedridden, as the old injuries from the crash began to flare up again. A bout of bronchitis turned to pneumonia.

Late one evening, after Daphne had said goodnight to Tommy and fallen into an exhausted sleep, the nurse knocked on her door.

'I think you should come and see Tommy. And hurry.'

Calling for her to ring the doctor, Daphne ran to his room, reached his bedside just in time to see Tommy turn his head and look at her with his beautiful clear green eyes; a faint smile and then he stopped breathing. She tried to give Tommy the kiss of life, pumping at his chest with the heel of her hand, but he was gone.

She sat by his bed, holding his dear hand, engulfed by a wave of grief. Then she made herself stand up, go to the phone and call the children.

By the end of the day, they had all arrived to say their last goodbyes. They stood together outside the house as the undertaker came to take Tommy away for the last time.

She choked back her tears, turning to face Tessa, Flavia and Kits. 'I don't want you to be sad,' she told them. 'You see, as I sat by his bed, I felt him there still. I saw him, a vision, standing on his boat at the head of the Fowey Estuary, his arms wide, a look of joy on his face. As if to say, I'll wait for you.'

CHAPTER 33

KILMARTH 1965

Wrapped in Tommy's old army redingote that she loved to wear so much, the faint scent of his cologne still perceptible in the worn woollen fabric, Daphne sometimes reflected on how life might have turned out if she had been able to understand and resist the trickster's path that Jim had encouraged her along. Although she could see that by temperament, by circumstance, she had been primed to be Jim's all-too-willing pupil.

If only she could go back twenty-five years, with the understanding of the human mind that she had now, its ways of hiding parts of oneself in the shadows. Then perhaps Christopher Puxley would still be married to his wife. Perhaps she would have been more content to support Tommy. Covent Garden might never have happened.

Perhaps. She knew that there was a darkness that lingered in the heart, ready to cause chaos, and she knew now the importance of fighting for and cherishing what matters – those we love.

She blamed herself for so much, but she still wished that she could take a knife and cut Jim out of the history of the du Mauriers like a canker. Jim had passed through and done incalculable damage, lives lost and ruined, leaving only grief and regrets for those whose lives he touched.

The last time she had spoken to Nico, he had said he was worried about her.

'I understand what you are saying,' Nico had said. 'But this isn't like you to be so very angry. One has to find a way to move past bitterness, Daphne. I don't want you to go down with the family curse of depression. You have to see past these things.'

Then Nico called again, something he'd discovered about Jim. Why didn't she come and visit them at the cottage and they could chat?

As she drove down to Kent, she wondered what it was that Nico wanted to tell her so badly. 'I know last time we spoke you were feeling rather fed up about Jim,' was all he'd said. 'I think this might go some way to explaining the man a little more.'

Jane had prepared a lavish tea in a sitting room with plump sofas and an inglenook fireplace stocked with baskets of logs. A Labrador settled next to Nico's armchair.

'How are you enjoying your new home?' asked Nico, passing Daphne the scones. 'Must have been quite a wrench to leave Menabilly after so long – and after you'd done so much to restore it.'

'Thank goodness Kilmarth came up, a wonderful old house nearby overlooking the sea. And I can still walk to Menabilly any time and stroll in its woods, so I do consider myself fortunate. But yes, it was very hard leaving her. But enough of me now, Nico, do tell your news.'

'The main news at the moment is that Nico's completely taken up with getting ready for his annual trip to the castle on Harris,' Jane chipped in.

'Best place in the world,' said Nico, his voice full of warm enthusiasm. 'Fantastic fishing and breathtakingly beautiful. When Jim took us there, I absolutely fell in love with the place. Been back there almost every year. Sadly, Jane's not able to come with me this time.'

'It's an awfully long way,' said Jane. 'All fishing at remote lochs and walking up mountains and since I'm recovering from a knee operation at the moment it's not a good idea. Next year, all being well...'

'I really shouldn't be leaving you,' said Nico with a concerned frown.

'Laura will be on hand here. You go and relive happy memories.'

'I've often wondered,' said Daphne, tentatively, 'how you managed to escape the melancholy that seemed to so badly affect your brothers, Nico?'

'I've thought about that,' he said, looking puzzled. 'And I don't have an explanation for you other than that we had very different experiences as boys. I was always just rather straightforward as a child, happy to play cricket or table tennis with Uncle Jim, or fish for hours. You have to remember that Jim was always incredibly good company for boys when he was in the mood to be, a fund of jokes and stories that had us doubled up with laughter.'

'So what do you think Peter meant when he talked about a world of shadows then?'

'Just that. Jim had an obsession with death. Reckoned he'd found a ghost, Mary Rose, in Harris that year. She became that famous play a few years later. You remember, we listened to the music for it with Michael in Jim's flat. Very eerie.'

'I do, yes. It does seem highly unsuitable for children and adolescents though, looking back? Especially boys who had lost their parents, their mother.'

'Of course, but we knew it was just a story. You see, even though his plays were full of ghosts, Jim didn't believe in an afterlife and ghosts any more than he did in magic.'

'And yet he had such a strong obsession with the departed. With death.'

'That's what I wanted to talk to you about. I had a letter from a researcher fellow. You know how mad everyone is to write about Jim still. He's been looking into Jim's time as a boy. In particular the death of his elder brother David.'

'You mean the brother who died in a skating accident. The one his mother adored. His mother was so overcome with grief when he died that she neglected six year-old Jim for a year. Explains the Peter Pan story, really, a small child knocking on the window of a mother who won't let him in. Clearly, the death of Jim's elder brother sent Jim off into a morbid place. I can see that.

'I don't mean to be harsh, but many people lose a sibling and their mother is consumed with grief for a while – but that's no excuse for subjecting the children in one's care to one's own morbid obsession with death.'

'That's true enough. I agree. But they say to know is to understand. You see, this researcher fellow, Mr Tobin, he's uncovered a mismatch in the accounts of the death of young David Barrie at thirteen. The official story, the one Jim always told everyone, is that six year-old Jim was at home when his brother was killed on the ice, when some child skated into David and caused him to crack his skull.'

'That's right.'

'Except it's not the whole story. According to Tobin and some recently uncovered letters, Jim was in fact visiting David at his boarding school that same day. It seems that the child to whom David loaned his skates was Jim. It was six-year-old Jim who came skidding across the ice and knocked his brother over as he stood watching. David cracked his skull on the ice and died shortly afterwards.'

'You're sure of this? Jim killed his brother David?'

'According to the letters.'

Daphne narrowed her eyes, remembering something. What was it? Then she saw Peter Pan on stage telling Wendy with feigned carelessness that he never remembered the people he killed.

The exact quest of Jim's life: to try not to remember that he had killed his brother.

'Once I've killed people, I forget them.'

'What did you say?'

'"I forget the people I kill," isn't that what Peter Pan says? 'The boy who could never grow up.' Daphne frowned, nodding to herself, thinking what this must have meant. 'Just as Jim could never grow up, always frozen in the moment when he killed his mother's most beloved child. The very reason why his mother refused to see him for months on end, froze him out of her heart.'

'It would certainly have maimed him psychologically. Responsible for his brother's death. His fault that his mother refused to love him. And imagine how it must be for a child, knowing that about himself, carrying that burden in secret. Clearly the family closed ranks to hide Jim's part, wanting no doubt to spare Jim a life of being known as his brother's killer. And as to the question of whether Jim should have been allowed to care for children in the half-dead state he was in. Probably not. But he was the one who stepped up. We can only try to understand and forgive. We all carry our own particular maiming.'

'You are the nicest person I know, Nico, but there are still things that shouldn't be excused.'

Daphne drove home feeling angry that Nico had tried to ambush her into being a little more forgiving of Jim. But that was Nico. Always cheerfully in a world of his own.

But as the miles went by, Daphne couldn't forget the little boy, hovering outside his mother's window, beating on the glass for her to open it. She felt a pity for that boy welling up, tears pricking her eyes. And for another child. She saw a small girl sitting alone, knowing that her mother can't find it in her heart to like her. Far easier to fly to a land of make-believe, alone in her room, than to try and understand why she always makes Mummy so cross and so tired, Mummy's arms filled with the bundle of Baby Jeanne.

Tears were dropping into her lap, for all the lost children, scattered throughout the years. She pulled up on the verge of a field, and let the tears flow, sobbing for them all.

CHAPTER 34

KIRRIEMUIR 1867

Six-year-old Jamie sits at the top of the stairs in the darkness, hugging his knees to his chest. His too-big knickerbockers come down to his shins. He can feel the scratchy tweed jacket drooping off his shoulders. His cheeks are wet from crying and cold as the snowy air outside. Through the skylight he can see the sky with its remorseless points of light. The bedroom door into his mother's room stands ajar, moonlight casting a grid of shadows from window struts.

He knows his mother is in there, lying ill with grief in her bed. But she doesn't want Jamie in there with her. *Oh, take him away.* Because it's only David she wants. And she can't have him, for David is dead at thirteen. Tall and blond and blue-eyed, and clever and happy and charming, David is gone. Gone, his way of standing legs apart and whistling breathily. Gone, his way of shimmying fast to the top of a tree to shake down cherries for Jamie. Gone, his way of boasting about himself – though no one minded such a thing from him.

They cannot believe he's left them. The draught blowing through the windows seems to carry his whistling, the wind rattling the roof tiles an echo of his quick footsteps on the stairs.

Just three days ago, so the story goes, the only story that Jamie is allowed to tell, in a winter colder than anyone could remember, David had been away at his boarding school, skating on a pond with his friends. Kind child that he was, he'd loaned his skates to another boy – no one knew whom but it was the very same child who had crashed into David as he stood watching at the pond's edge. He'd made David fall back and crack his skull on the ice.

Mother had just been setting out for the train with Jamie, so the story goes on, to see David when the telegram came. She'd fallen to the ground, had to be carried up to her room.

Now the curtains of the box bed stay closed. His big sister Jane Anne creeps in to light the fire. The tray goes up to her room but comes down again with the broth untouched. Mother still won't see anyone. Won't see Jamie.

So Jamie had made a vow to himself. He'd find a way, somehow, to make Mother happy again, a way to make her love him again, even though she doesn't want to. That afternoon he'd found David's old suit from the dresser drawer, pulled it on. Practised David's whistle to make sure it sounded right. Holding tight on to the too-big knickerbockers, the jacket sleeves folding round his wrists, Jamie had crept into his mother's room. In bare feet, legs apart, Jamie stood and whistled a tune. Breathy, careless, just the way David used to.

He could tell Mother was listening. Then a frail, cracked voice. Incredulous. Hopeful.

'Is that you?'

'Aye, it's me, Mother.'

'Is it really you?'

She'd struggled up quickly, pushed back the curtain. And what did she see? A child too small for his age, a head too large for its body, a wide forehead in the white moonlight and a small pointed chin. Nothing of David's athletic height, nothing of the one destined to become a minister and his mother's prize.

'Oh, it's just you.' Hope drained from her voice. The curtain fell back.

Clutching Davey's trousers to his waist he'd crept out, a little ghost haunting his own home.

So here he waits at the top of the stairs, cheeks wet. A shaft of yellow light as the door below opens. The creak of the wooden treads as dour sister Jane Anne comes up with a candle. She makes him go down to the kitchen, drink hot milk and get into his nightclothes that she'd left warming by the fire.

Later, he lies awake, listening out for his mother on the other side of the wall, thinking, thinking, of a way to make her smile again – should he tell a joke, stand on his head?

Just as he'll lie like this each night throughout the rest of his life, at school, as a young man in London – asking what tricks he can perform, what games he can play, how to charm them all into an affection for him – being, as he knows he is, so deeply, deeply unlovable.

Because he knows who killed David. Knows very well. But that's a secret so deep and terrible that he's not allowed to speak of it. No one will. No one must know. Sometimes, it's a secret so deep that he wonders if he dreamed it after all, if some other boy did crash into Davey.

But now he must find how to make Mother love him. And he does, in a way. After months of bringing Mother jokes and tricks, he finds what brings her back to him – his stories, especially the ones they both like best, stories about herself.

Propped up on the feather pillows, the ties of her night bonnet knotted under her chin, she listens as Jamie tells the story she told him of her childhood, of a motherless little girl of eight who used to wander the lanes of old Kirriemuir at twilight, a lamp in one hand, carrying her father's supper to the mine gate in a tin pail; she loves the stories of that little girl in her too-big apron who had to keep house for her brother and her father.

How Jamie longed to meet that child, see her coming towards him through the lanes of Kirriemuir carrying her pail. She would take his hand gently, call him her dearest Jamie and ask him how he was. He felt such love for that little mother child – mother to a lost boy. But his mother grows tired of him. That's enough of him telling her his stories or reading *Treasure Island* or *Kidnapped* to her again.

Over a year passes by and his mother still not up, Jamie is sent away to a boarding school. No one hugs Jamie, or puts a kiss on his brow before he sleeps, or notices when he cries in the dark.

Night after night Jamie lies in his bed and longs to be home. He dreams of floating home across dark fields and forests until he can see the white cottage in the moonlight. He hovers outside Mother's window, tries to find a way in. Bangs on the glass with his fists. But there's only silence. The window is locked and barred from inside.

And each time he wakes in tears. Sorry for the great mistake he made, the reason why his mother cannot love him. All her love has gone to a land far beyond death where David will always be the beloved golden one, the boy who can never grow up.

One day he'll become so rich and successful that he'll be able to go home and show his mother how well he can take care of her. He'll tell her stories and plays and make up games for her until he's so famous that she can't but love him, or something very like it.

And he'll grow, but not enough, always with the small body and too-big head, secretly hating mothers, knowing nothing of love or poetry or romance or music, trading only in whimsy, satire and make-believe, forever playing his trickster's games, crowing, *Look at me, cock of the walk. I'll make you follow.*

Sick at heart.

Until one day, he meets some real boys, swaddled in their parents' love, and tries to warm his cold soul at their hearth. Tries to grasp the shadow of what it is to be loved unconditionally even as it fades from his hands.

CHAPTER 35

KILMARTH 1970

It had been a hard blow when the time came for the Rashleighs to take back the lease for Menabilly. She moved to the dower house, a grey stone building overlooking the sea with light-filled rooms. In time, Daphne has begun to love Kilmarth almost as much as Menabilly.

Lying on the grass in the garden, Daphne places her hands behind her head, crosses her feet and stares up into the blue sky. It's an excellent lawn for playing cricket with her troop of blonde-haired grandsons and her one granddaughter when the family all arrive for the summer holidays. Long afternoons together at their secret beach or walking in the Menabilly woods where she still had the Rashleighs' permission to go as often as she wishes. Daphne's hair is completely white now and her skin is more lined than she would like, but here, lying on the summer grass, a sense of peace washes over her. She feels at ease with herself, at one with the world, a moment of pure happiness and contentment.

It's been five years since Tommy passed away, his stout heart gradually becoming too frail to support his body, and she misses him every day. But for now she has books to write, and Tessa, Flavia and Kits, along with her eight grandchildren, are often at the house. She speaks on the phone daily with Angela and friends.

She still insists on a walk every day.

She gets up slowly from the grass with the help of her stick, calls for her Westie to come, and sets off down the fields towards the sea. Reaching the path down to Par Beach, she stops, shades her eyes at the sunlit water and makes out the figure of a boy, dashing in and out of the waves, throwing a stick for a large dog. He's a boy of twelve or thirteen, mischievous and cocky, his clothes soaked. She recognizes the son of her friend Mary Varcoe. She waves to him, and he waves back, running away along the beach.

Far out to sea, a low light is striking the water, a pool of silver on a field of turquoise blue. She breathes in the warm air with its scents of gorse flowers. Thinks again of the day Tommy died. The moment when, as she'd sat by his bed, bereft, she'd seen him, so very clearly, waiting for her at the head of Fowey Estuary, arms wide open, his dear smile.

It's not time yet, but she won't be afraid when it does come, when she'll find him again and the two of them will set sail in *Marie Louise*, passing over the horizon to begin their adventures again – find again all those who were lost.

AUTHOR'S NOTE

In her later years Daphne wrote two novels with underlying themes of the tension between fantasy and reality. *The Flight of the Falcon* is set among the towers of a small Italian hilltop town, Urbino. It is an allegorical tale filled with vertiginous steps and dramatic falls, images inspired by Jung's dream imagery around the tension between flights of fantastical imagination and the gravitational pull of reality. It was written as a thriller but the deeper meaning was there for those who chose to see it. She also wrote *The House on the Strand* based on her home, Kilmarth, where a drug that allows time travel ends in tragedy.

Daphne is known as a romantic, Gothic novelist, with a talent for writing page-turners, and for her evocative descriptions, but she is also fearless in exploring human psychology. She faced mental breakdowns in her life but was able to recover her balance by reading Jung and Adler, also writing her way back to sanity through her stories and novels. The timeless psychological truths at the heart of her stories, and the excellence of her writing, mean that Daphne du Maurier will always have new generations of avid readers, and new adaptations of her stories will continue to be made for the screen.

ACKNOWLEDGEMENTS

I would like to thank Christian Browning for his permission to use the Daphne du Maurier archive at Exeter University and for his kind help in reading *The Mischief Makers* to spot any glaring errors. Thanks too to the staff at Exeter University Archives who were all so helpful and welcoming.

I was fortunate to be able to spend time in a cottage on the Menabilly estate walking the same paths and beaches as Daphne once did, and I would like to thank Sir Richard Rashleigh for his hospitality. I was also lucky enough to stay in Amhuinnsuidhe Castle, now a hotel, on Harris for a night and visit Loch Voshimid and Mary Rose's island as guests of Mr and Mrs Scarr-Hall.

My curiosity about Daphne's connection to J. M. Barrie was sparked by Piers Dudgeon's excellent biography of the du Mauriers, *Captivated*. Piers's book on J. M. Barrie, *The Real Peter Pan*, and Andrew Birkin's book, *J. M. Barrie and the Lost Boys*, were also invaluable biographies of Barrie and the Llewelyn Davies boys. I consulted a wide range of excellent biographies of Daphne's life, including the brilliant ones by Margaret Forster, Tatiana de Rosnay, and Jane Dunn. Daphne's daughter, Flavia Leng's, autobiography, *A Daughter's Memoir*, gave a wonderful window into life at Menabilly. Angela du Maurier's autobiography, *It's Only the Sister*, contained many helpful insights. Oriel Mallet's *Letters From*

Menabilly were invaluable. Daphne's autobiography, *Myself When Young*, offered a superb picture of her years up until marriage. Daphne's own books and stories informed much of the book's plot regarding her reactions to J. M. Barrie. I was indebted to Daphne's grandson Rupert Tower for his chapter on Daphne du Maurier in his and Christopher Perry's book, *Jung's Shadow Concept*. Thank you to Tom Varco at the Four Turnings Farm Shop for his help. Many thanks especially to Piers Dudgeon and Hans Kuyper for their research into the possibility that J M Barrie was the child who killed his own brother David – a theory that Daphne would not have been aware at the time of but which is included in the novel for dramatic purposes for the reader to better understand Barrie.

Many, many thanks to my agent Jenny Hewson of Lutyens & Rubinstein for her amazing support and her wisdom. Sarah de Souza at Corvus Atlantic was a very patient and wise editor, and I am very grateful for all her help and hard work. Mary Chamberlain my copy-editor worked tirelessly, and any remaining errors are mine. Many thanks also to editor Sarah Hodgson and to the book designer and all the marketing team at Atlantic who work so hard to bring books to the world.

I would like to thank Kathy and Andrew Welch for their hospitality and for a quiet place to write in Majorca at a critical time.

I'm so grateful to Josh who is always ready to visit new places, however far flung, in the name of research. And a big thank you to all the family who came to share the cottage in Menabilly over the weeks we were there, Hugh, Alison, Isaac, Luke, Asher, Kirsty, Hans Peter, Magnus, George and Anna, and a big thank you too for all the family's support over the past three years of writing *The Mischief Makers*.